MW01043576

THE CROWING
OF
THE BEAST

HETTIE ASHWIN

To David
enjoy

Hettie

Published by Slipperygrip 2015

First edition: Morris Publishing Australia 2013
Second edition: Slipperygrip 2015

ISBN-13:978-1511799249

www.hettieashwin.blogspot.com
www.slipperygripcolumn.blogspot.com

Books by Hettie Ashwin

<u>Humour</u>
Literary Licence
The Reluctant Messiah
Mr Tripp buys a Lifestyle
Barney's Test
The Truffle War

<u>Thrilllers</u>
The Mask of Deceit

<u>Short Stories</u>
A Shilling on the Bar
After the Rains & Other stories

THE CROWING OF THE BEAST

The greatest revolutionary changes on this earth would not have been thinkable if their motive force, instead of fanatical, yes, hysterical passion, had been merely the bourgeois virtues of law and order.

Adolf Hitler (Mein Kampf)

CHAPTER ONE

The Gendarme rubbed the palm of his hand over his riot visor, smearing the blood splat to one side. What he saw made him grip his baton tighter.

Blood sprayed from the victim's face as the boot ground down, repeatedly. What once was recognisable was fast becoming a bloodied mess. Small bits of flesh stuck to the sole of the polished steel-cap. The perpetrator lifted his boot for another attack and lost his footing in the congealing pool of blood and bone. He stumbled,

"You fuckin' Jewish cunt," he yelled, as his spittle rained down on his dying victim.

Protesters threw themselves at the line of riot shields. Their shouts drowned out any cries of help, as the skin-heads raged through the throng picking off the innocent. The pack hunted; their hatred a weapon no shield could deflect. A woman screamed as she was punched in the face and pushed to the ground. Her blood stained hands splayed out to cushion her fall and were trampled by the crowd. The protesters lunged forward at the police line, their banners turned to lances. A shot rang out. People fled, blinded by panic, trampling those who weren't quick enough. And then the pack mobilized in an orgy of blood and hate, kicking, stomping, and bashing those left behind.

The papers described the scene in horrific terms – massacre and racial murder – and said Paris lost the last vestiges of civility that day. The death of Andre Darlan was testament to what Paris had become, the papers cried, as his only crime was being a Jew.

***

George Nozette picked up the newspaper from his desk and read the headlines again. The three inch letters screamed at him, 'Race Riot Shame'. He skimmed the details of the demonstration, as he had seen the whole thing on the television for the last twenty-four hours. He had mixed feelings about the reason the Jewry of Paris was protesting. He well understood in this modern world one was expected to be tolerant, and George counted himself a politically correct citizen, but somewhere in his gut, he felt the Jews had a point. Who wants a Mosque right next to a Synagogue?

The paper took the moral stand, but still they described the slaughter, the riot Gendarmerie, the injured, and the blood in graphic detail – ending with the death of Mr Darlan in front of the Synagogue on Rue de la Victoire. Social commentators dared to use the words Neo-Fascist, describing the riot as a malaise of the ills of society. The editorial condemned them as a small group of misguided youth. But anyone who had seen the television footage knew these thugs weren't misguided youth; they were a reincarnation of evil of the worst kind. Their brown shirts, their skin heads, and their belief in a symbol that everyone thought had died in a bunker at the end of the Second World War, made them idealists of the worst kind. Amoral and ready for a fight.

Janelle interrupted, "Coffee, Mr Nozette?"

"Yes, why not?" George said then asked, "Is Mr Simeoni in yet?"

"No, not yet." George knew his partner in their law firm would be a little late. George had never known a time when Bernard wasn't late. He never arrived until after Janelle, their

2

secretary, had made coffee. He turned to page three and the full spread of pictures. Bodies lay on the ground in one photo, another showed a Gendarme with blood over his visor, and another the retreating band of thugs as they ran from the military intervention of plastic bullets, water cannons and tear gas. It looked like a war.

Janelle came in with his coffee and peered over his shoulder to look at the pictures.

"Awful, isn't it?"

"Yes."

"They said the man who died was only in his 40's. With a wife and two children. And he didn't do anything. He was just..." Janelle bit her lip.

"A Jew."

"Yes," she answered a little embarrassed, knowing her employers were also Jews.

"I thought the world had finished with all this." George folded the paper and threw it on an empty chair. "So," he began, "what's on the agenda today Janelle?" As far as George Nozette was concerned, the news might as well be on the moon. It didn't affect his daily routine, his family, or his life. He drank his coffee and listened while Janelle outlined his appointments for the day, preparing himself for a full day of legal matters. Legal matters that to him meant bread and butter, but to the clients meant they could buy their apartment, realise their husband's will, grant some relative the power of attorney, or try to stay out of gaol.

"Good morning, George." Bernard popped his head around the corner of the office door and grinned. "Traffic is..." he trailed off, and then continued, "All the streets are cordoned off after the riot. Just chaos."

"Ah, I see."

"Well, what does the day bring?" Bernard asked as he straightened his tie. He absentmindedly brushed his trousers and preened his expensive suit. Bernard was the expert in paperwork and research, and with his fastidious temperament, he was well suited to the job. The firm of Nozette & Simeoni did well in the small end of town. They had carved a niche and resolutely stuck to the small holding.

"We have that domestic violence case at 3:30. She said she wants to go to mediation now. All that work, and now she changes her mind!" George said, scrolling down the list on his computer.

"I had a feeling about that one. And remember we need that payment for the divorce. The accountant is starting to get fidgety," Bernard replied. George searched through the mess of papers on his desk to confirm the payment.

"How can you find anything in there?" Bernard pointed to the pile of papers, folders, post-it notes, and lunch wrappers.

"It's a system," George replied. "Anyway, Janelle keeps me up to date." They discussed their various daily appointments and the schedule was set.

It was around lunch time when Bernard came into George's office. He went to sit on the chair and spied the paper.

"Did you see this on the television?"

"Yes."

"What do you think?" Bernard asked.

"I think..." George started, "I think that it will all be over in a week, people will forget, we will go on with our lives and..."

"Mr Darlan's widow will not forget George. She will not forget her husband's head was smashed, his face pulped by a Neo-Nazi heel all because he was a Jew."

"Do you really think anything will change? People are crippled by the GFC. We are sharing our world with seven billion people. Today it's thugs in brown shirts; tomorrow it's famine in Africa. It all seems so terrible now, but in a week it will be forgotten. I have forgotten it already, Bernard."

"Yes, I know, but... he was a Jew, George.

"He was a man in the wrong place at the wrong time. Jew or no Jew." George sat back and pulled on his moustache. Bernard moved the paper and sat down. The tension in the air made Bernard fidgety. He looked at their certificates to practice law.

George caught him and said, "Bernard, don't bring it up."

"It's just that I..."

"Okay. So we made an error. That was a long time ago."

"I know," Bernard began, "Markus was innocent. It wasn't our fault. The evidence was corrupted. I know all that, but he still went to prison. We didn't do enough. He still committed suicide... because of our error." Bernard slumped in the seat and looked at his partner. They had been fresh and hungry for cases, and, in their enthusiasm, they overlooked the obvious. Markus Depardieu was an innocent man. He deserved justice and didn't get it. It was a black mark that made the two lawyers even more determined to uphold the law, no matter what the costs. Every case they took now was a small step in assuaging their guilt. Bernard sighed, "I don't think they will ever catch the murderer. The crowd was huge and I heard the CCTV was smashed. You know, I doubt if anyone will get a fair trial if they are caught, because the public and police are baying for blood, not justice." He flicked through the paper. "Look, three whole pages of it. It seems there is a demonstration or riot every week now. Someone is always disaffected by something. Is no-one happy with their lot these days?" Bernard posed the rhetorical question and shrugged his shoulders. "But still... life goes on, as you say George, life goes on." Janelle brought in their lunch from the local cafe and the men ate in silence – Bernard reading the paper, and George doing the crossword.

That night, and for the next three nights, the rioting in the streets continued. The gradual escalation of violence turned to looting, and those whose religious outrage sparked the riot, were pushed aside as opportunists and gangs from the underbelly of society wreaked havoc.

Politicians implored the public to stay calm, but some heroic citizenry banded together to quell the disturbed nights, but the violence, the arson and the looting populous took no notice. The authorities had lost their edge and the gangs knew it.

The Commissioner of Police appeared on the television and was heard to say that these crimes would not go unpunished. They had information, arrests were imminent, and justice would be served. It was a convincing performance, but the jaded public were not so easily swayed and had little faith in the French Police Department.

**

George's prediction was right. People did forget. The police promised they were dealing with the murder of Mr Darlan, but after two weeks, there were other things to occupy the front pages of the papers; politicians in disgrace, World Cup scandals, and visiting celebrities all fired the public's imagination. Nozette & Simeoni forgot as they carried on with conveyance work, wills, and jobs for ordinary people with ordinary lives – until the phone rang on a rainy Wednesday at 3pm.

Janelle put the fateful call through.

"Mr Simeoni, a Mr Tag on the line,"

Bernard waited, and then asked, "How can I help you, Mr Tag?"

CHAPTER TWO

Bernard threaded his way through the noisy mob to the crowded front desk of the police station. He hated going to the duty officer and waiting in line like a criminal. He felt he should have been afforded some respect, but there was little in evidence. A woman, who was holding a screaming baby, stared at him, oblivious to the child's wailing. He smiled at her.

"What you looking at?" she spat the words. Bernard looked away as the woman was joined by an extended family of about twelve. He pushed to the front of the queue and handed his card through the grill, "Er, excuse me. I'm here to see a Mr Tag." The officer on duty read the card and made a phone call, as Bernard tried not to look in the woman's direction.

"That way Mr Simeoni. Through the side door; on the green light." The officer pointed to a door at the end of the waiting room. Bernard waited, briefcase in hand, until the green light flashed then pushed the door open and stepped through to relative sanity.

"That woman is crazy," he said to the waiting officer as the door closed and locked. He brushed himself down and adjusted his tie.

"We get them all in here, Sir. That lot are gypsies. Nowhere to go and nothing to do but create more problems for us. Now, you are here for...?"

"Mr Tag."

The officer flicked though his manifest, "Right, follow me."

Bernard was led through a maze of corridors with police officers scurrying to and fro and lines of suspected looters who stood, as they waited to be interviewed.

"The riots have stretched the Force to its limits," the officer said, squeezing past a nasty bottle-neck of young thugs. Bernard passed them with his eyes firmly fixed on the officer in front. He was led to interview room one. He had been there before on many occasions, for petty criminals hoping for justice, and he knew the drill. He signed the register, and was patted down, before he was shown inside. When the door opened, he expected to see an overworked detective, a cup of coffee, and a man who usually is repentant and hoping to forget it all by the next working week. But in interview room one, things were different this day.

"Afternoon Mr Simeoni, I am Detective Inspector Pallis." Bernard shook the Inspector's hand and smiled.

"It's quite busy out there isn't it?" Bernard said referring to the crowded corridors and the gypsies.

"We sweep the streets, but they still come back." Bernard watched as Pallis narrowed his eyes and pursed his lips into a sneer.

"It's a problem."

"Hhummmp." Pallis ended the conversation. He looked at Tag. Your client." the Inspector nodded, by way of introduction, in the direction of the man sitting at the table. The other two police officers in the room shifted on their feet. Bernard studied the sitting figure. He had a shaved head, which wasn't so remarkable, except for his tattoo of a winged dagger on one side, and some barbed wire drawn around his neck. His face was heavily pierced and he had a spike for jewellery in his left ear. He looked up and his stare was blank. Bernard tried to get a response and smiled.

"He picked you from the phone book. Said he wanted representation."

"I see. From the phone book?" Bernard scratched the back of his neck and took a deep breath. "Well... may I have a few moments alone with my client Detective Inspector?"

"Yes," the Inspector said, then added, "Mr Simeoni would you like coffee?"

"Thank you. And maybe something for Mr Tag?" He looked expectantly at his client.

Tag nodded.

"Two coffees please, thank you." Pallis flicked his head at one of the officers and threw a look of disgust at Tag and left. Bernard and Tag were alone.

"Now, Mr Tag, if I am to act on your behalf, you need to sign this, and this, and this." Bernard produced the necessary documents from his briefcase and laid them on the table. And if I am to act, you must instruct me." Tag looked at the papers and shuffled them on the table, and then he picked up the pen Bernard had provided, and signed. His rough hand gripped the pen awkwardly. Bernard studied the tattoos on Tag's knuckles as he wrote his name.

"Heinz is it?" Bernard asked looking over the signature.

"Yes."

"Good." Bernard took the papers and tapped them into a neat pile on the interview desk. "Now Heinz, what is this all about?" Bernard tried to remain professional, but Tag had an air about him. He seemed agitated and tight as a coiled spring ready to snap. "Heinz?" Bernard asked again glancing at Tag's forearms for telltale drug use.

"Fuckin' questioning me. I wasn't even there."

"Where?" An officer opened the door, interrupting the conversation, and Pallis followed the second officer carrying two cups into the room.

"All set?"

"Well, I guess we can hear what you have to say." Bernard looked to his client, but Tag's face showed little emotion. Pallis sat down and drew his chair in close and picked up a paper clip, turning it over with his fingers, then began to pull it apart.

"We have reason to believe Mr Tag was involved in the murder of Mr Darlan on the 24th of November at Rue de la Victoire in the 9th arrondissement. We would like to know Mr Tag's where-abouts on that day?" The Inspector sat back in his chair with a look of satisfaction. Bernard swallowed hard. He took another look at his client and things started to fall into place. The shaved head, the brooding look of hate, the tattoos. Pallis lifted an eyebrow and smirked.

"My client informs me he was not in the vicinity."

"Not in the vicinity." Pallis reiterated the statement. "You may tell your client that he was identified by one of our officers in Rue de la Victoire." Without warning Tag jumped up, his chair fell to the floor and the two coffees followed. The room stood still and then Tag grabbed Pallis's jacket. He pulled the Inspector across the interview table and spat in his face. Bernard, flustered, staggered back as the two officers pounced on Tag and threw him to the floor. One thrust his knee down on Tag's back, and his breath left him in one gasp. The other officer raised his baton and brought it down on Tag's shoulder blades. Bernard watched, mesmerized until Pallis shouted, "Get him out of here, NOW."

Tag was hauled up, his hands cuffed behind his back. He spat, "Fuck you," as he was pushed through the doorway.

"Well, Mr Simeoni," Inspector Pallis said as he wiped the spittle from his cheek, "Good luck to you. That..." and here he looked to the door, "That piece of filth doesn't need your council, he needs a bullet."

"We shall see, Inspector."

"If I had been at Rue de la Victoire that thing would not be walking out of here today."

Bernard studied the Inspector. His contempt left a sour taste in the air. There was a no nonsense approach to the man

10

with his thick head of black hair ar
fidgeted constantly and it seemed he (
still.

"Thank you, Inspector." Bernard k
assess the situation. They could hold
any real evidence, although his littl
interview room would earn him anothe
sentiments of the police, he didn't ho
getting out of there without at least one broken rib. Bernard
looked over to the Inspector who was straightening his
clothes.

"From the phone book you say?"

"Yes. From the phone book. It looks like it's your lucky
day Mr Simeoni." Somehow, Bernard didn't feel that lucky.

There were some formalities to attend to, and then, when
Bernard had been handed the paperwork regarding Tag and
his alleged crimes, he once again walked through the front
counter crowd and left.

"Not lucky at all," he said to himself as he drove back to
the office to break the news.

***

"What's his name again?" George asked.

"Tag, Heinz Tag. I did a bit of digging. He's on Facebook,
but you're not going to like it."

"What?"

"He... calls himself the Warrior of the Apocalypse. He
has the same symbol that's on his Facebook page tattooed on
his head."

"Sounds deluded. I would guess the police think he is
their man? I can't see him getting any justice with that
profile."

...ector Pallis seems to think he fits the bill. ... though. He is a dead man walking," Bernard ... firm of Nozette & Simeoni prided themselves on ...ioning the rights of the individual. Their ideals, ...ned over the years after their rocky start with the Markus Depardieu case, often sat uncomfortably in the real world, with graft and corruption almost a second economy. But they resolutely stuck to their principles, upheld the law, and fought for justice in the legal system.

"So, what next?" George asked. "He obviously needs council, but I wonder if we are the right council. This isn't drink-driving or shoplifting is it?"

"Well... no, but I think, no matter what Mr Tag has or hasn't done, he deserves to preserve his rights don't you?"

George listened then nodded and played with his moustache. "Bernard," George looked his partner in the eye, "What is your opinion of Tag? Is he...?"

"Just a man in the wrong place at the wrong time?" Bernard finished the sentence.

"Touché Bernard. But the question remains."

"So it does, George, so it does."

The conversation was interrupted by the telephone. Janelle put the call through and Bernard picked up.

"Hello?" The caller was from the newspaper and Bernard motioned to George to pick up and listen.

"We have reliable information Mr Simeoni that you are representing a suspect in the murder of Mr Darlan. Is this correct?"

"That is not for public discussion." Bernard gave a quizzical look to George.

"What is his name?" the reporter probed.

"I am not discussing anything with you at this time. If you care to make an appointment with my secretary..."

"Who is paying for his defence?"

"I have stated my position. Now, if that is all, good day," and Bernard hung up. The men looked at one another when the phone rang again. Janelle said it was the press from another paper, and what should she do, because she had three more on the line.

"Just say no comment at this time, Janelle. It's all we can do," George answered.

"Shit Bernard," he said as he hung up. "This is..." but George couldn't think of the right adjective to describe the growing fear that they were in for a battle of mammoth proportions. The phone rang hot for the rest of the afternoon with the media machine on the hunt and looking for anything that could be loosely construed as fact. Bernard and George tried to concentrate on their bread and butter cases, but with every ring of the phone in the outer office, the tension built – until George told Janelle they would be finishing early and to just go home. When she had left, the men came together, and George pulled out a bottle of wine from the kitchenette fridge saying, "I think we deserve this, Bernard, don't you?" Bernard nodded and watched the wine fill his glass.

"To justice," George said and Bernard concurred, "To justice."

After George had left the office, Bernard began his research. He poured himself a whisky and went over the police paperwork, made several lists to get the evidence in perspective, then studied the video footage of the riot. Seeing the police in their riot armour and the Neo-Nazi gang cut a swathe through the crowd, he felt sick at the gratuitous violence. The gang had come armed with vicious weapons, iron bars, and chains designed to maim. It was a sickly study in controlled hatred. Bernard tried not to let his emotions get in the way of his study. He played the riot over and over, watching for the spark that started the violence.

Bernard finally decided to turn out his study light at around 3 am. His research had thrown up some startling information. Information that he knew might cause considerable trouble for the firm. Information that might help their client – and one startling fact.

CHAPTER THREE

It was a cold Thursday morning, with the chance of rain, the paper said. George sat at his kitchen table and opened the newspaper to the second page. The headlines made him spill his juice.

"What is it?" his wife Audrea asked, as she grabbed a sponge.

"Look at this." George spread the paper on the table and read, "Law firm takes on Neo-Nazi supporter. Nozette and Simeoni...," and he read on to Audrea. The article described the suspect as possibly having affiliations with the Neo-Nazi group, and the group's illegal conduct over their short, less than illustrious, history.

"The story didn't mention Tag by name, so things haven't moved to a formal charge," George surmised. And when he read it over one more time, it really didn't say much, except that they were acting for a person of interest. The paper didn't know if he was a supporter, or paid up member, but were drawing a very long bow in connection to the murder.

"What does it all mean?" Audrea fussed over their two children and looked at George.

"It's just another media beat up," George said, "They get hold of something and run away with it. Don't worry Audrea, it'll all blow over."

"But is it true George? A Neo-Nazi?" Audrea studied her husband's face for the truth.

"He may be. But that is not the issue Audrea. Doesn't he deserve a fair trial?"

"George, how can you. What of your faith?"

"What of justice? Doesn't that count for something?" George folded the paper and stood up to face his wife. "You have him convicted already, just by association."

"Well... I," Audrea stammered. "I just..." she let the conversation hang in the kitchen as the children ate their breakfast.

"It is early days Audrea. This thing will die down. He is just a man. A man that may have been in the wrong place at the wrong time. That is all." With that pronouncement, George kissed his family goodbye and drove to work, pondering the implications of the press. They had the capacity to annihilate a reputation if they put their collective minds to the task. A duel with the media wasn't a prospect he relished.

Once in the office, he went through his usual routine of reviewing the paperwork, putting the urn on, and watering his few stubborn windowsill plants.

Janelle was punctual and busied herself making coffee. "Good morning, Mr Nozette. Coffee?"

George nodded and stood by the window picking a few dead leaves off his plants. A loud thud on the window glass startled him. He staggered back. What looked like thick red paint dripped down the pane from an explosion.

Janelle ran into the room, "What was that?"

"Stay back, Janelle." George held her by the arm as they looked at the window. The stain congealed on the outer sill. After a minute or two, George crept to the window and looked out. The street was empty.

"Mr Nozette?"

He turned and saw the look of alarm on Janelle's face.

"I think we might call the police, don't you?"

Janelle nodded and rushed out of the office to her desk.

The police arrived at the same time as Bernard. He nodded to the men and held the door open.

"What is all this about gentlemen?"

One of the officers had begun to speak, when George came down the stairs and answered the question, "We have been vandalized, Bernard. On the window upstairs. A bomb."

"A bomb?" Bernard asked his eyes wide.

"A paint bomb," George explained.

"What?"

"A paint bomb was thrown at the window. Come." George led the posse upstairs to his office. On the window, the drying red paint cast an eerie glow in the room. Statements were made, a camera was produced, pictures taken, and then the two officers left. Janelle was instructed to engage a window cleaner. There was a palatable tension in the air.

"Did you see the paper, Bernard?"

"Yes, I did. So, I'm guessing that…" He pointed to the window. "is why we are now targets."

"Exactly. But more to the point; is Tag a Neo-Nazi supporter?" George asked. Bernard sucked his breath in through his teeth. "Well?" George perched on the edge of his desk.

"It looks like it," Bernard answered. "I did some digging late last night, and our Mr Tag belongs to a group with all the signs. They don't actually say 'Neo-Nazi', that is a press beat-up, but their objectives are pretty obvious. Their web site is full of veiled threats and metaphors. My guess is that they just, only just, circumvent the web censors." Bernard crossed to the window and looked down the street. There was the usual traffic, a few shoppers, and everything looked normal. He looked over to the building opposite and caught a glimpse of a figure moving from the window. It was an accounting firm and their business was very staid and ordinary, but that furtive movement made him uneasy.

"What else?" George asked. Bernard told him about the news footage that showed the police line with riot shields and then one officer with blood on his visor. "The News footage played that particular segment over and over," he said. Then, holding the best for last, he told him Tag had been in the rat house.

"The rat house?"

"Mental institution. He was in for drug rehab. A bit... you know." Bernard raised his eye brow and smirked.

"Well, we could use that. Delusional and easily brainwashed."

"Maybe," Bernard said staring out the window.

"So are you going to see Tag today, Bernard?" George asked, startling Bernard back to the office and the conversation. "We need to establish some sort of case." He sat down. "And a rapport."

Bernard nodded. "We need a strategy for disclosure."

It was George's turn to nod. The men knew that the police would have public opinion on their side, and their need to show an outcome sometimes outweighed the need for a fair trial.

"Our Mr Tag may be his own worst enemy. By what you have told me, he doesn't seem to care what happens. No self-preservation at all." They decided that another interview was necessary and George said he would go, to get a feel for their client. Before Bernard left George's office, he briefed him on his other research.

"And good luck trying to get more that two words out of him," Bernard said. He made himself comfortable in his own office and set to work researching the Neo-Nazi group and its affiliations. And how Tag fitted into the scheme of things. The interview with Tag was slated for the afternoon. After lunch, when George was just about to leave, Janelle put a call through.

"A gentleman, Mr Nozette, he didn't want to leave his name." George waited and then a soft German accent came on the line.

"Mr Nozette, I understand you will be representing Mr Tag."

"Who is this?"

"A concerned individual. I represent a group who would like to put our monies at your disposal."

"A group? You know I cannot take money from an outlawed group."

"No one is suggesting such a thing."

"Of course not," George said as his brain was working overtime.

The man with the German accent continued, "So, if you can furnish my interests with your banking details, we can make a deposit and ensure your costs are kept up to date."

"Yes, yes of course Mr ...?"

"Thank you, Mr Nozette. We will be in touch."

"Yes, thank you, I will pass you over to our secretary for the necessary. Good day, Sir."

George went into Bernard's office and related the conversation. His version included some speculation as to the caller.

"If it is the Neo-Nazi group and their money, I'm not sure it is legal," George said.

"And if it is just a concerned individual, well who are we to complain? I wouldn't suppose Mr Tag has any money." And so it was decided they would keep the deposit in their account and work pro-bono until things became a little clearer.

"By the way," Bernard said, "those accountants across the way, do they have all the offices on the second floor?"

"I don't know. Why?"

"Oh, nothing really. I just thought I saw someone looking at the window."

"Not surprising really, is it, Bernard. Paint bombs, police, and the newspaper. We may be next to a bakery and a chiropodist, but we are news."

"Yes, I guess you're right. Well... good luck, George. The Angel of the Apocalypse awaits."

"Thanks, I'll remember that."

As George walked to the underground car park, he mentally prepared himself for the interview to come. The drive was through heavy traffic. He took a more convoluted route, not noticing a motorbike, which followed his trail through the back streets. At the police station, he handed over his card and waited for the green light. When the door opened, he followed the officer to the interview room and waited. Presently, Tag was escorted into the room, manhandled to a seat, and told to sit. His handcuffs banged against the table as he sat down.

"Can we be alone?" George asked the officer. The officer nodded and indicated he would be just outside the locked door. George put his briefcase on the table and waited, pulling on his moustache. Then, with the door shut, he looked at Tag. Heinz had given up all his piercings and now had a large bruise over his left eye and an extended ear lobe to take the place of his spike.

"Are you alright?" George asked, then realising he hadn't introduced himself, he said, "George Nozette, of Nozette and Simeoni. You met Mr Simeoni yesterday." George held out his hand. Tag inclined his head.

"Now, we need your co-operation on this, Mr Tag. The charges are quite serious. Do you understand?" Tag inhaled and stared at George. "First we must establish if you were at the demonstration. Were you?" He looked at Tag who was fidgeting with his cuffs.

"Heinz?" Tag looked blank. George tried again. "If you have a credible alibi then the police need something else. They say they can place you at Rue de la Victoire. An officer can identify you at the scene."

"So what if I was?"

"Well... think of it as snakes and ladders, Tag. They have moved one place, now we have a move, without going down, only up. So you were there?" Tag nodded. "Good. Now did you take an active part in the riot?" Tag looked at George. He controlled his breathing and narrowed his eyes in a look of contempt. George pulled on his moustache and waited, flicking a quick look at the officer outside the door. "You know someone has bankrolled your defence. Your fees are taken care of." George though if Tag knew he had an ally he might be more inclined to talk. "Whatever you say will be in confidence."

Tag sat back and for the first time he smirked, and George knew he had broken the ice.

"What happened to your head?" George indicated the bruise.

"What do you think, smart lawyer." Tag said, then turned and looked at the officer on the other side of the door.

"Do you want to file a complaint?" George pulled out a legal pad and held his pen at the ready.

Tag huffed.

"Oh yeah, sure." He spat his sarcasm across the table. George let the moment pass.

"So, do you want to tell me what you were doing at Rue de la Victoire?" The story that George heard made the hairs on the back of his neck stand on end. Tag peppered his short story with hatred and contempt for the police, Jews and just about everyone else. His motive was racial, and his pack mentality evident in his regurgitated rhetoric. When the interview was over George felt drained. He alerted the officer at the door. Tag was led back to the holding cell, while George walked out with more than a few questions on his mind and a moral issue that hung over the case like the Sword of Damocles. He drove back to the office thinking of all he had heard. Tag might not have been particularly skilful at expressing himself, but he had a belief that was entrenched. He was single minded in his objectives, or the instilled objectives of the group, and couldn't see beyond his racist views. As George pulled into the garage and cut the engine, he sat in the car thinking. A motorbike stopped at the underground entrance and the rider looked at the stationary car for a moment and then sped away. George, unaware of the incident, walked to the office. He knew he had to enlighten Bernard about what they had signed up for by representing Tag.

Janelle greeted Nozette with a frazzled look. She had been on the phone all day fielding calls from all over the world regarding their representation of the suspect involved in the murder of Mr Darlan. It seemed the media were hot on the story, as it had fired the public imagination, and was being debated worldwide on every social medium.

"Mr Nozette, I need help. I can't do this…" She pointed to her phone with three red lights. "… and do my job." George went over to the telephone cord and pulled it from the connection.

"Solved. Only email, Janelle. Go out and get a new mobile phone. Then let our clients, and only our clients, know the new number. If we get personal callers, take their details and then make an appointment. And Janelle…"

"Yes."

"Don't worry." George smiled and walked to Bernard's office. It was a long afternoon as the two lawyers talked over the growing media, their client, and their strategy. The one thing they both agreed on was that Tag deserved a fair hearing. As yet, he hadn't been formally charged, except for the assault on Detective Inspector Pallis, and the public prosecutor had yet to be named. As the day drew to a close, George made coffee and steeled himself to broach the subject he had been dreading.

"Bernard," he began, "there is a slight problem."

"What else?" Bernard asked sipping his coffee.

"Well, Tag being the Angel of the Apocalypse and all that crap, well... he's not exactly," George stumbled with the words.

"What is it?"

"He doesn't know that we are..."

"God, get it out."

George took a deep breath. "He doesn't know we are Jews."

"So?"

"Well, how would it look, Jews defend Neo-Nazi. It's not exactly kosher."

Bernard smiled at the last word. "We're not exactly practicing, are we? When was the last time you went to synagogue?"

"Yes, I know all that. But still...?" George said, pouring himself another cup.

"Well, he need never know. If we don't advertise the fact, and we never do anyway, then there is nothing to worry about. Is there?"

"If you put it like that, but if the press get hold of it, it will be different."

"Fuck the press. They print crap anyway." Bernard felt aggrieved that they had to put their lives up for scrutiny just because they were doing their job. "Tag, for all his sins, deserves justice and Nozette and Simeoni are the ones that will give him justice."

"Nice speech, Bernard. Let's just hope the press will see it that way." As the men finished their late afternoon coffee, they knew they were on the side of justice, but they privately doubted anyone else would think that way.

CHAPTER FOUR

Tag's morning in court for assault didn't attract too much attention from the press. The police had spent the last two days sweeping the suburbs and the housing estates. The courts were awash with people charged with looting, rioting, public disorder, receiving stolen goods – the list went on. Nozette and Simeoni arrived in good time, only to discover they were number 143. Bernard spied a friend from another law firm in the crowd and hailed her, "Simone." He held out his hand. "What do you make of all this?"

"Hi," she began, "I'm flat out. We were called in late yesterday. All five courts have been sitting throughout the night trying to get through the mess." She saw Bernard's ticket. "Oh, I see you have a number. There is a reasonable amount of no shows. God knows where they are. There're so many cracks in the system. You should get through reasonably quickly." Simone smiled.

"Good luck with that," he said pointing the sheaf of papers in her arms.

She shrugged her shoulders and was distracted by the announcement of her number. "Must go." She began to walk away, then turned and said, "Judge Remillio is in Court three and he's on the war-path. We're all trying hard to avoid that number." Simone chuckled then strode away.

Bernard turned to George, "Just chaos," he said, then brushed his suit down and adjusted his cuff links.

The overflow from the holding cells was milling around in the corridors and George tried to find Tag. He looked at the crowd of accused, from all races, backgrounds, and walks of life.

"Just thieves," an old lawyer said to George. He had bags under his eyes and looked like he had a lifetime of overwork on his face. "They all have an excuse, but nothing excuses their guilt. Most of it was caught on CCTV." He rubbed his morning stubble and shifted his papers in his arms. George nodded and glanced down the line.

"The thing to be afraid of is the opportunist that takes advantage of the disaffected. They…" The old man nodded in the direction of the line. "… think they have a right to behave badly." He licked his lips and took a cup of coffee from an orderly. "Rights come with responsibilities. Try telling them that." He drank his drink and George excused himself. He found Bernard and shook his head. "Nothing."

"Well, I guess we just wait," Bernard said fingering the number he was given. They studied the line, noting some who seemed nonplussed by their appearance in court. Veterans of the system, who had done the rounds more than once. As the morning wore on, the corridor thinned. There was a quiet hush of voices. When someone gave a small laugh, the room visibly stiffened. A man swung around to find the perpetrator, and Bernard saw his crazed eyes. The heavy set man growled, lunged at the youth, and landed a punch straight on his nose. The young lad keeled over onto the floor and the three officers on duty waded into the fight. Shouts were thrown at the police and then someone jumped on an officer. The officer grabbed his Taser and fired at his attacker. The two fell to the ground, only to be attacked once again by the angry mob. The police were hopelessly outnumbered in the corridor and they panicked. A fresh-faced gendarme flayed his gun about trying to terrorise the crowd. Someone knocked it out of his hand. Bernard and George stepped back from the fracas and watched as the crowd descended – their frenzied attack a mob mentality. The young officer screamed and George took up his call for help. He thrust forward into the crowd and began pulling off the assailants by their clothes, their hair, and anything he could grab.

"Bernard, help," George yelled, but Bernard was rooted to the spot unable to move. He watched as punches were thrown and George was accidently Tasered. As his friend slumped to the floor and lay still, Bernard roused himself and swung his briefcase around, trying to get to his partner and pull him away. He hit a woman in the back and she went down. A young man drew his hand back for a punch. Bernard raised his case and thwacked his arm. He lost his balance, tripped over the fallen woman, and landed on his knees. Bernard tried to balance. He saw George's feet and bent down to pull. Something hit him in the back. Winded, he sprawled to the floor. There was a loud bang and Bernard looked up to see reinforcements arrive. They swarmed over the rabble using their truncheons to beat off the thugs. Bernard saw some dogs jump into the mix. He was scrabbling around, trying to rouse George when an officer grabbed him by the collar and hoicked him up.

"I'm a lawyer. I'm a lawyer," Bernard shouted as the gendarme wrenched his arm behind his back. He looked down at George, who was just coming around.

"He's a lawyer too," Bernard yelled over the barking of the dogs. George managed to get on his hands and knees and then stood up. He tried to focus and staggered, leaning on Bernard for support.

"In his pocket," Bernard said. The officer frisked George, found his credentials, and let go his grip on Bernard. The crowd were thrashed back into line, one truncheon at a time, and eventually order was restored. George stood back and watched the dogs patrol the corridor, then the beaten young officer was taken away on a stretcher. Bernard sighed and straightened his clothes.

"Are you alright?"

"Yeah, I feel crazy though. Fifty thousand volts is crazy stuff." He stumbled and Bernard held his arm and led him to a seat.

"Sit here, I have to get my briefcase." Bernard hunted around the room and found his prize. "Now we wait," he said.

George rubbed his neck and wondered at the stupidity of the crowd. How they thought they could get away with assault in the courthouse was just madness.

"I think the whole friggin' world is mad, Bernard, the whole world." George lifted his shirt and looked at the growing bruise on his hip.

The word sent down from Judge Remillio was that the hearings would resume, and anyone found out of order would forgo their one chance at liberty. The crowd were subdued now as they waited, the dogs an extra incentive to behave.

A clerk walked the corridors giving out numbers and allocations for the courts. He spied Bernard's number and looked at his list.

"Court three, Judge Remillio." He then asked for particulars.

George furnished him with the paperwork and they sat and waited.

"Remillio will crucify Tag, you know that don't you?" Bernard said and George nodded in agreement. Nozette and Simeoni sat through the rest of the morning round and heard the same plea of 'an opportunistic act of stupidity' over and over, but nothing could disguise the intent when some of the accused were found with trucks full of electrical goods and furniture. One woman had looted three flat screen televisions.

"That's pretty stupid," George whispered to Bernard as the woman, who was sobbing, was led away. Tag was finally called. Bernard looked to the gallery of press who were drinking coffee out of paper cups and seemed disinterested in case 143. The Judge was tired and listened to the charge with his eyes closed. Bernard stood and waited for the word 'murder'. When it was announced, he felt the press prick up and the courtroom bristle with anticipation. George stole a glance at the gallery as Bernard outlined his defence in the hope of bail. The Judge listened, impassive to the speech, and then frowned. He read some notes on his desk and sighed. He looked at Tag, whose eye was puffed from a punch and who sported a split lip. Bernard waited on Judge Remillio's word, hoping for a miracle.

The Judicial system and the Police had other ideas and Tag was held on 'non-specified' charges. As he was led away back to the cells, he threw a look at the lawyers that no-one could mistake as friendly. George and Bernard went straight over to the court secretary and made an appointment with the presiding judge.

"Yet again, we wait," George said looking at his watch. "How can they just throw that into the mix? Non-specific charges. What the hell does that mean?"

Bernard shrugged his shoulders. "My guess is it is something to do with those new terrorism laws. Held for questioning and they don't have to say a thing. National Security crap."

"Crap is right. And all we can do is wait."

The Judiciary of Paris were overworked and the backlog of cases to be heard took all morning so George said, "I'll go back to the office and get on with things," then added, "I need to do something about this," he pointed to his hip. "We should try and keep up with our other work, even though Tag is taking precedence."

George left Bernard sitting on a wooden bench and began the three block walk to the car park. He fossicked for the keys. As he opened the Citroen door, he saw a motorbike with a rider waiting on the other side of the road. As he gazed at him, something clicked. He had seen a rider the other day at the office car park. Coincidence? He sat in his car and waited, watching for his tail to make a move. The rider sat still, his blinker flashing as if ready to move off. After a minute of the stalemate, George pulled out of the parking space and joined the traffic. The bike moved out.

George took all the major roads, watching the bike in his rear vision mirror. Just as was near to Montparnasse Railway station, he swerved and took a side street. He caught a glimpse of the bike as it tried to weave through the traffic and was stopped at a light. George thumped the steering wheel in victory, thinking he had outsmarted the tail, but the thought of someone following him was enough for George to begin to sweat.

"This is not a game. This is not a game," he repeated to himself to gather some courage. He pulled into his designated parking spot in the underground car park and sat in the car for about five minutes trying to compose himself. This wasn't a detective movie or James Bond, but real life. Nozette took a deep breath and walked quickly down the street to the office, watching for any suspicious behaviour. The door to the stairway and the relative safety of the office was only 300 metres from the car park, but to George it felt like a marathon. He broke into a trot and almost fell into the stairway. He took the stairs two at a time, then came up short as a gentleman was just beginning to descend.

"Excuse me, sorry," George said side-stepping onto the landing. "Did you come to see someone in particular?" The man took a step back and looked at George.

"I'm George Nozette, can I help you?" The man shifted his briefcase to his left hand and held out his right.

"Duval. Pierre Duval," Mr Duval said shaking George's hand. George tried to recollect a client with the name, but he came up blank.

"How can I help you, Mr Duval?"

"Well, Mr Nozette, it is more how I can help you," Duval said smiling and withdrawing his hand. The two men walked into the reception and Janelle looked up, surprised to see the stranger again. George ushered his visitor into his office, hurriedly cleared a seat, then indicated for him to sit.

"What's this about, Mr Duval?" He looked at the thick set stranger with close cropped hair. His whole demeanour seemed to be one of strength, but it was his eyes that made George look away. Duval's grey eyes bored into their subject, and George felt they could pluck at his very soul. He glanced at the floor and avoided direct contact.

"Have you ever heard of the N.A.T.A. Mr Nozette?" Duval said as he sat down. George shook his head and sat down behind his desk, wincing as his body reacted to the pain.

"We are an agency which protects." Duval adjusted his briefcase on his lap.

"Protects? What do you mean Mr Duval?"

"We have reason to believe," Duval went on, "that Nozette and Simeoni are in contact with some radical groups." George swallowed and bit his lip. It wasn't a pleasant interview. He tried to think on his feet, but it seemed Duval had done his homework.

"Radical?"

"Let's not play games, Mr Nozette. I think we both know what's meant by radical."

George shifted in his chair and picked up a pen. "And who did you say NATA was?"

"National Anti-Terrorism Agency."

"I've never heard of your agency, Mr Duval."

Duval smiled. "Are you surprised about that Mr Nozette?"

George tapped the pen on his desk, and spied his notes from the telephone conversation about Tag's fees. He casually moved his pen around and covered the scrawl on the post-it note.

"Well, I guess not. But..." George began.

Duval interrupted, "We will be in contact. If anything seems out of the ordinary, let me know." Duval handed over his card and George absently read the details.

"So you're looking for someone or something?"

"Not necessarily. Just doing my job, that's all. The Agency likes to tick all the boxes, Mr Nozette. It's as simple as that."

"And if I said, for instance, that I thought I was being followed," George said.

Duval smiled. "Well, we would reassure you that we probably know. And that, if you were being followed, you should think of it more in the nature of protection."

"So, what you are saying is that it was the NATA." George frowned.

"I'm not saying that at all. This is just your hypothetical, Mr Nozette isn't it?"

"Yes, yes, just a hypothetical."

Duval stood up. "Remember Mr Nozette, anything that isn't quite right. Anything at all." He shook George's hand and let himself out. George went to the kitchenette and reached for the whisky. Janelle interrupted him and he put the drink away, thinking to save it for when Bernard returned. He certainly had some interesting news to relate and they might just need a drink at the end of it.

"Mr Nozette, I am going to the post now. Is there anything you need?"

"No, nothing." George answered, and then thought he might warn Janelle to be careful. Of what he didn't quite know, but he felt he ought to say something.

"Just there and back Janelle. What with the paint bomb and everything else, we don't want to take any chances."

"Yes, right."

George was left alone. Duval's visit played on his mind, so he went to the window, and turning Duval's card over in his hand, watched Janelle walk down the street and into the car park. He scanned the street for suspicious characters, but chided himself that he wouldn't know a suspicious character if he tripped over one. He looked over to his desk and saw about half a dozen pressing jobs to be done. His computer had gone to screen saver and pictures of his children scrolled across the screen. He watched his family enjoying their holiday, then pressed resume. He decided to knuckle down over his bread and butter cases and put Tag on hold.

He was bent over his desk, when he heard the outer office door open.

"Janelle?" There was no answer. George walked over to his door and then thought better of opening it straight away. He grabbed an umbrella and then flung the door open, to see Bernard flicking through the post.

"What's that?" Bernard asked. George put his umbrella down and breathed a sigh of relief.

"I thought it was..."

"What?"

"Nothing, I'll explain it all later. Where's Janelle?"

"I met her on the stairs, hence the post. She went to the bathroom. What's up with you, George?"

"Look, I..." George started. "Come into my office, we need to talk about Tag."

"You are right on that one. We really do need to talk, George. I..." Bernard started, then stopped as George held up his hand. He went to the stairs, looked out, and then beckoned Bernard. They walked into his office and George shut the door.

"What the hell is the matter with you?"

"Bernard, we are involved in something big." George related the conversation he had had with Duval and its ambiguous nature. "And he was most insistent that we should tell him if we notice anything that might be out of the ordinary. You know; anything that doesn't seem right."

"Well we haven't, have we?" Bernard could see George was on edge.

"Well, not exactly, but I thought I was being followed this morning. A rider on a motorbike. And I said as much to Duval." George filled Bernard in on the details. As much as the men wanted to see Tag get a fair deal, the trouble he was causing, the publicity that the firm gained and now the NATA's involvement all transpired to put the men on edge.

"So what's on the court front? What is that non-specific?"

George's question made Bernard raise his eyebrow. He explained that the non-specific was as he thought. It was grounds to keep Tag under lock and key so he could help them with inquiries regarding national security.

"National bloody Security. What the hell is that?"

"They don't have to say.

"And who is 'they'?" George asked.

Bernard shrugged his shoulders. "All top secret stuff. They won't say and I am not allowed to ask. It's as if a steel trapdoor has shut and Tag is on the other side. They said I could have an interview if I submit to their criteria."

"And that is?" George's anger was rising.

"It will be recorded."

"What? How can they do that? We have a privilege. They know that."

Bernard went on to point out that, if someone is held under the anti-terrorism laws they can just disappear off the radar.

"Like that." Bernard clicked his fingers.

"What the fuck?"

Bernard nodded at George. "Exactly George. What the fuck?"

***

The afternoon was a mishmash of questions and legal wrangling. The lawyers had never been on the sharp end of the new terrorist act that was passed surreptitiously. The public had heard of the debate but it was couched in terms that made it clear it was going though, no matter who the detractors. And with phrases like 'for the good of the nation' and 'the safety of the French way of life', no one would have dared argue with its sweeping measures and its blanket of secrecy. The attack of 9/11 gave Governments the mandate they needed to erode civil liberties and the power to control the populous.

Now Nozette and Simeoni felt they were up against something phantom-like, and it didn't feel right. They tried to keep their other cases current, but Tag seemed to take their collective energy and suck their drive, making work difficult. As the afternoon wore on, the turbidity of the air finally ground any real work to a halt.

Bernard walked into George's office and seeing he wasn't doing anything productive, he asked,

"Shall we call a hiatus on the other cases? I have nothing pressing for the next week anyway. I won't be able to get anything done with this Tag case hanging over me."

George looked at Bernard and sat back pushing the papers on his desk away from him.

"I know what you mean. I can't get past the fact that this has blown up in our faces. If we are on the back foot on this one, can you imagine how Tag must be feeling?" George proceeded to list the obstacles in their way.

"1. We have a man who the police want as their man. Whether he is guilty or not seems immaterial to them. 2. We have an eye witness, who we think didn't see anything, and

35

again the police will say he did. 3. We have the media breathing down our necks," and here George shook his head and added, "which I particularly don't like, and 4. Our client is a self-confessed anti-Semitic and doesn't know he is being represented by two Jewish lawyers. So in my estimation we are just about up shit creek. What do you think?"

Bernard laughed. If there was a funny side to it, George failed to see it.

"That's about the size of it. But don't forget the NATA. They really are the big boys in all this. That Mr Duval, if that was his name. Who is he really representing? His own interests, our interests, or …?"

"Exactly." George sat back and swung around in his chair.

"They did a good job on the window. But you know what?" Bernard shook his head. "As the guy was cleaning, I suddenly thought that it all might be a ruse. You know; the paint was only a ploy so that someone could get close and plant a listening devise or something. That's how paranoid I am now," George said.

"Well, I guess it could be a possibility. I wondered if that figure I saw across the road was someone looking in on us. It makes you jumpy as hell, doesn't it?" The men remained silent each thinking of the endless possibilities in the situation. Suddenly, George jumped up and strode to the window.

"Did you see that?"

"What?" Bernard followed him to look out to the street.

"Over there, a figure, in the window opposite. I saw someone with a camera." The men looked out at the street and the building. Straining to see something, they let their imaginations run loose.

"Look, I think we need to get our act together. We have to think laterally in all this."

"Laterally? What the hell is that?" George asked. Bernard frowned as he peered across the street.

"Well, we have to think of what might happen and take steps so it doesn't."

"Meaning?" George peered out the window and squinted.

"Well, think of the worst case scenario." Bernard said.

"Worst case scenario. Well, we die."

"Or, we get found out as two Jewish lawyers defending a Neo-Nazi supporter. We would be finished. Kaput." Bernard drew his finger across his neck. "So we have to stop that from happening before it starts. And…"

"Easier said than done. What else. Hang on. What about being spied upon? Should we limit their access?"

"Now you're talking." George pulled down the blind in his office and then they walked to Bernard's office and did the same. The men decided they needed to make themselves less of a target. To that end, they created an elaborate plan to leave at staggered intervals and not to park in their underground spaces for the foreseeable future.

"And how do we keep our Jewishness a secret?" Bernard asked.

"We never mention it. We don't draw attention to ourselves, or our families. No-one really cared before, and so realistically, why should they care now?" It seemed logical and so they felt they had done all they could to limit their vulnerability, and packed up for the night.

As they were walking down the stairs, there was a thud on the outer door and both men stopped.

"What was that?" Bernard asked. They waited for some moments and then crept to the door and listened. Nothing. Gently Bernard opened it and saw what had made the noise. Someone had spray painted a Swastika on the door in black paint, and thrown the spray paint can when the deed was done.

"So now it begins," Bernard said. "They know." Who exactly 'they' were, the men were not quite sure. But with this flagrant act, the firm of Nozette and Simeoni were definitely on the map. They cleaned up the graffiti as best they could in the fading light of the evening and George said he would come early the next morning to check over the building. The less conspicuous they were the better. It would be a hard battle to keep the public arbitrators at bay. Leaving the car park at staggered intervals, the men drove home, each with more than a few concerns. They privately knew that this case would make or break the firm and hoped for the former over the latter. George took an extra-long route to his family home, checking all the time in his rear vision mirror, but everything in his heightened state seemed a threat and it was with great difficulty that his remained calm.

His house was in one of the new, better placed areas of Paris, quiet and middle class. The last thing the district needed was vigilantism. His wife and children were comfortable and respectable. He had worked hard to afford the suburban lifestyle. He felt a certain apprehension that they might be dragged into the maelstrom, and so he vowed to shield them from the uglier side of his work.

Bernard had married well. His career wife was from a wealthy family and they lived on the high end of modest. George often chided him that he should retire and be a kept man, but Bernard liked the work, and felt he should contribute to the marriage. As he drove into his apartment building car park, he took one look behind him. Paranoia took the place of common sense. His building had a gated entrance and only those with a code could go past the driveway gate. No-one could get him on the 4th floor, still, he had an uneasy feeling as he stepped into the lift and pressed the button. Gabrielle would not be home, he knew that. She was always late, working at her family business. He let himself into his apartment and saw the phone blinking a missed call. He pressed play and a hard, angry voice came on the line.

"You will fuckin' rot in hell. Nazi lover. Rot in hell." Bernard pressed off and shivered. To be assaulted in his own home made him feel even more vulnerable. He pulled out his mobile phone and rang George.

"So you got one too," George said. Audrea answered the phone and copped the abuse. We have to change our numbers. This thing is getting out of hand."

"That is an understatement. Did you ring the police?"

"Well… I was going to, and then I thought not."

"Ah, I see. And I'm guessing Mr Duval will not be on your list either."

"You got it, Bernard. I think we need to keep this vitriol to ourselves. I have told Audrea not to answer the phone. I'm even thinking of sending her and the kids away for a bit."

"That's a good idea. I might suggest the same to Gabrielle." They talked about the logistics of secrecy. It was agreed that the men should distance themselves from the authorities, and their families, until all this was finished, one way or the other.

CHAPTER FIVE

The morning dawned with a cold crisp feel to the air, and a heavy frost on the ground. George stood at his kitchen window and looked at the fine layer of frost, which was particularly clean and clear. His children would be waking up soon and the day would begin, but at this early hour, he had the house to himself and the quiet to think. He padded in his sock feet to the front door and opened it, expecting to see his paper. What he saw was a set of footprints. Footprints that walked around the house, stopped at the windows, and then disappeared on the concrete drive. George walked the few steps to the path and turned to view what the intruder had viewed. His bedroom window; his children's windows; and the lounge room. It was a violation that he would not put up with; whatever the cost. He ran inside and shut the door, then opened it again, grabbed the paper and slammed the front door. The noise woke the whole family. It was a frenetic morning as George arranged for his family to visit Audrea's mother and father in the Alps. He rang Bernard and explained the situation. Taking precautions, just in case his phone was being monitored, he decided he didn't need to get into details.

In an effort to thwart those who would harm Nozette and Simeoni, George took his Land Cruiser to the office, thinking that his second car might not be in their sights. The drive to work was the usual, a tedious affair of traffic snarls and endless waiting. This morning George was grateful for the long drive as it gave him time to think. He ruminated over the recent events and tried to get some logic into his apprehension. The traffic cleared within a five minute drive to Rue De Maine. George took one look over his shoulder, drove his Land Cruiser in record time, and parked in the firm's space. He waited a minute or two, then, when it was all clear, walked the block to the office. The outside of their modest building was clear of any signs of vigilantism, which George thought could only be a good sign. Perhaps, he mused, this thing was blowing over, and the anger metered out to the firm was at an end.

The morning routine was as always, and it was just after 9am when Bernard came in. He went straight to George's office.

"I swear the traffic is getting worse. And now I couldn't get a park in the car park. I had to park in the lane and you know what that means. Feeding the meter every 4 hours. God, I hate the city sometimes."

"Well, at least you arrived in one piece," George said.

Bernard walked over to the window and looked down at the lane and his parked car, then he turned to George and asked, "So, what did you decide to do with Audrea and the kids?"

"They are going to her family, in Bonneville. Straight down the freeway. The kids love it. There might even be a little snow. The weather is certainly turning. I'm sure they will be well out of it in the mountains." Bernard nodded and told George of their plans. Gabrielle and Bernard had agreed that she would live in her parent's apartment on the other side of Paris.

"They have security and she can still work." He shrugged his shoulders, knowing Gabrielle would not give up her work easily. George then asked Janelle for more coffee and began to explain the footprints outside his house. He countered his concern with his musings that they might have seen the last of the public reprobation as the office was clean when he arrived. Bernard wasn't quite sure.

Their next plan of action was to apply for another interview with Tag. Not that they needed any more to convince them of his anti-Semitic views, but they wanted to test the resolve of the NATA and the police department. George drafted up some questions he might ask Tag. Bernard thought that if he contacted Duval and said he wanted to meet him for a talk, he might be out of the way when the interview was taking place. So it was around midday when George, with his appointment confirmed, left for the police station and an hour later when Duval stepped into Bernard's office. Bernard stood up and the men shook hands.

"So nice to meet you, Mr Simeoni. Mr Nozette and you have a nice little business here." Duval smiled.

"Yes, we do well. Nothing too complicated really, just your run-of-the mill legal stuff."

Duval nodded and sat down.

"Coffee?"

"Why not."

Bernard asked Janelle to attend to their drinks.

"So, Mr Simeoni, what was it you wanted to discuss? Something worrying you?"

Bernard sat down behind his desk, put the tips of his fingers together, and drew breath.

"Well, Mr Duval, George, Mr Nozette, and I were wondering what..." Bernard looked at the NATA agent, "What powers exactly does your agency have in relation to our client? The Police have their anti-terrorism laws, which are all encompassing, but what is your role?" Bernard laced his fingers and laid them on his desk.

"Well, you are under a misapprehension Mr Simeoni. We are not interested in your client. He is... shall we say, just a pawn in the game. No Mr Simeoni, your client is not on our agenda."

"Who then?"

"Look, I am not at liberty to say. But I will tell you that things aren't as clear cut as you would suppose. There are players in the game who have a lot at stake. Players that cannot be named."

Bernard interjected. He was getting sick of the metaphors and began to get agitated, "You are talking in riddles. What the hell do you mean to come in here and spout all this game and players crap? If you are not interested in our client, then what do you want?"

"I'm sorry if I have offended you, Mr Simeoni. NATA is a security organisation. We follow subversive activity. Your man belongs to a group that interests us. That's all."

"What group… who?"

"I know you are not a stupid man, Mr Simeoni. I think you know what organisations we are talking about."

"The…" Bernard stumbled with the right words. "The Neo-Nazis?" Duval nodded.

Janelle brought in their coffee and the men relaxed a little. Bernard polished his glasses as he studied Duval. The agent wasn't tall, but he had a manner that made him seem big. He seemed very in control, and Bernard felt that every word he said would be stored and used later.

Duval missed nothing with his piercing stare. He finished his coffee and said, "Maybe they, the group, will contact you. If they do, we would like to know. That's all there is to it really."

"Well, why the hell didn't you say so in the first place? All that game rubbish is just that. Rubbish."

"Well, if you think of anything that might be of help, let me know." Duval stood up and walked to the door, and Bernard followed.

"Mr Simeoni," Janelle interrupted. "I need to go to the post office, but my car is in the garage."

"Take mine," Bernard said and he handed her the keys from his pocket, "it is in the lane, right on the corner. I couldn't get a park this morning. Some idiot was in the firm's space."

"Thank you, sir," Janelle said as she shouldered her handbag and walked down the stairs.

"A nice looking girl. Has she worked here long?"

"Yes, since the beginning. I don't know what we would do without her. A great value to the firm." Bernard watched her walk down the stairs and then indicated Duval should follow.

Duval had parked a few doors down from the office and so Bernard walked him to his car. The Audi stood out amongst the Fords, Citroens, and Japanese imports.

"An Audi TTS Coupé, very nice. I was hankering for one of these." Bernard bent down and looked inside.

Duval sat in the driver's seat and leaned over. "Get in and have a look," he said.

Bernard opened the passenger side door and sat down. He felt he deserved a car with this sort of power and styling.

"It is the new model. I've had it a week."

"Very nice, and the standard silver too," Bernard said running his hands over the leather interior. He looked down the street to his Peugeot 207 parked in the lane and watched as Janelle put the blinker on to pull out. A black Toyota Kluger SUV drove by, and there, right in front of his unbelieving eyes, his car was raked with automatic machine gun fire. The Kluger burnt rubber as its back wheels skidded to get traction, burst onto Rue de Maine and headed for the main road.

"What the...?" Bernard couldn't quite figure what had just happened. Then the truth dawned and the blood drained from his face as he thought of Janelle. He made to get out of the car when Duval turned on the engine and pulled out into the street, then did a skid U turn and ramming the Audi into gear gave chase to the SUV.

"What the hell, Janelle was in that car. Let me out you fucking idiot. My secretary was in that car."

"Shut up. Put your seat belt on."

"No, you have to let me out. Janelle was in my car." He tried to grab the steering wheel when Duval, in a lightening reaction, grabbed Bernard's wrist and twisted.

"Ow, get off me. You're a fucking maniac." Duval threw Bernard's arm down and took the wheel. Bernard leaned over and grabbed a fistful of Duval's jacket.

"That was my car." Then the words hit Bernard and he realized the gunfire was meant for him. He let go of Duval and closed his eyes then put his head in his hands.

"Oh, fuck," was all he could utter. He looked up as the Audi skidded around the end of Rue de Maine and into the traffic, the engine revving down the gears, as Duval drove after the Toyota. The black SUV forced its way through the lanes, trying to drop the Audi tail. Bernard now hung on as Duval followed, bluffing his way into the small spaces between the cars. The Kluger went from the inside lane to a right turn, creating a pile up. The Audi shot through a gap and followed, narrowly missing a pedestrian.

"What about Janelle?" Bernard shouted. "You bastard! What about Janelle?"

Duval fossicked in his coat pocket and threw a mobile phone at Bernard, "Ring." The car suddenly swung left.

"Shit, I dropped it." Bernard groped around. The car mounted a kerb and he hit his head on the dashboard. "Fuck," he said as he sat up and rubbed his head. He opened the iPhone and then tried to think who to ring.

"The police?" he shouted at Duval over the revving engine. Their car took a sharp left turn mirroring the SUV manoeuvrer into a one way street. The turbo screamed as Duval threw the gearbox into third and the rev counter needle hit 7000 rpm. The street ended abruptly in a 90 degree turn and the Toyota, with its wide turning circle, mounted the footpath. As it accelerated, it scraped its way along a brick wall. Bernard hung on to his seat belt as the Audi took the corner low in second. Then he heard the sirens.

"Ring this number." Duval dictated a number and Bernard tried to listen, "Who is this?" the voice on the other end asked.

"They want to know who it is," Bernard yelled over the engine.

"Jesus Simeoni, tell them."

"Duval," Bernard answered, then looked around at the sound of sirens and saw three police cars following.

"The Police." Bernard pointed to the back window.

"Hang on." Duval threw the Audi over a curb. The jolt made Bernard's glasses fly off. The SUV took the off-road conditions better than the low slung Audi. Duval hammered the engine and saw that the Toyota was heading for the overpass. He swung off the road. The police cars did the same. One of the police cars tried to match the speed of the Audi and pass, but Duval threw the wheel to the left and pushed the car into a railing. The Police Renault scraped along the fence and finished up wrapping its bonnet around a street lamp. Bernard tried to retrieve his glasses. He was thrown violently to the side of the car, as the Audi skidded to a halt, doing a 180 degree turn in the road. The second Renault tried to stop, but the sudden change in direction caught them and they swerved and hit a delivery van. The Renault rolled several times and Bernard thought he saw three or four other cars plough into the ensuing mess.

As the Audi sped away to take a side turn, Bernard looked up to see that they and the SUV would merge in seconds. He glanced at Duval who was concentrating and then realised he was still holding the phone. He tried to listen but the line was disconnected.

"They've hung up." He signalled the phone to Duval.

"Watch out!" Duval shouted, as he rammed the gears home and put the Audi one car behind the black Toyota.

"In the glove compartment," he said, swerving into the offside lane to get alongside the SUV. Bernard pulled open the compartment and saw a gun.

"Use it."

"What?"

"Fucking use it!" Duval shouted. Bernard took the PPK and squinted at the weapon.

"I...I don't know how. I haven't got my glasses." He tried to excuse himself of the task.

"Safety latch off." Duval took the gun and flicked the catch. He pushed it into Bernard's lap. "Grow some balls. Use it." Bernard took up the gun and Duval pushed the window button down as he threw the Audi into fourth and waited for an opening.

"Now!"

Bernard extended his arm and the gun was caught in the wind. It waved about. He grabbed it with his left hand and aimed at the Kruger.

"Now, for God's sake. Fire!"

Bernard pulled sharply on the trigger and let off a shot. It hit the side panel of the car. The sudden recoil made him drop the gun and it clattered down the road.

"Jesus," Bernard said as the Audi took an opening and came up next to the Toyota – a lane apart.

"Under the seat." Duval shouted over the wind and the turbo. Bernard lent forward and felt under his seat. A shot was fired at the Audi and Bernard sat up holding a semi-automatic Glock.

"What the..." Bernard nursed the gun as the Audi drew closer to its target. He looked over his shoulder at the last police car and then he heard a helicopter.

"They're firing on us." He swivelled around in his seat and tried to look up. Then he saw two police on BMW motorbikes coming from behind.

"Safety catch," Duval shouted. Bernard nodded and fiddled with the gun.

"Ready," he said. The Audi TTu coupe used its engine muscle and gained some ground on the SUV and Bernard waited for the cue.

"Now!"

He tried to aim and pulled the trigger. A spray of gunfire hit the car and the Toyota cannoned into a motorbike rider. It quickly recovered and pulled off at the next side street and they tried to follow, creating a car pileup, which blocked the police vehicle.

"They are heading for the tunnel. Christ."

"What, what's wrong?"

"The tunnel is no good. There are too many variables on the other side. Shit." Duval hit the steering wheel.

The Audi slammed down into second as it took a corner gaining on the SUV. The black car sped off into the tunnel approach with the Audi jumping lanes to catch up.

The traffic in the tunnel was moving fast but the SUV seemed to be able to weave through the gaps. By the time the incline began, signalling the exit, the Audi was too far behind. When they reached the other side, the SUV was gone in the merging traffic. Duval, for the second time, hit the steering wheel.

"Shit."

Bernard relaxed and started to breathe again. His heart was racing, the bump on his head throbbed, and he suddenly felt sick at the thought of Janelle. Duval breathed deeply and slowed the car to match the traffic conditions.

"What now?" Bernard asked. Duval ignored his question and when the first turnoff arrived, he swung off the road and found a park. After the frenetic drive, the two men sat still, each gradually coming down from an adrenalin rush. Bernard watched the traffic for a moment, then his emotions caught up with him, and he grabbed Duval's jacket collar.

"You fuckin' idiot." He wrenched the collar, pulling at the agent. "You're mad."

Duval grabbed his hand and twisted it into a painful hold. Bernard wanted to punch him. The wail of sirens caught his attention. Police cars appeared from all directions, screeching to a halt and surrounding the car. The Gendarmes tumbled out and pulled their weapons on the two men. Bernard opened the door, stepped out with his hands up, and was immediately tackled to the ground. His face was pushed to the road and a set of handcuff latched onto his wrists, which were pulled to his back. Duval slowly got out of the car holding his credentials in the air. One of the officers took the ID keeping his gun trained on the NATA agent. Another car pulled up and an officer stepped out.

"Restrain them," he said. Two officers grabbed Duval's arms and he was cuffed.

"Sir?" A Gendarme asked when Bernard and Duval were standing under guard.

"I want them under lock and key, you understand."

"Sir," the Gendarme answered, then marched the two men to a waiting Renault police car. Once in the car Bernard began to shake as the adrenalin high dissipated.

"Breathe deeply," Duval said. Bernard tried to take the advice and took gulping breaths until he calmed down.

"Look, don't say anything. Leave it to me. Do you understand?" Bernard nodded.

As the men were escorted into the police station, Bernard saw George leaving.

"George," he yelled.

Immediately, the officer thumped the butt of his gun into Bernard's back. "Quiet."

Bernard winced and walked on, not daring to look back. The men were led into the holding cell, their cuffs released, and then the iron door slammed shut.

"What now smart guy?" Bernard said rubbing his wrists.

"Oh, why don't you just fucking shut up?" Duval said. Bernard turned his back on the agent and closed his eyes.

Nothing happened for about an hour and then they heard voices and the door opened.

"Simeoni?"

"Yes." Bernard stood up.

"This way." Bernard gave Duval a withering stare and followed the officer through the corridors of cells to a flight of steps. They tramped up one floor. The officer stopped at an interview room.

"Through here."

"Thank you." The room was furnished with a table and two chairs and Bernard sat down. He waited; tidying himself and straightening his clothes, and presently Detective Inspector Pallis walked in and sat down.

"We have met before."

"Yes, I'm Bernard Simeoni. I was acting for my client."

"Ah, yes. Tag."

Bernard nodded and under stress went to polish his glasses only at the last minute remembering they were still in the Audi somewhere. "And how do you now come to be in a car creating havoc in the city?"

"Well..." Bernard began then stopped as Pallis' phone rang. The Detective Inspector stood up and walked out of the room to take the call. Bernard sat back and watched the officer left to guard him. He thought it might have been the same man who escorted him to Tag. He was thinking of striking up a conversation when the door opened.

"It seems," Pallis began as he re-joined Bernard, "It seems that you are free to go."

"What?" Bernard asked. He didn't know what was going on.

"Free. To. Go." Pallis said the words one at a time and Bernard noticed he wasn't happy with the events.

"But…"

"Merde! Just get out of here, now." Pallis opened the door and waited. Bernard walked out, and was led to the back entrance. As he stood wondering what to do next, Duval appeared.

"How did this happen?" Bernard asked. Duval smiled.

"Let's just call it spheres of influence."

"What the hell does that mean, spheres of influence? More riddles."

Duval shrugged his shoulders and pulled out a cigarette.

"Oh, just forget it," Bernard said getting angry with the way he was being treated. "I suppose I will read all about it tomorrow in the papers."

"I doubt it." Duval said as he lit up.

"What? We just carved up the city centre, had shots fired at us, and I lost a gun on the ring road, the police arrest us, and then for no apparent reason let us go, and you say it won't hit the papers."

"Yes."

Bernard stood dumbfounded as Duval dragged on his Gauloises. "I will be in touch Mr Simeoni." A car pulled up and he climbed inside. He leaned out of the window, "Salut," the agent said, then was driven away. Bernard stood on the footpath. He felt drained and incapable of a decision.

"Sir?"

"Yes," he answered to a woman officer.

"Would you like a taxi?"

The taxi dropped him off at the end of Rue de Maine. There was incident tape over the end of the street and the scene brought back the vision of his Peugeot riddled with bullet holes. Bernard walked up to a Gendarme and introduced himself. The Gendarme lifted the barrier and escorted him to a small group of men in front of his office street door.

"This is Mr Simeoni, Sir," the Gendarme said and then left.

Bernard started, "Is ... was there anyone who survived?" He swallowed and looked over to his Peugeot. "Anyone?" Bernard said.

The Sergeant in charge shook his head then looked over to the ambulance that had parked some way down the street. Bernard started walking towards the van. Each step seemed agonizingly slow as he passed the familiar shops he had seen a hundred times and not noticed. When he reached the ambulance, the ambulance officer looked over to the Sergeant. When he got the nod, he explained that the victim would have died instantly.

Bernard heard the words but nothing seemed to stick. He sat down on the back step of the vehicle and held his head in his hands. *How could this be happening?* he thought. *How could any of this be real? A few days ago, they were doing divorces and now this.* He sat still for a long time, the coffee the ambulance officer had brought to him going cold.

"Mr Simeoni?" Bernard looked up. "We suspect that the gun-fire was meant for you."

"Oh, brilliant deduction, Sergeant." Bernard's sarcasm hit the officer with its raw emotion.

"And," the sergeant went on, "we would like to know why you fled the scene."

"Fled, Fled," Bernard yelled. "I didn't just leave. I was..." and here Bernard stumbled. He didn't know if he should tell anyone about NATA and Duval. He didn't know if he should say anything at all. And when he thought about it, he didn't know if he would be believed if he did.

CHAPTER SIX

Bernard sat at his office desk and downed a second whiskey as George filled his own glass. The Sergeant watched the two men.

"If you would like, we can do this later." The sergeant stood at the door.

"Yes, later. We need to..." George looked at the reception, "we need to just sort a few things first. Oh, by the way, will you contact Janelle's family or..."

"We will take care of that, Sir. Anything else?"

"No, nothing. It's just such a shock, that's all. Thank you, Sergeant Renard," George said reading the officers name tag. The policeman let himself out and finally the men were alone. Bernard sat back and rubbed his face with his hands.

"I can't believe it. I just can't believe it, George."

"When I heard about it at the station I thought they had made a mistake. Nozette and Simeoni is a small law firm. Not this stuff. Not shootings, threats, and God knows what else." George sat down and looked at the floor.

"What have we got ourselves into?" Bernard asked. He went to polish his glasses and realised they were still missing.

"I lost my glasses. My spare pair is at home."

"Perhaps we should go home. There is nothing to do here just now, and I don't feel like doing anything anyway."

"George, do you think we should see Janelle's family. I mean later this evening. I feel we have to do something."

"She was from Rouen. No family here at all."

"I didn't even know." Bernard shook his head. "I didn't even know that much about her."

54

"Bernard, I know it's not the time, but do you want to know what Tag had to say."

"Go on." Bernard listened with his eyes shut. George related his interview with Tag, saying the police were trying to fabricate a case, but although Tag was at the demonstration, there was scant evidence that he was the murderer.

"And unless they find his boots, it is just one policeman with an obscured view because of blood on his visor against a number of people who saw Tag running through the crowd on the opposite side of the street."

Bernard looked up at his partner, "Do you think he killed Darlan?"

"Let's just say he looks like the type that could have. The police are really pushing this. The media are crying out for some sort of revenge. Tag doesn't have much going for him. And to make matters worse, it seems that if they can't get the murder up and running, they are going to shackle him with terrorist activities. One way or another, Tag is their man. But Bernard, you know me. I still think he deserves a fair trial."

Bernard nodded. The two men decided to go home and as Bernard's car had been impounded, George offered to drive him. The journey gave Bernard ample time to relive his car chase and George listened with an incredulous look.

"But, was it kind of exciting?"

"Well... I think I was too scared to enjoy it. That Duval is a skilled driver, but I wouldn't want to repeat it."

George pulled up at the security gate of Bernard's apartment and Bernard opened his door, "See you tomorrow George. And, be careful." He shut the door and swiped his card on the gate security. Once inside the compound, Bernard turned and watched George drive off, his Land Cruiser merging with the traffic. It was twilight when George finally pulled into his driveway. It was only when he was sitting down with a glass of red wine and a CD playing, that he finally relaxed. *Tomorrow would be a trying day,* he thought. Tag's future was decided on two options. Charge him with the murder or let him go. George really didn't have an idea what the police might do, but he knew whatever happened it would be a feast for the media. He poured himself a second glass and planned to ring his wife after a hot shower, but the day's events caught up with him and he fell asleep on the settee before his glass was half empty.

The office seemed empty as George went through his morning routine. He kept thinking yesterday was just a dream, or more like a nightmare, and Janelle would walk through the door. It was not to be, he told himself, and made his own coffee. He sat down and tried to concentrate on his work, but quickly gave it away and stood by the window watching the street come to life. Bernard's car had been towed away and the whole area cleaned, so no traces were left of the tragedy. He was standing at the window when Bernard came in and poured himself a coffee.

"Bernard, you're early," George said.

"Well, it was bound to happen one day, wasn't it?" The men laughed and then talked about the day ahead. Tag, they guessed, could only reasonably be held for 36 hours, even under the terrorism legislation, and his assault on Pallis wasn't due for weeks. The workload of the legal system was at breaking point. Cases were being deferred, others suspended, so Nozette and Simeoni would be put on a list like everyone else. George had submitted his summary for consideration and the Public Prosecutor's office had done the same. It was up to the Judge to decide if Tag had charges to answer.

"I'm not really hopeful. Although he was there, and there isn't any real evidence to say he was involved in the crime, they have their witness." Bernard pulled off his glasses and rubbed his eyes.

"I think we have a chance. They have to charge him, and I really don't think they will risk it unless they are damn sure, and I have a hunch they don't have anything substantial at all."

"I hope you're right, Bernard, I just hope you're right."

Number three court was closed to the public as the two lawyers walked to their seats. They had seen the Judge was one of the hard-liners on crime. Judge Venier took his seat in the committal proceedings. The court asked the public council several questions and they were answered with the same arguments Nozette and Simeoni had heard before. Then they in turn were asked if they had a case to answer. George answered all the questions trying to allude to Tag's inalienable human rights, and the spurious non-specified charge. He finished and sat down, pulling on his moustache.

"I have considered this matter before the court and..." Bernard and George heard the words, and knew only a miracle or a bargain with the devil would get Tag out of trouble. The case was put on the list and then the Prosecution asked that Tag be kept in custody. George didn't object, knowing Tag was safer inside the system than out.

As Judge Venier shuffled his papers, the clerk handed him a note. He seemed to take a long time to read the small scrap of paper. Then he scrunched it in his hand and took a long breath.

"Bail is granted at 100,000 Euros." Bernard looked at George and frowned. He was about to whisper to his partner when the Judge stood up and left. They watched him leave and the Public Prosecutor hurry after him.

"What was all that about?" Bernard asked as he closed his briefcase. George shrugged his shoulders.

"I have no idea." Then he spied the screwed up piece of paper on the floor near the Judge's chair. He walked over and smoothed out the scrap of yellow paper. Bernard looked over his shoulder,

"What does it say?" George read the cryptic note. *Let the dog run. R.*

"Who is running this show George? Who is R?" George looked up trying to think of anyone higher up that might just call the shots to a Judge.

"I don't know, Bernard. I can't even begin to imagine." The more pressing question George wanted to know the answer to was who was going to put up the surety for Tag.

"Well, if he hasn't the percentage then he will have to stay." Bernard still thought Tag being behind lock and key was the best solution.

"But he does have the funds. I only have to make a phone call and his benefactor will step in." Bernard looked hard at George. The last thing he wanted or needed was an association that might stir NATA into action.

"Well, we should go and tell our client the news. Perhaps he might have a bank account. And if 'R' wants him to run, well maybe, George, we shouldn't rock the boat."

It was decided that they would go together to break the news. So around two in the afternoon, they confronted Tag in the visitor's room at the gaol and explained the situation, leaving out the salient point regarding the standover tactics of the mysterious 'R'.

Tag sat back in his chair and drummed his fingers on the plastic table. He looked pleased and as his eyes darted from one lawyer to the other. He ran his tongue over his teeth with a smirk.

"So we were wondering if you have any funds, Heinz?"

"Not me, but it will come."

"Who?" Bernard asked leaning a little closer.

"Who do you fuckin' think." Tag's vitriol startled Bernard and he fell back in his seat. "Ring this number." Tag said and then rolled over his forearm to reveal a tattooed number on the inside of his elbow. George copied the number down on

58

a post-it note and wondered at a man who carries a telephone number tattooed on his arm.

"If this person can deposit the percentage by the end of the day, Heinz, you will be out of here," George said, glancing at the white walls and the wire mesh over the doors and windows. He then went on to explain the procedure for trial and the number of interviews they might need, the witnesses, the accomplices and other evidence when Tag put his hand up to stop.

"You think this is a game? The world will be watching. I will tell the truth to the world. I am a soldier in the war."

"What war, Heinz?" Bernard asked.

Tag stood up and yelled, "The war against the Jews. The war against the Muslims. The war against the fuckin' world." A guard appeared, and with a quick jab with his baton, Tag was pulled away and out the door.

"What just happened in there?" Bernard asked as they walked across the car park.

"It's a showcase. We will be complicit in a showcase of racial hatred. And the world will be watching." George stopped as he went to put the key in the door. "Bernard, the entire world will be watching."

CHAPTER SEVEN

Money appeared after the firm made the call. George looked over the application document and read the guarantor name.

"Dietrich Technologies." He recalled the brief conversation on the phone to someone who was willing to put up the bail.

"Do not hesitate to contact us," the voice said, and "You have our resources at your disposal." Was it an invitation, George pondered, to align the firm with their ideals, or Tag's ideals? Bernard said it felt like bad money, and they wondered, not for the first time, who was calling the shots. The thought of double dealing and the NATA or 'R' putting up bail to see where Tag would lead them, crossed Bernard's mind, and so it seemed prudent to say nothing, and listen to everything.

Somehow, the press had found out about Tag's release and George jostled with the small crowd to find a parking spot.

Tag was escorted to the front gate of the gaol and George hailed him as the press moved in with cameras and microphones, "Do you want a lift Heinz?" George escorted Tag over to his waiting car. Tag was still wearing his same clothes from his interview. With his piercings re-installed on his face, he was a menacing figure.

"Yeah," he said.

"Don't give them anything Heinz. Nothing," George warned.

A cameraman tried to walk in front of the pair and tripped over in the scrum. He fell heavily as others stepped over him to get a word or a picture. Tag stopped walking and punched the air with a cynical smile on his face. '*It was the picture that defined the man and all he stood for*', the papers later reported. '*A portrait of racism*'. The press pack scrambled after the couple until George pulled away in his car, and joining the ring road, headed into the city.

"Where do you want to go?" George asked.

Tag's paperwork had indicated an address on the other side of the city, but George doubted very much if that was their destination.

"Gare de Nord," Tag replied, and then he settled into the passenger seat, and looked out the window, signalling the end of the conversation. It was at least an hour drive through the traffic when the Land Cruiser finally pulled up at the train station.

"Tag," George started, "don't do anything stupid, and..." George looked at Heinz, "We have to know where you are, it's a requirement. You wouldn't want your guarantor to lose that money, would you?"

Tag sniffed and gave George a cold hard stare. "Fuck you."

George watched him swagger across the concourse and he was soon swallowed up in the human traffic. It was if the man had a death wish. He couldn't imagine what Tag was thinking about his appearance in court. He wondered if he thought much of anything at all, when his vocabulary was so limited. The Land Cruiser pulled out into the traffic and a small Renault followed its lead, and didn't give up until George had pulled into his underground parking space and cut the engine.

"So, how did it go?" Bernard asked as he met George in reception.

"The press were there. We will be on the news I expect."

"Did Tag behave himself?" George related the incident and voiced his doubts as to Tag's mental stability. Bernard nodded in agreement. Then they heard the outer door open and footfalls on the stairs.

The frosted glass door to reception opened and Duval smiled. "Good afternoon gentlemen."

George and Bernard exchanged a look.

"What is it you want from us now?" Bernard asked. Duval shifted out of the doorway. George asked if they all might retire to his office.

"Well, we have some questions that need answers," Duval said.

Bernard sat down heavily in the only spare chair and did not try to hide his contempt for Duval. "Questions? Well we have a few questions of our own, don't we, George?"

George swung lazily in his chair and pulled on his moustache. "You first, Mr Duval."

"Where is Tag?"

George explained that all Tag's documents were in order and his known address was on those documents. Where he was at this precise time was anyone's guess. "Having coffee or a hot shower I would suppose."

Duval walked to the window and looked down on the street.

"And this Dietrich Technologies, who did you speak to?"

George swivelled around to face the agent. "A Mr Dietrich."

"Ah, yes, Mr Dietrich." Duval turned and faced the two men, "Have you heard of the FFZ?"

Bernard shook his head and George said, "No."

"The Freedom Fighters for Zion. They are..." Duval hesitated then leant on the window sill. "They are a group of radicals. A well organised group of radicals that have, we believe, powerful backing."

"From who?" Bernard asked.

"That is not important. What is important is that the FFZ want your Tag. They want to stop him and his kind. They want to ..." He looked at Bernard and continued, "To stop anyone who has an interest in Tag and his Neo-Nazis." Duval let the words sink in.

"What do you mean by stop?"

"Eliminate anything or anyone." The room fell silent as Duval's words left a pall of dread in the air.

"Are you offering us protection, Mr Duval?" George asked.

"Let's just say I am offering you an opportunity. We, NATA, want to gather information. You may be able to assist."

Bernard stood up as he put two and two together and came up with six. "Bait, he wants us as bait." Bernard threw the accusation at the NATA agent.

"Well, Mr Duval. Is that what you are suggesting?"

Duval then indicated that they would be watching the lawyers and that NATA would monitor their movements, and he personally would guarantee their safety.

"And where were you when our secretary was shot? Where was your safety net then?" Bernard stood up and faced the agent. "If this FFZ can shoot Janelle in the middle of the day, on a busy street, I don't like your chances Mr Duval."

"Forget about her, she was nothing."

Bernard counted the dismissal, "Nothing! Nothing to you maybe, but she was our colleague, our friend. You come in here, telling us we are targets then dismiss our secretary as collateral damage. And you want us to trust you. I don't think so."

George stood, signalling the end of the interview and Duval walked to the door.

"Remember gentlemen, I may be the only ally you have." He left the office and the men waited until they heard the outer door close.

"Bloody NATA. I wouldn't trust him George. He has too much influence. Too many agendas and we really don't know too much about him other than he drives like a maniac and has two automatic weapons in his car. For God's sake, who drives with automatic weapons under the seat?"

George perched on the edge of his desk, "Perhaps we should do a little checking. I know the clerk downtown. He might be able to verify something."

"George, this is NATA. They don't even divulge their own birthday to their mother. I don't like it, but I guess … well, what choice do we have, although I'm not happy about it." George looked through his open door to the empty seat in reception and thought Bernard was right, they needed an ally, but Duval and his callous attitude was the last one he would have chosen.

Bernard went to work on the computer. He reasoned if the FFZ were as all powerful as NATA supposed, then they might have some sort of legitimate front. He pressed search on Google and came up with a page of hits. Trawling through the list, he finally came to something that sounded like it had all the right connections. The FFZ consisted of a hierarchy with military commanders. Their slogan of 'We will never lie down again' sounded like jingoistic rubbish, but if it was put in the context of Jewish freedom fighters then all the speeches on the site began to make sense. George read their aims and objectives with interest, and the more he read the more he thought the FFZ were in Duval's words 'a radical organisation'. Who was funding them was a mystery and the web site stopped short of asking for donations, but if Bernard knew anything about Jews, he knew they loved a good cause.

The men gathered in front of the television in George's office for the evening news and watched Tag's performance.

The newsreader seemed to know all the details, the possible trial date, the defence, the price of bail and then there was an interview with a psychologist and other experts.

"They are trotting out everyone. I doubt if we will actually get a jury by the time this media circus is finished." Bernard sat back in his chair and sipped a whisky. Every channel had the same news and the same views.

"Imagine what it will be like at trial." George stood and turned the television off. "Tag will get his audience all right. I'm just not sure if he will get his message across."

"I just hope the court questions him so that he doesn't get a chance." Bernard said. The men sat silent, listening to the evening rain and then George stood up to leave.

"Well, I guess we had better call it a night Bernard. I'm going to see the family at…" Bernard held up his hand to stop George. He pointed to his ear and then indicated George should say no more. It would have seemed improbable, just a short time ago, that they might be bugged, but now it was a threat they considered real.

"Well, I'll be gone for the weekend. If anything happens, well, just give me a ring, Bernard." George thought for a moment and then added, "Just ring me anyway. Shall we say at 6pm both days?" Bernard nodded and they packed up their things and left the building together.

"Do you want a lift?" George asked as they stood under the awning out of the rain. Bernard shook his head.

"I have taxi card. It will go on expenses." He rang the taxi number and watched as George ran the few metres to the car park. It was dark and cold as Bernard waited the few minutes for his ride. He paced up and down under the veranda when a light caught his eye in the building opposite. He stopped walking and looked up to see a figure in the window. The dark shadow stood still, maybe watching, Bernard thought, and so he stepped back next to the wall in the dark and waited. He hoped it was NATA. He thought back to the figure he had seen before and tried to fathom the timeline. Was it before or after he met Duval? He convinced himself it was before and tried to be rational about the revelation. He took another look at the window. The light went out just as his taxi pulled around the corner. Bernard stepped into the light of the street lamp and hailed his ride. He had the whole weekend ahead of him to figure things out. Being methodical, he knew if he put everything down, the possibilities, the facts, the timeline and the people involved things might be a little clearer.

It was still raining when the taxi pulled up to his apartment. Bernard ran the few metres to the security gate and then once under the gatehouse portico, swiped his card. He waited for the latch to release when he felt someone behind him. Quickly, he turned around, and was confronted by a very wet man.

"Can I help you?" Bernard asked.

"I'm just waiting for my friend to come out. Apartment fifteen."

Bernard had let the latch lock again and so re-swiped his card. The gate once again opened and he stepped inside.

"Well at least it is dry under here." He opened his post box and picked out his letters not noticing the man watching. He dashed to the foyer and was soon in his apartment pouring himself a wine and looking for something to eat. It was only later, when he was reading his mail, he realised that apartment fifteen was empty. It hadn't been let for some time. Bernard thought of the wet man. He wouldn't be able to describe him – it was dark. His voice was nothing of note, and then Bernard thought about what he might be doing in the portico. It only took a moment to realise that the man was waiting for him. Waiting possibly, to see where he lived, and to verify if he was at home. It was a theory that seemed not only credible, but frighteningly real to Bernard. He went to call George but knew that he would still be in traffic. The suburbs might have space but the commute was horrendous, especially on a Friday. So with nothing to do but wait, Bernard closed the blinds and called his wife on Skype. She was staying with her parents and Bernard knew they'd be eating fashionably late. He put through a call and waited. It wasn't long before Gabrielle came on the line and he began to tell her about his day. She had seen the news and was fearful of Bernard's safety.

"Look, I just think you need to say there for a few days, maybe even a couple of weeks. These things can get really ugly. I think I'm under surveillance and..." Bernard didn't quite know how to say that his life, according to Duval, was in danger. He skipped over the threats, then his wife said she had had a call from his mother.

"What did she want?"

"Bernard," Gabrielle began, "she wants you to go over. She is having an operation and she feels it won't go well."

"What? What sort of operation? The last time I visited in Israel she was fine."

"Bernard, call her, she will explain everything." Gabrielle said.

It was too late to call, Bernard thought, *and if it was urgent, then she would call back.* He promised himself he would find out all about it tomorrow. It didn't occur to Bernard that a trip to Israel might show his true colours, and the world might come to know he was Jewish.

***

George pulled into his driveway just as the rain stopped. He had toyed with the idea of driving through the night to visit his family, but decided that it was too wet and wild for driving in the mountains. He busied himself with packing a small bag and then tried to go to sleep. It wasn't going to happen, and so he threw his bag into the Land Rover around midnight and started the long drive. Once on the freeway, he engaged the cruise control and the kilometres flew by. George forgot his dilemmas and concentrated on seeing his family. He didn't think to look behind him as he turned off for the climb to Bonneville. The Citroen, which had been following him since Paris, pulled back at a discreet distance as George took the familiar roads. Audrea's parents lived on a farming block at the foot of the mountains and as George drove up the winding road, he imagined the surprised look on his wife's face. The mountains looked spectacular in the moonlight. They had had the first falls of snow just the week before and George thought they looked almost new. He turned into the steep driveway and then pulled into the patch of dirt near the garage, the wheels crunching on the frosty ground, and cut the engine. The Citroen stayed back, it's headlights off, as George walked around the back of the house and let himself in. He had spent nearly every winter at his in-laws and knew the house well. He tiptoed to the bedroom and slipped inside, then sat on the side of the bed to look at his wife sleeping. Audrea opened her eyes in fright, and then smiled as she recognised her husband. It only took a moment for George to undress and sidle up to his wife in bed. He caressed her back and then her breasts, rubbing his hands over her nipples as she snuggled into his body. The goose doona wrapped itself around their bodies as George made love to his wife in the early morning. She wrapped her arms around his back pulling him closer and George responded, biting her neck as he became fully aroused. Their bodies heaved under the quilt in orgasm and then they lay still.

The weak morning sun cast a pale light on the doona as George and Audrea slept. Their door flew open and two boisterous children ran in and jumped on the bed, surprised at finding their papa. George knew it was the right decision to visit his family. It was only when he went to collect more firewood from the outer shed and saw, through the trees, a car parked down the road, that he questioned that decision. He gathered the wood in the barrow and made his way back to the house, thinking he would fetch the binoculars and walk to the knoll higher up, before the car disappeared.

"Where are you going?" Audrea asked as she cleared the breakfast dishes away.

"Just out for a walk. Nowhere in particular," George said.

"Take the kids with you then."

"No!" George said, startling his wife. "They need to stay here."

"George?"

"It's nothing, really. I just want to take a look at something." He put on his hiking boots and jacket and began the short climb to the outcrop at the back of the house. Once in position, he looked through the binoculars and found the car. The occupant was watching the house. George noted the number plate and thought he would tell Duval on Monday. He climbed down trying to think of a way to get rid of the spy. Audrea's father was a hunter and George had seen a shotgun in his study. He felt he needed insurance for his family and so he went in search of the gun. He was loading it when his father-in-law interrupted him.

"What is all this?"

"Look Franc, I can't explain too much, but some stuff has been happening at work. We have a case which is... difficult. There are people who don't want us to take it on."

"I see. And a gun will stop them?"

"Well, no. But I just want to be prepared. I think they followed me here." Franc took the gun from George.

"I will go. Where are they?"

"I don't want to get you involved Franc."

"It seems you already have. They are here."

George looked out of the study window, but the copse of trees blocked his view.

"On the road, just down from the woodshed. Be careful. These are desperate people, Franc. Just tell them to go." George watched Franc walk out of the study and then ran to the upstairs window for a better view of the confrontation. He saw Franc talking to the occupant of the car and then the car reversed down the road to a passing point, turned, and drove away.

"He was a police officer," Franc told George as they met in the kitchen, "From the bureau."

"The Bureau of what?"

Franc shrugged his shoulders. "I don't know. Perhaps you had better sit down, George, and tell us everything. We cannot help you if we do not know." George felt he should respect Tag's client privilege. He had never discussed his work with Audrea's parents and they never asked. He sized up his options and realised that it was only fair they should know, as his visit made them unwitting targets. He asked Claudine and Franc to sit down and began. Audrea listened in while making coffee.

"So you see," George ended, "We really didn't have a choice."

Franc reared up from his seat. "How can you? How can you?'" he yelled. "You are a disgrace to your faith. Don't you think being a Jew means anything?" Claudine pulled at her husband's arm, but Franc threw her off. "You, a Jew, defending that... that monster." He stood still, the veins in his neck standing out, as he tried to control his anger.

"Doesn't every man deserve justice, Franc? Doesn't that mean something in this world?"

"Justice. You talk of justice. Claudine's family... where was their justice at the hands of the very same people. There will be no justice for them." Claudine pulled a tissue from her sleeve and wiped her eyes.

"Papa. Please," Audrea pleaded.

"And you." He rounded on his daughter. "Did you know of this? What of your faith? Have we taught you nothing?" Franc banged his fist on the kitchen table and Audrea jumped.

"Get out. Get out of my house," he shouted at George.

"I thought we were finished with this hatred. I thought the world had become more civilized." George said.

"Tell that to your friend. His kind will always despise us."

"And it works both ways, Franc."

"Get out."

"Papa." Audrea grabbed George's arm. "George, say something."

"He has said enough already. He is not welcome in my house." Franc spat on the kitchen floor and strode out of the room.

"I'm going." George snarled and pulled away from his wife. "You stay here Audrea, with the children; it's not safe in the city."

Audrea stood, stunned at the anger, and watched her husband leave. George gathered his bags and his skis, said a quick goodbye to his children, who were playing with the chickens, and left. As he drove down the drive, he saw Franc standing like a sentinel on the front porch and his anger welled up again. He put his foot down and spun the wheels on the light covering of snow and drove down the mountain road as fast as he dared, muttering to himself, trying to vindicate his position.

He cursed the whole situation and as he came to the junction in the road, "To hell with them," he said and turned left to the ski slopes. He always liked to ski. Audrea and he met on the slopes, and in his mood, he knew the invigorating exercise could only be cathartic. The Land Cruiser took the mountain road with ease and as George pulled into the parking bay, he looked up to see a good covering of snow on one of his favourite runs.

His anger melted away as he strapped on his boots and zipped up his jacket. Franc would come around, he felt sure. He took the vehicular train to the top. The run wasn't too crowded as the season had just started, and school holidays weren't for another week, so George could see a good line right to the first ridge. He breathed deeply, snapped on his goggles, and pushed off. It was as if a switch had been snapped in his brain and he forgot what was waiting for him in Paris. He skied with skill and an athleticism that seemed effortless. The powder snow was perfect as he flew down the mountain.

At the ridge, a large tree had been felled to warn of a rock fall and George swung around the obstacle and stopped. He looked at the next run. It was empty and a bit patchy this early in the year, but just on the edge of the tree line, the snow seemed a little deeper. He went to push off when something whizzed by his shoulder and thwacked into the fallen tree. George turned and looked up the mountain, but the sun was in his eyes, and the glare made it impossible to see anything with any detail. He pushed off; heading for the tree-line, then saw a figure in the trees. Instinct told him that this wasn't a coincidence. As he glided down the hillside, the figure followed, keeping to the cover. George kept his eye on the character, and then lost him in the thicket. A bullet kicked up the snow about a metre from his ski and George sprang into action.

"Shit." He crouched low and looked around for an exit. He zigzagged across the slope to put some distance between himself and his assassin. Some trees on the other side of the run afforded cover and George made the choice to run for it. The snow was lumpy at this altitude and he used all his skill to keep upright. A quick glance back saw a dark figure in pursuit. His attacker had the advantage of cross country skis, and George knew this would give an edge, so he hunkered down and dug his stocks in, while he looked for a good path to follow.

The terrain had big snow drifts in places and George hit one at speed, ploughed into the bank, and fell. Lying in the snow, he wondered if it all was just a bad dream. *How could this be happening?* he thought He chanced a look and saw his assailant. George watched as the person stopped and pulled a rifle from their shoulder and took aim. He needed to move, fast. With a sideways slide he extricated himself and crouched, then in one movement, he poled himself headfirst down the slope.

The speed was tremendous as he crouched against the wind, trying to put some distance between his assassin and himself. With the trees just metres away he made a final push and slew to a halt behind a big fir. He couldn't see the gunman. His heart was beating fast and his breath came in short gasps, as he watched the slope.

Time was elastic as he stood still straining to see anything that might give him a clue as to their position. Then, he saw it – a skier gliding low across the last bit of open snow to his copse of trees. *It was make or break,* George thought, and so, while he still had some advantage of distance, he made the decision to go. The trees were quite close together and George concentrated hard to slalom between them. He looked back. The other skier was in hot pursuit. Once he found George's tracks, he traced them with ease. George looked back once more, then made a push for the nursery slopes. When the kiosk was about fifty metres away, he glanced over his shoulder and saw his assailant fall.

The skier tumbled over, his poles flaying about, and then one of his skis snapped and he lay still. George stopped and watched. The man didn't move. He retraced his run and found the man face down in the snow, a growing patch of red seeping from his side. He had been shot. George turned quickly and powered through the trees not daring to think about the other shooter. The gentle descent on the end of the run made him push harder to reach the kiosk.

The crowds were thin, but enough safety for George to mingle as he made his way to the car park pulling his hat and jacket off along the way. Then with a glance back, and feeling confident that he was relatively safe, he strapped his skis on the roof rack and jumped in the car. He shoved it into gear and sped out of the car park and down the road.

It wasn't until he reached the town centre that he began to shake. The enormity of the situation caught up with him. He pulled over to the side of the road and sat still, trying to come to terms with the feeling that someone was trying to assassinate him. After about ten minutes, he had regained his composure and headed for a roadhouse. The coffee was average, but its warming effect helped George to calm down. A second cup and George was ready to begin the drive back to Paris. He pulled into the traffic and looked behind him, just in case. All was clear, and feeling satisfied that he wasn't being followed; he drove at a leisurely pace. He made plans on the trip, the first being to see Duval and explain that he and Bernard needed some sort of visible protection. How receptive Mr Duval would be to the suggestions George didn't know, but he would insist.

There were road works holding up the traffic and as George waited, he hunted around for some food in the car. His children sometimes had muesli bars or chocolate. He swivelled around to the back seat and then looked up to see a black Mercedes about five or six cars back. Why he thought it was sinister he couldn't say, but he felt sick with apprehension. The light turned green and he sped through the road works, and past a sharp bend, then took the first right up a steep incline.

The road was narrow but in good condition. George followed the twists and turns and came to a junction. He took a quick look behind, and finding it was clear, he turned on the GPS and surveyed his options. Left, the road began snaking its way over the top; right, the road went back down to the one he had just left. He quickly looked at the fuel gauge and judging he had plenty, he swung left and climbed.

The road had magnificent views of the mountains. In happier times, he would have loved to stop and admire the scenery, but now he looked down and saw the unmistakable black car coming up the road. The GPS advised the conditions could be treacherous, with ice in the winter months, and so George engaged the 4WD and prayed the sun still had some warmth. He slowed for a hairpin corner and then saw the Mercedes just one bend away. Forgetting his caution, he floored the Land Cruiser and shot up the steep incline, the engine screamed as it tried to wring all the power it could from second gear. George looked in the rear vision mirror. The other car was gaining. He studied the GPS. A turning showed after the next bend. He took it, sliding his back wheels on the loose gravel. The road went down rapidly.

The Land Cruiser wasted no time in covering the distance to the small bridge over a ravine. George turned to see the car flying down the road after him. He pushed the gears to their limit to get up speed. The Mercedes caught up and bumped his back fender. The jolt made the Land Cruiser skid to the side of the road and knock over several snow poles. George had regained control when he was hit again. He grabbed the wheel, his knuckles white with the effort, and swore. The Rover wouldn't go any faster as the road began to climb. The menacing black car hit him again and then the Cruiser seemed to drag. George tried to change down the gears. Nothing was responding. He realised that the

Mercedes must be caught on his tow bar. He was dragging the thing up a twenty-five per cent incline.

He threw the Cruiser into second, veered over to the road edge and tried to lock the breaks. He cursed the ABS system and all the safety features he had optioned up. The slewing action was enough to swing the stuck Mercedes off the road and disengaged its tenuous hold from the tow ball. George watched as it's back hung over the mountainside.

He slammed his car into reverse and pushed. Suddenly, one of his skis came loose, and like a javelin, it speared the wind-shield of the car and hit the driver square in the face. He could hear the Mercedes lose control, its engine revving. He looked in his mirror to see the driver slumped back in his seat. Slowly, George pushed the black car and it inched over the precipice until the force of gravity was too great. It and began to slide. George grated the Cruiser into first and spun the wheels to get out of the way. He watched as the Mercedes gathered speed then flipped over and over crashing though trees and finally hit a rocky outcrop.

It was over. He sat for a long time in the car. At first, he felt strangely euphoric – the victor. But as he sat, the feeling that he had wilfully killed someone crept into his conscience.

"They tried to kill me," he said to himself for some sort of justification. He didn't know whether he should ring the local police and say it was an accident. He didn't know whether he should say anything at all. But one thing he did know was that he would have to live with his decision for the rest of his life.

CHAPTER EIGHT

It was dark by the time George reached the outskirts of Paris. The stress of the day lay heavy on his body. All he wanted to do was sleep. The drive back to the city had been silent – his mind and body exhausted. He shook his head to focus. Reasoning that Bernard wasn't safe, he rang him. He pulled up outside the apartment around nine pm.

Bernard met him at the underground security gate and let him in with a pass key. With the car safely parked, the two men walked to the elevator. It was only when the coffee was made that George began to talk. Bernard listened, staring at his friend. George was always the capable one. The one who knew how to fix any situation, but now he saw his friend was on a knife edge.

"Where are your family?" Bernard asked. George then related the fight he had with his in-laws and the black cloud that hung over the relationship. Bernard laced the second coffee with a whiskey, but by the time he came back, George had succumbed to sleep.

It was at one am when the phone rang. Bernard lumbered into the study and in the dark picked up the call. He listened half asleep as the caller relayed the news. It wasn't what Bernard wanted to hear at one am or at any time, but as he grunted and made noises in the affirmative he was awake enough to realise he had a duty.

George woke up with a crick in his neck and a blanket sliding off his hip. He looked around and things began to fall into place. He looked at his watch. At seven am on a normal morning he would be in traffic, now he was in Bernard's apartment. He walked to the window and pulled the curtains to reveal a light snow shower. He watched the flakes whirl around and disappear to the ground. It would be cold today. His mind suddenly flashed back to the mountain side and the tumbling car, the man's bloodied face and the sound of the vehicle smashing through the trees. George shuddered.

"Are you cold?" Bernard padded into the lounge room in his dressing gown and slippers.

"No," George said turning from the window then added, "I guess since I'm in the city we should go to the office."

"Ah, well ... George," Bernard began, "I need to talk about that."

"What?"

"Well, it seems my dear old Mother is ailing. She is having an operation. And well ... she wants me to be there."

"And where is there?"

"Israel," Bernard said wrapping his gown a little tighter around his girth.

"Israel? Is that wise? Just think about it for a minute Bernard. If you are seen going to Israel for whatever reason, don't you think someone will notice. And when they notice it won't take long to put two and two together and come up with Jew." Bernard looked at the floor.

"But, I could just be going for business, or a holiday."

"I don't buy it and neither will the media." George stopped and looked at his friend. "We are dead." George drew his finger across his throat. "Dead, if we are found to be Jews."

"It's just that she has cancer and this is the last straw, if you know what I mean. She sounded so small and frightened last night on the phone."

"I'm sorry. Of course you must go. But we have to be careful." Thinking on his feet George suggested a stopover somewhere to confuse the issue. It was decided that Cyprus might be good. From there he could catch the ferry to Haifa in Israel. The more convoluted the route the better.

George drove Bernard to the airport and elicited a promise that he wouldn't be too long. In the car, they decided that George would contact Duval and explain what had happened.

"Just go and see him. Tell him what happened. The chances are that he already knows anyway. Look how I just walked out of the police station, no questions asked." Bernard looked out the window at the grey sky.

It was a job George didn't relish. "What if I just say it was an accident? For God's sake Bernard, a man died."

"Duval's not stupid, George. I think we need to..." Bernard tried to think of the right word. "To... I want to say trust, but I don't think our relationship stretches that far." He looked at George, "I don't know what, or who, he is really is George, but we need someone on the inside." George nodded, swung the car into the drop off zone, and stopped.

"I usually had a good nose for people, but Duval is decidedly off."

"Well, I trust you George. You will think of something." With that, Bernard collected his luggage, shut the door of the car, and leaned in the window. "See you in a week or so."

George watched Bernard walk to the concourse, his own mind turning over the situation. It wasn't that Duval seemed to know all the answers, or that he was one step ahead of them, it was the way he seemed to manipulate the situation. *With Bernard away*, George thought, *they would only have one person to worry about – besides Tag – and neither George nor Bernard knew where Tag might be.* He drove away planning what he would say and what he would keep to himself.

CHAPTER NINE

Business Class was so much nicer than economy, Bernard thought, as he settled back and sipped his wine. The ticket to Cyprus was cheaper than expected and he had been upgraded. He relaxed for the first time since Tag had come into their lives and tried to remember Tel Aviv and his mother's apartment. Fifteen years was a long time he mused.

The flight stopped at Munich then a few hours later descended into winter warmth and olive groves. Once out of the terminal at Larnaka airport, Bernard hailed a taxi and was deposited at his hotel. The hotel ran a travel agency, and with a little coaxing, Bernard managed to book a ticket on the ferry. The ship only left Limmasol twice a week for Haifa and so Bernard had two days to wait before his sea voyage. He gathered a few pamphlets from the hotel lobby and went for a walk in search of a taverna and something to eat.

The taverna was a modern establishment and the menu reasonably extensive giving Bernard more than one reason to stay until the sun had well and truly set. He had ordered another drink, and had sat back to bask in the warmth, when his mobile phone rang. It was George. Bernard relayed his arrangements regarding the ferry, and then George told him about Duval. Bernard listened, occasionally muttering, until George had finished.

"And it would be prudent to stay in contact," Bernard advised, adding, "Anything might happen."

"That is more than likely," George said. "The papers are full of moral outrage and vigilantism."

Bernard shivered at the thought of someone shooting at him. He felt a coward in the face of George's ordeal and wondered how he would cope in the same conditions. Bernard ended the conversation with, "Until tomorrow, George." He watched the last rays of sun dip below the horizon and tried to clear his mind. It wasn't an easy task.

The walk back to his hotel was pleasant and it was only when he was in bed that he went over George's conversation with Duval. It seems Duval had known of the incident on the mountain side and it was reported as a tragic accident. George was astounded at the capacity of NATA to clear away a death. Duval had said the man following was with the FFZ, but as George pointed out to Bernard, it all seemed just a little too convenient to blame the FFZ for everything.

"But who else would want us dead?" Bernard had said, and George couldn't answer that one. Duval explained that the men would have discreet protection, but George thought that meant hanging them out for bait and waiting for the vultures to arrive.

"He doesn't know where Tag is either," George said. Bernard thought this was an outright lie. Duval had tentacles of enquiry everywhere and if he couldn't find Tag, he wasn't trying. It just wasn't believable. George thought so too and so he said he would try and find Tag. And the biggest mystery was the shooter. Duval denied any knowledge of the incident on the slopes, and then he seemed cagey.

Bernard turned out the light and tried to put all his work out of his mind and concentrate on his mother – the matriarch of the Simeoni family and very much a Jew. He wondered how he could get away with being secular in a religious nation and how his Mother would take his lapse.

With two clear days, in Cyprus Bernard set about acting the tourist. The town was busy with back packers and holiday makers. He joined the throng and went shopping. A Fedora caught his eye and he bought it, placing it at a jaunty angle. He purchased treats for his Mother and other odds and ends that might brighten her day. *It was,* he thought, *a million miles away from Paris and the trouble.* He began to enjoy himself, treating himself to little luxuries and good food.

On his last day, he gathered some pamphlets and did the tourist trail. The Island had a wealth of history and Bernard meandered through the street to end at the old church of Ayios Lazaros. He read the description in his pamphlet. *Ayios Lazaros was built in the 9th century to house the reputed tomb of Lazarus, the man raised from the dead by Jesus. Reconstructed in the 17th century, it is the most impressive sight in the town of Larnaka.* He sat down in the quiet of the cool dark church and wondered how he had lost his belief. How did he slip so that his faith meant so little? His Mother had been faithful. Was everything so important these days that he didn't have the time, or was he just lazy?

The question played on his mind. Then he thought of the case. Why did he take on such a controversial case? Was it his ego? All these questions raced around in his mind. He could only think of one certainty – justice mattered. That was why he went into law. He had a moral belief that justice counted for something in the world. It was something that he would never take for granted. He knew George felt the same way and in their small firm, they had strived for justice in every case. That was his faith, a belief in justice. He sat back to look up at the cupola when a noise made him look around to see a lone figure take a seat near the door. It only took a moment for the real world to intrude. Immediately he felt apprehensive. He stood up and consulted his map. The tomb was down a flight of steps. Bernard followed the signs while listening for footsteps behind him. He stood in the crypt and waited, sweat beading on his face and neck. A man appeared at the doorway and then descended to stand next to him,

"Some things are never meant to die, don't you think?"

"Pardon," Bernard said.

"He came back. It's like history, it repeats itself no matter what we do to the contrary, don't you think?" Bernard wiped his brow and squinted in the darkness.

"I'm not quite sure I follow." The man shrugged his shoulders and left Bernard alone. Bernard suddenly felt afraid. Was this fellow trying to tell him something? Was he following Bernard's movements? He dashed up the steps and into the church. A group of German tourists had arrived. Flustered, he left the dark, incense laced sanctuary of the church and burst into the daylight scrunching his eyes against the sun. He walked across the road to a taverna and a refreshing drink. *Things were clearer in the daylight,* he thought, *and his encounter was just a co-incidence, nothing more.*

The sun was just starting to dip. Bernard ordered another drink and had sat back to watch the people promenade in the early evening when his phone rang. His mother wanted to know when he would be arriving. She said she was arranging to get his cousin to pick him up from the airport. Much to his Mother's consternation, Bernard explained that he was taking the ferry and would be arriving in Haifa and then catching a bus. She couldn't understand why. Bernard had to weave a lie to make it all sound plausible. After he had hung up, he thought his lie would come in handy and repeated it to himself. *The old adage that if you repeat the lie often enough, it becomes the truth might just work,* he mused.

The ferry left late in the evening for the overnight trip to Haifa. It was a large car-carrying ship and seemed to have all the occupants of Cyprus clambering to get on board with their overstuffed bags, dozens of children and live chickens in cages. Bernard walked the gang plank and found his cabin for the crossing. He had a porthole, which he considered a bonus, as the smell of the room made him feel sick before they had even cast off. The ferry was due to leave at midnight so Bernard quickly made himself comfortable and settled in for the night. He lay still listening to the noises of the boat. Then, remembering George's encounter, he climbed out of bed and made sure the door was locked.

"Insurance," he said to himself as he closed his eyes and drifted off to sleep.

**

The port of Haifa was a mishmash of commercial vessels and fishing trawlers and people, hundreds of people. Bernard watched the activity from the upper deck. He looked for a rank of taxis or buses but nothing was evident.

"Where do you go?" a woman standing next to him asked.

"I'm going to Tel Aviv, and you?"

"Here, this is my home," she said smiling. Bernard smiled back.

"You couldn't tell me where to catch the bus could you?" She quickly explained how to get to the main bus station, and then said, "I will take you there. I have a car." Bernard tried to say no but the woman wouldn't hear of it and so they walked off the ferry together. After a passport check and a few quick questions that Bernard answered by including his convenient excuse, he met Marta on the other side of the barrier and they walked to her car. The drive through the chaotic traffic gave Marta ample time to pump Bernard for information about his trip. He once again repeated his excuse for not flying and then told her about his aging mother and her health.

"It is a worry. I'm live in Paris; she is here."

"Yes, I can imagine it would be. And tell me Bernard. What do you do in Paris?"

"I'm a lawyer."

"Really. Do you know about that case that was in the papers? The one about the death of that Jew?" Marta took her eyes off the busy road and looked at her passenger. Bernard swallowed and tried to stay calm.

"That was in your papers too?"

"Oh yes, It was quite a story. That sort of thing is, here, for obvious reasons."

Bernard nodded. He studied the young woman. She seemed genuine. Her questions could be innocent, but Bernard felt they were probing. He tried to change the subject but she stopped talking and concentrated on the traffic.

"Well, here we are."

Bernard stepped out of the car and thanked Marta.

"No trouble at all, Mr Simeoni, no trouble at all." Bernard watched the car pull away and then it hit him. He tried to remember if he had said his last name. He was sure he had just introduced himself as Bernard. *The woman was very inquisitive,* he thought, *and she wanted to pump him for information, he was sure of it*. Who she worked for, Bernard was yet to discover. He stepped up his awareness and bought his bus ticket for Tel Aviv.

The two hour trip was cramped and Bernard wished he had taken the train, then he revised that, and wished he had flown. All his subterfuge with his travel arrangements and still he had the distinct feeling he was being watched. He had made up his mind that the woman *was* trying to get information and he made what little facts he had fit his conspiracy theory. As the bus lurched from town to village and every stop in between, Bernard watched the vista roll by.

For all the news items of unrest and troubles, Bernard saw daily life as it had always been. There were young soldiers doing their service, Arabs, Israelis farming and working and the country seemed quite normal. The suburbs of the capital were a sprawling mass that swallowed up the bus as it ground to a halt in the horrendous traffic. Everyone groaned and Bernard knew they would be in the snarl of cars for some time.

When the bus finally pulled into the main terminal, everyone was desperate to get off. Bernard was herded along. When he alighted, he was pushed and his new fedora fell off. He struggled with his bags and heard someone say, "Here you are." A gentleman had his hat and proffered it to him.

"Thanks." Bernard placed his hat on his head and went to thank the Good Samaritan. He took a step back as he thought he recognised the same man who was in the church in Larnaka.

"Not a problem. These crowds can be murder if you don't keep moving." Bernard was sure he knew that voice. He smiled and took a good look at the face of the man. It was craggy with many worn lines around the mouth. His eyes were dark and Bernard felt uneasy as the stranger grabbed his stare and returned it.

"Where are you going?"

"I'm..." Bernard began and then thought better of it. He looked about and saw a billboard advertising a well-known hotel. He threw the name of the hotel into the conversation and then picked up his bags.

"Thanks again," he said and started to walk inside the bus terminal. Once inside he found a phone booth and with the door closed, he rang George.

"All that trouble and I'm sure I'm being followed," he told George.

"Well, who could it be? Just think about it for a minute Bernard."

"George, I'm in a Jewish state defending a Neo-Nazi supporter. Everyone hates me. I'm probably on a hit list already." Bernard began to sweat as he played out his assassination in his mind.

"Look, stay calm. I guess all you can do is see your mother and then get out of there. Perhaps they are just keeping you under surveillance so that you don't cause trouble. You know the state is a little paranoid." George said they should contact each other later that night and rang off. Bernard exited the booth and then remembered he had to call his cousin.

His mother's apartment was on the ground floor of a four story block. She had bought it years ago when the suburb was considered out of town, but now it was close enough to be called city living. Bernard saw her waiting at the door and noticed that in the intervening years his mother had grown very old. She was smaller than he remembered and looked quite frail, leaning on her walking frame. Catherine Simeoni smiled at her son and moved aside to let him pass. Bernard bent low and kissed his mother then watched her slowly turn and shuffle into the lounge room and sit down. They stared at one another and then Catherine asked, "Bernard, is it you who is defending that man?"

Bernard was shocked at the direct question. She may be frail but her brain was like a steel trap. His mother had always been forthright and now she stared at her son and expected an honest answer. He took a deep breath and answered in the affirmative, then added that he felt it was his duty to find justice in a very one sided argument. Catherine nodded and Bernard felt the more times he said it the easier it was to believe.

CHAPTER TEN

The apartment was small but well kept. Bernard unpacked and then asked the most important question.

"What do the Doctors say?"

Catherine came straight to the point. "I am old, it is to be expected. I have six months at most. It is they say – advanced."

"Why didn't you tell me before?" Bernard took his mother's hand.

"You still have life, what good would it do to come here and watch me die." Her directness startled Bernard, but he said no more.

The hospital appointment was one day away and Bernard was encouraged to re-visit Tel Aviv and his few relatives while they waited. It would be a chance to catch up, his Mother said.

Winter in Tel Aviv was a wonderfully sunny day. Bernard heard the forecast on the radio and decided to walk to the city centre. He felt he needed the exercise as Gabrielle had commented recently on his weight. He took a map and set off promising to be back to meet his cousins in the afternoon.

The inner city suburbs were crowded with apartments and the streets full of people going about their daily business. Things had quickened since his last visit and as he walked, the streetscape seemed familiar. He remembered shops that now were car parks and car parks that were now apartments.

A cafe came into view and Bernard stopped for a coffee. He chose to sit outside, and looking around, saw two men stop and look in a shop window. They seemed furtive while trying to remain casual. Bernard watched them for a long time and they eventually moved on.

His coffee arrived and he began to rationalize his feelings. He knew he was being paranoid, but after all that had happened, he felt he had the right to be on edge. He wondered for the second time if he might have the courage of George if he was in a tight situation. George was always the strong one, the one to take charge. He, on the other hand, was the thinker. He was the one in the relationship who so often found a solution.

He stood up, and after paying his bill, walked on glancing back every so often, almost in the hope of catching someone, but there was nothing out of the ordinary. He had begun to enjoy his walk when someone grabbed his arm. He struggled and looked at a squat man with an iron grip.

"Hey, let go of me," Bernard wrenched his arm away and people nearby stopped and stared. The sudden movement gave Bernard time to sprint into an alleyway and then he opened the first door he came to and rushed up a flight of stairs. On the first floor, he looked down and saw the outer door opening and the little man begin to run after him.

Panic mixed with adrenalin gave Bernard the push he needed and he banged open a fire door and found himself in another stair well. Taking the stairs two at a time, he descended and then threw his shoulder at another fire door. The door sprang open and Bernard was on the street once more. He quickly surveyed his surroundings and tried to walk casually down the street, puffing at his sudden exertion. At a large intersection, Bernard mingled with the crowd crossing the street. Half way across, he turned and joined the group going back the way he had just come. Scanning the crowd, he saw them. The two men were looking ahead, and with his subterfuge, missed him.

Bernard reached the footpath and then took the first turning on the left. The small one way street was lined with parked cars and he hugged the building until the street ended at a market. He stopped and caught his breath. As far as he could tell, he hadn't been followed and he felt proud about that.

The market was busy with shoppers, delivery trucks Bernard joined the throng. He wove his way into the aisles, past the fruit and vegetables, and began to drop his guard. A very large stand of pomelos caught his eye and he stopped, thinking he might buy some, when he was grabbed from behind. Someone twisted his arm behind his back. Bernard fought back and thrust his elbow into his attacker's chest. The force was enough to break his abductors hold, and Bernard swung around to face a big, square jawed man. Bernard had seen that face before.

Stunned, he took a step back and in that moment the man grabbed his hand and started to crush his knuckles. Bernard buckled under the pain, and in his weak moment, his tormenter once again twisted his arm and started him walking towards the exit. Bernard complied as his hand throbbed in the vice like hold. Once in the sunshine two more men appeared. Bernard was roughly bundled into a waiting car.

He was thrown onto the back seat. A squat man sat on him as the car sped away into the traffic. He heard the traffic, the horns, the buses and trucks, but every time he went to twist his neck to look up, his captors pushed his head down. He tried to stay calm, but vivid scenarios ran around in his head. Was he being kidnapped to be killed? – for ransom, for torture? That last one made him sweat. He knew he didn't know anything, but his torturers didn't know that. Bernard decided he would try to bargain with them when the time came. He had saved a bit of money, and Gabrielle had her own money. He was sure he could buy his way out. He figured that his mother and cousins would call the police when he didn't come home.

The car came to a stop and Bernard thought they were still in traffic. He could see the door handle. He gradually brought his left arm up. With a deft movement, he grabbed the handle and pulled. The door flew open. In the panic, his captor jumped up and Bernard slithered onto the road. He shoved the door shut with his foot and then scrabbled to his feet. He was in the middle of a busy intersection and a bus missed him by centimetres as he staggered across the road. His assailants jumped out of the car. But the traffic was too thick. By the time they reached the other side of the road, Bernard was gone.

As his taxi stopped outside Catherine's apartment, Bernard scanned the residence for anything suspicious. When it looked all clear, he paid the driver, strode to the front door, and knocked. His mother answered. Once inside Bernard collapsed onto the lounge. His dishevelled appearance, and his general malaise had his mother asking questions, but Bernard thought at this stage that the less she knew the better. He concocted a story about a mugging and went for a shower.

When the relatives had been and gone, Bernard retired to his room and rang George. He related the whole episode with as little embellishment as possible, ending with his fear that they wouldn't stop until they had him.

"Do you have any ideas who they were?" George asked.

"No more than you," Bernard answered.

"I think it was the same person at the bus station and I think he was the same guy at the church in Larnaka. They all look alike ... but then I can't be sure. It was dark at the church, it was busy at the bus station, and I was scared to death at the market. It doesn't help when you are trying to remember a face." Bernard laughed. Then George brought him up to date on Tag. It seemed that Tag had called in every day as his bail required, but where he disappeared after that George couldn't say.

"He just vanishes off the face of the earth. I waited for him at the police station and then dropped him off in the city," George said.

"Someone must be looking after him."

"I asked him, but you know how talkative he can be," George ended sarcastically.

"Anything else?"

"I also contacted a few police officers on duty. They said their vision was obscured because of the placards. And they said the Gendarme who claims to have seen the murder, actually had blood all over his visor. So much for the prosecution's star witness." George felt he had achieved a great breakthrough and hoped it would be enough to cast doubt in the jury's mind. "If we don't have to call Tag, then his vitriol won't be heard."

Bernard agreed. "And what of your family?"

"Fine," George said trying to skip the details. "And your mother?" Bernard filled him in and then rang off. He rang Gabrielle but there was no answer. *Typical,* he thought. *She was probably working and wouldn't think to ring him.* Work always came first with Gabrielle. He sat back thinking on their marriage. It was a convenience at best. They had all the trappings of a life together, but he felt a spark was missing. He shrugged off his melancholia and went to bed.

"Tomorrow," he said to himself, "I will ring tomorrow."

***

The morning began with rain. Bernard looked out of his window to a leaden sky with no prospect of a break. He had discussed his mother's impending operation with his cousins and Ira, his cousin on his mother's side, who was to take them to the hospital at two pm.

Catherine looked weary as they helped her out of the car and into a waiting wheel chair. He knew her feelings on the outcome and her wish that she wanted to die at home, not in a sterile hospital.

"You know you don't have to have this operation," Bernard said as they wheeled her into her room.

Catherine looked at her son, "I know, but I need this. I have one more job to do."

"What. What could you possibly need to do?" Catherine looked at Bernard and he understood. She had always lamented his lapse from religion. He was a disappointment to her. He left her to settle in and Ira took him back to the apartment, with a promise to pick him up tomorrow for a visit. Bernard sat down and with an early afternoon whisky, poured over the photo albums his mother had kept all these years. There was scant history of the war years but the pictures after made up for those missing. He relived his whole childhood in Kodak snaps. He was enjoying the memories when there was a knock at the door. When he opened the door, three men manhandled him to the tile floor. Bernard gasped for air as the fall winded him, then his attackers hoicked him up. He felt the rain on his face as they dragged him to a waiting car. This time, they took no chances. He was handcuffed with a plastic cable tie and shoved to the foot-well of the back seat. The drive was long and hot. Bernard felt helpless. When they stopped, Bernard was bullied out of the car and into an echoing corridor, then down a flight of stairs and through a large metal door.

The room was stark except for two chairs and a table. The walls were peeling and the smell was of dank decay and fear. The big man threw Bernard into one chair, cable tied his ankles to the legs of the chair and left. The light was bright and unforgiving as Bernard looked around. He felt bile rising in his throat and swallowed hard. He coughed and swallowed again. He guessed the time around three or four pm and waited, licking his lips of the last remnants of whisky.

Bernard woke with a start as the door opened. He was amazed that he had slept at all. Now he had no idea of the time. Was he asleep for hours or just a few minutes? Then he remembered that when he was shoved into the car, he felt a sharp pain in his leg. *They must have drugged him,* he thought. The door banged shut. A man walked to the other chair and Bernard tried to see if he had a watch. He didn't know why, but he thought the time crucially important. Without some sort of anchor, he felt he had no control at all.

"I am En Saliki," the swarthy thick set man said. Bernard looked at his face trying to place its ethnicity. He looked eastern European, perhaps Slavic. Bernard nodded.

"Do you know who I represent?"

Bernard shook his head. He felt unable to answer. His face wouldn't respond with the words he wanted to say.

"Mr Simeoni," Saliki began, "Why are you here?"

"Because ... you ... kidnapped ... me." Bernard enunciated the words one at a time, trying to speak with clarity.

"Mr Simeoni, why are you in Israel?"

Bernard thought about the question. If they knew his name, where he was living, then he reasoned they would know why he came.

"You can tell me." He slurred the words

"Ah ... I see. You might need persuasion."

The veiled threat of torture brought Bernard into a sweat. "I'm here see mother. She ... operation," he blurted out.

"Yes, we know. But your *other* motive."

"None." Bernard dribbled as he tried to speak. He could think clearly but his whole body felt alien.

"Well we think otherwise. You are a very hot topic here Mr Simeoni. Your clientele in Paris makes you my business. And I don't like your company."

"Tag?"

"Ah, I see we are on the same page now. Yes, Mr Tag. We don't particularly like his company either." Saliki smiled showing a row of white teeth evenly spaces with one gold tooth to break the line.

"We?" Bernard said looking Saliki in the face.

"We are the conscience of Israel. We hold back the tide of terrorism, Mr Simeoni."

Bernard was confused. These riddles sounded like he was being held by an Israeli Government sanctioned organisation. He took a punt on his next question. "Are … you … working … for … the … Government?" He took great pains with his words.

"That is not your business. What you do need to know Mr Simeoni is that we do not want your kind here."

"My kind?"

"If you know what is good for you, you will leave. We will give you 24 hours to get back to Paris."

"But… my mother?"

"Forget her. If you value your life, you will leave. There are people here with long memories and even longer knives." Saliki licked his lips and brought out a cigar from his breast pocket. He slowly pulled the Montecristo from its tubular holder and taking it gently between his fingers he ran it under his nose. Bernard watched as Saliki savoured the moment. Then a box of matches was produced and he lit up. The aroma lingered on the air and it reminded Bernard of his father. Mr Simeoni senior had smoked cigars when he got the chance. Bernard always associated the pungent smell with an absent father. He closed his eyes trying to concentrate on the moment rather than on the past.

"This is not a warning Mr Simeoni. Do not underestimate our resources."

"But, I'm a Jew." Bernard said the words as a defence, and they seem to resonate within him. He held up his faith and repeated his vow. "I'm a Jew."

Saliki leant forward on the table. "That very fact will get you killed. Nothing has changed in the world, Mr Simeoni." The cigar smoke wafted over the words as Saliki exhaled once more. "Nothing."

CHAPTER ELEVEN

Bernard was shoved into the street. The rain had stopped and he stood on the wet pavement rubbing his wrist. His watch showed eight-thirty pm. He began to walk without thought of direction, running the interrogation through his mind. What were Saliki's motives he wondered? He was trying to remember everything that happened, when a dream flashed through his brain. He remembered Saliki saying, "Let him run, we will follow." Bernard rubbed his eyes and stretched his memory. He was sure he had heard those words. Perhaps in his drugged state they had been talking in the room. The memory made sense he reasoned. Why else would they just let him walk away? They were using him. Bernard walked in a daze, trying to make sense of it all. At an intersection, he hailed a taxi and found he was a good 40-minutes-drive from his mother's apartment.

The door was open when he arrived and he cautiously made his way inside. Everything seemed to be as he left it. The drug was wearing off, and so with Saliki's words echoing in his head, he rang George and left a message on the answering machine. Then he rang Gabrielle and left another message, letting her know he would be home in a day or two. He knew he wouldn't be able to see his mother; she would still be in surgery. It grieved him not to be able to say goodbye. With his bags packed, he pulled out his iPhone and trawled the internet for a flight, any flight leaving for Paris. There was one at midnight.

The airport was jammed with people. They were sleeping on the floor, all the seats were taken, and the place smelt of stale humanity. As Bernard picked his way to check-in, he heard the announcement. A volcanic ash plume was grounding all flights over Europe. He groaned, knowing Saliki would not take a mere volcano as an excuse. The ground crew were trying to pack passengers onto other flights, but most were resigned to their fate. Bernard scanned the departure board and found a flight going to Marrakech It would be below the ash cloud the woman behind the counter said and leaving in one hour. For Bernard that was reason enough.

The six hour flight was fully booked and although Bernard had tried to upgrade to business class, he was stuck in economy. He closed his eyes and tried to sleep but with his mind in turmoil at his sudden departure, he just sat and wrestled with his conscience.

The flight arrived in good time and Bernard exited the plane to the chaotic bustle of Morocco. Nothing seemed to be happening with any order or thought, and everyone shouted. Bleary eyed and in need of some creature comforts Bernard walked through passport control and headed straight for the taxi stand.

"Hilton," he said. He sat in the front seat and hung on, as the car careered into the morning traffic. Watching the hustle of vehicles, Bernard felt safe in the knowledge that if he was being followed, they would have a hard time. His driver smiled and without warning changed lanes. The taxi disappeared down a narrow street and re-appeared right in front of the Hilton Hotel. The concierge took control of Bernard's bag and it was only about ten minutes later that he was having a hot shower and letting his worries wash away with the dirty water.

Room service was prompt and Bernard thought the steak breakfast delicious, as he ate in peace and quiet. While he ate, he jotted down what he knew and who he had met. It was a comprehensive list with a lot of unanswered questions. When he looked over his work there seemed to be one common denominator. Everyone, including the Paris police had let him go. And the only reason he could think of for such an act was the fact that they didn't have any clues themselves as to the associations of the Neo-Nazi group.

The police were hoping for a lead, NATA were looking for a communication or a meeting, and the Israeli Secret Service with En Saliki wanted the big guns in the picture. It seemed to Bernard that he and George were the bait and everyone wanted the big fish. Then he remembered the FFZ. They just wanted to stop the whole damn show and didn't care who they killed to achieve their ends. He finished his meal and sat back. It would all end tomorrow he mused, if he dropped the Tag case. Just tell the court that they feel compromised and he would need new council. All it would take would be a phone call.

As if on cue, his mobile phone rang and it was Gabrielle. She didn't sound happy and as Bernard tried to sooth her anger, he felt more than a little aggrieved at her callous attitude. Her main concern was the apartment and the plants.

"Thank you for thinking of my mother," Bernard said sarcastically. Gabrielle calmed down and told Bernard that she was going back to the apartment. Living at her parent's house was inconvenient and she didn't see any real threats.

"Look Gabrielle, I can't explain it all over the phone, it's too complicated, but I would suggest you reconsider. It will only be for a few weeks." He could hear her exasperation and knew he was backing a lost cause. They hung up and a pall of indifference lingered on the line. His call to his mother was in a different tone altogether. Ira came on the line when the hospital patched him through to Catherine's room. She had come out of the operation and all was good news Bernard's cousin explained.

"Why did you leave?" The question needed an answer. Bernard didn't know what to say. How could anything take precedence over his mother? Any excuse would be a bad one.

"I was called away by the Government, you understand." Ira made a noise that didn't sound like he believed Bernard. The conversation petered out and Bernard hung up. He told himself it would all be resolved, his mother would get better, Gabrielle would remember why she married him and one day, sooner Bernard hoped than later, Tag would be finished, one way or another.

Bernard turned on the television in time to see the news and the watched with disappointment the havoc the ash cloud was creating. Everything was grounded. There was no way he could get back to France by air. If he had any hope of going home it wouldn't be for days or even weeks. He didn't feel tired and Morocco seemed a world away from Israel and France so he donned his fedora, his walking shoes, and a comfortable pair of trousers and shirt and went out.

The streets were full of people and traffic. It was invigorating to be anonymous on the streets and walk without fear. He sought out the Souk and decided to buy presents for everyone. After all, he said to himself, I'm here I might as well enjoy myself. The covered market was made up of thousands of little alley ways and annexes. Bernard wandered aimlessly, picking up trinkets along the way, when a jewellery store caught his eye. He admired the necklaces on offer and knew Gabrielle well enough to know she would love one particular piece that had an Art Deco styling. The shop keeper sidled up to Bernard and began to ply his trade when a voice interrupted the spiel.

"He will rob you if you don't watch out."

Bernard turned to see a tall slim well-dressed woman smiling at him. "It doesn't seem that expensive really," Bernard said. The woman flicked her long dark hair over her shoulder and bit her bottom lip. She said something in Arabic and the shopkeeper bowed and disappeared into his shop.

"What did you say to him?"

"I told him I was the Souk police. We have laws here in regard to ripping off tourists."

Bernard smiled. "Bernard Simeoni." He held out his hand.

"Nasra Ziati." She took his hand with a firm grip and shook it.

"Are you with the police?"

"No," Nasra laughed, "but he doesn't know that. If you want real jewellery then I can show you where to buy it." Then she added, "At a decent price."

"So you work for another shop, poaching customers. Is that it?"

"No," Nasra laughed again, "I just feel that a tourist should have a memorable experience in Marrakech, and not be taken for a ride. Come on."

Bernard watched her as she confidently walked through the souk. Her lithe body moved easily under her white cotton trousers and fine linen shirt. She strode with purpose, and yet to look at her, it seemed she was strolling and nothing could touch her. Once or twice, she grabbed Bernard's hand, to steer him across a walkway or street, and the action was so natural he didn't think it strange or presumptuous. They reached another entrance to the market and burst into the sunlight. Bernard squinted and Nasra pulled a pair of sunglasses from her head, and threading her arm through his, led him across the busy street.

He fleetingly wondered why he was following, like a lamb to the slaughter. He knew nothing about her, he may have known her for all of three minutes, and yet he felt an attraction that went beyond sexual.

"You're not kidnapping me are you?" he said jokingly.

Nasra smiled, showing her perfect white teeth, and beckoned him with her hand. "In here." She stepped into a small shop wedged between a cafe and a barber. Bernard rubbed his eyes until they were accustomed to the dark and then saw the cabinets filled with antique jewels. He walked around studying the cabinets.

"This is very nice." He pointed to an Art Deco pendant. Nasra asked the price in Arabic and translated.

"He says it is only in American Dollars, $300,"

"That seems a lot."

Nasra looked at the pendant. She did some negotiating and announced the new price of $180.

"It is a good price," she said. "Your wife will be a lucky woman."

Bernard nodded. "A bit of a peace offering, really." Bernard pulled out some Euros and counting them with a calculator, the shopkeeper was satisfied.

"Now would you like coffee?"

"Well... yes, but I mustn't keep you Miss Ziati. I'm sure you have other tourists to rescue."

Nasra smiled once again and Bernard knew he liked this woman and her open face and laughing nature. "Coffee is on me," Bernard said. They walked easily side by side. Presently they came to a pastry shop with tables outside.

"Here. Their pastries are the best in Marrakech," Nasra said taking a seat. Bernard sat and Nasra ordered. It wasn't long before they were sipping thick sweet coffee and eating honey almond cakes. Bernard enjoyed the experience. He chatted freely about his work in Paris, his involvement in a high profile case, his mother, and his wife. He wasn't sure why he unburdened himself so readily, but Nasra seemed to be a willing listener and the coffee was very good.

The afternoon was whiled away, shopping and walking, until they found themselves back at the Hilton. It seemed they had talked all the day and yet he didn't know a thing about his companion.

"Do you want to come up? We could have a drink if you like?" Bernard asked. Once in his hotel room Bernard laid his shopping out on the bed. He had far too much to fit into his suitcase and laughingly said he would have to go shopping tomorrow for a new case. Nasra sat on the edge of the bed and looked around the room.

"Drink?"

She nodded and watched Bernard bend down to the mini bar. "Whisky or Brandy? No wait we have Vodka." He stood up and held the little bottle. A beam of red light hit the bottle and refracted over Bernard's shirt. Nasra lunged at Bernard, and with one quick movement grabbed his shirt and pulled him off his feet. She fell back on the floor and Bernard fell on top of her still holding the Vodka bottle in his hand.

"What the?" He tried to regain his breath. Nasra was still holding his shirt, her grip tightening as Bernard struggled.

"Stay down," she said. "Don't move." Bernard's eyes widened as he tried to figure out what was happening.

"What is it?" he whispered.

"Laser sight. From the window."

Bernard twisted his head and looked to the window. The curtains were pulled back and there was a building across the street.

"Keep still," she mouthed the word then put her finger to her lips.

Bernard froze as Nasra scanned the walls for the tell-tale red sights dot. After a minute, she relaxed a little and Bernard felt her breathing under his chest. He pushed a few stray hairs away from her face and then she closed her eyes. He kissed one eye and then the other. Nasra opened her eyes, pulled his head close to her, her hand at the back of his neck, and sought his lips. Her breath was warm and sweet and Bernard responded to the advance by tracing his finger down her neck and undoing her blouse.

"Is it safe?" Bernard asked as he slipped her shirt off her shoulders.

"Safe for whom?" Nasra replied, taking his hands and kissing his fingers. Bernard leant on his elbow, untucked her shirt, and stroked her firm belly all the way down to her trousers.

"Is this a peace accord between the Jews and the Arabs?" Bernard asked, then tenderly bit her breast. Nasra gasped.

"We need further negotiations. Every concession will be hard won." She licked his ear.

It was a mutual sexual encounter and neither were about to let their prejudices get in the way. Nasra kissed Bernard hard and then began to undress him. Bernard found her zip on her trousers and they were soon naked on the floor. Nothing held their bodies in check as Bernard fulfilled his carnal desires and Nasra made love to the limit of his endurance. Their bodies fell into a natural rhythm as she arched her back time and again, as he held her hips and thrust. Sweat mingled with their lovemaking until they were physically spent and lying still, side by side on the carpet. Nasra leant over and kissed Bernard on the forehead.

"Vodka did you say?"

Bernard laughed and propped himself up on his elbow. "Vodka it is, but first..." he looked into Nasra's dark eyes, "Who are you?"

The question hung in the air as she pulled herself up and leant back on the end of the bed.

"Well?"

"I am Nasra Ziati. I told you."

"Yes, but who... who do you work for, Nasra?" Bernard cupped her firm breast in his hand.

"Ah, I see. I am working for the Government."

"Which one?" Bernard said getting frustrated with the riddles.

"Our Government, Bernard." Nasra stood up and walked to the window. She pulled the curtains across and snapped on the occasional lamp. Bernard rose and sat on the end of the bed, admiring her casual stance.

"Look, I'm being honest here," Nasra began, "I am working for NATA."

"Bloody NATA. I'm sick to death of you people." He threw his anger at Nasra as she put on the complementary robe. "You come in and just take control. No thought for anyone. I suppose you were in the plan, all this was in the plan."

"No," Nasra said.

"Bullshit. You people will do anything to get an advantage. I've been shot at, followed, scared out of my wits, interrogated by who knows who and now you expect me to believe this," he pointed to the discarded clothes on the floor, "this was just... well, this just happened. I don't buy it." He took the other robe she offered and wrapped himself up tight.

"Bernard," she began, "I was told to keep you safe. I..." she faulted. "What happened wasn't in the plan. It just happened that's all. You were in someone's sights. They are tracking you."

"Who are *they*", Bernard ran his fingers through his hair, picked up his glasses, then began to rub them furiously.

"We are not sure. But they know where you are." She came and sat down next to him on the bed. "And I think I know how."

Bernard put his glasses down and sighed.

Nasra pushed him on the bed and began to undo his robe. He reached up to pull her down and she stopped.

"No, keep still."

"What?"

"I think you must have a micro dot on you somewhere. It is the only way they could be here so soon." She pulled off his robe and looked intently at his naked body.

"It is a tracking GPS. Very small. Almost invisible."

"God ... how?"

"I don't know. Perhaps in the street. Or anywhere really." She began to look at his toes.

"Sometimes they show up with talc. Do you have talc?"

"Yes, in my bag." With the talc spread all over his body, Nasra began her inspection. Bernard thought in different circumstances he wouldn't be able to control himself, but now he lay still as she searched her way over his body.

"Not there for God's sake."

"It had been known to happen." Nasra knelt on the bed and took him in her mouth. Bernard succumbed to her ministrations, living very much in the here and now. She practiced her lustful art, and then when Bernard was about to climax she stopped and smiled.

"Not fair." Bernard groaned.

"Negotiations rarely are," Nasra replied and continued her search. She worked her way over his neck then smiled, "I have it." She levered the dot with her nail from the back of his ear.

"How the hell did it get there?"

"They know all the tricks." Then Bernard remembered his hat. He thought the wind had blown it off and the man retrieved it for him.

"I lost my hat and this guy gave it back to me." Nasra nodded.

"That is all it takes. He put it on the inside and the next thing you know you are in someone's sights."

"There might be more than one. You need to shower and scrub." She led him into the bathroom and then removed her robe. "I will scrub you."

Bernard grabbed the soap. "Whatever you say Nasra, whatever you say." Nasra worked her way over his body as Bernard gave into his desires. He fleetingly thought of Gabrielle, but tried to reason with himself that their marriage was failing anyway, and this woman saved his life. It was only natural he should feel this way.

"Is this the Stockholm syndrome?" he asked when they were towelling each other off.

"Not quite. That is when the hostage falls for the captor. I'm not your captor Bernard." Bernard felt captivated by Nasra all the same.

As they drank from the mini bar, Nasra looked at the micro dot she had stuck to the hotel stationary pack.

"We need to get rid of this." She addressed an envelope, and put the dot on the underside of the stamp and called room service. The letter was taken away and Bernard finally relaxed.

"Can I make a call?" he asked Nasra as they lay on the bed.

"Not wise." She took the phone and pulled out the battery. Bernard lay still for a minute or two and then looked at her directly and asked, "Who was trying to shoot at me?"

"Well, we think it is the Israeli Secret Service." Bernard thought back to his interrogation.

"I'm sure I heard them say they wanted me at large. Some guy called En Saliki said, 'let him run', or something similar. I think they drugged me."

Nasra thought on the information. "Listen, things look clear to you but they are much more complicated. Have you heard of the FFZ?"

Bernard nodded.

"Well... there is a mole in the Israeli Service." She saw the look of consternation on Bernard's face.

"They know about it. But it suits their purpose."

"But then, who wants me killed? The FFZ or the service."

"We are not sure. At this stage, we think both. Your defence of Tag is very political. The Service has, we think, an elite squad. A sort of trouble-shooting hit squad. They have the same objectives as the FFZ, or they may even be the FFZ under a different guise."

"And their objectives are?"

"To never lie down again," Nasra ended.

"So what does the NATA want?"

"We want to..." Nasra looked at Bernard, her stare trying to penetrate into his mind. "We want to break the FFZ. And..." she kissed him, "to keep you safe." She smiled.

"Does it bother you that I'm defending Tag?" Bernard asked as Nasra lay back on the bed.

"No, but... of all the people to defend. Why did you take him on?"

"Because no matter what he has or hasn't done, every man deserves justice," Bernard said. His mind fleetingly thought of the Depardieu case. He sat up and swung his legs over the side of the bed. "There is only one thing we as humans need to act upon and that is injustice. Tag may be guilty, but he must be tried by the law, not popular opinion."

"You must see you will be coloured as a sympathiser."

Bernard turned to face Nasra. "I'm not the first Jew to be pilloried for my convictions." He sat back down on the side of the bed,

"Now ... about that peace accord. Should we go over the fine print again? I feel deep and meaningful negotiations coming on." Nasra grabbed his arm, pulled him close, and kissed him.

CHAPTER TWELVE

Bernard woke up to an empty bed. He sat up and looked into the bathroom but Nasra was gone. He turned on the television to find that the airports were still closed to European traffic and the experts were saying it could be another week. Things were looking grim. The phone rang and Bernard put the remote control down to answer.

"Where are you?" he asked Nasra.

"Look, you need to pack and meet me in the lobby in an hour." She ended with, "I'll explain later."

Bernard packed and then looked at all his presents. They were never going to fit. He made the decision to post them to his office address and called room service. He shoved all the gifts in one big bag and carried it down to reception, then looked at his watch. He was early so sat down to wait the twenty minutes.

The lobby was sparsely populated and Bernard casually people-watched. There were men in suits, women in fashionable clothes and several Arabs. No one seemed interested in him or in any particular hurry. Things in Morocco had their own pace he decided. A party of Arab men entered the lobby from the elevator and converged on the desk all talking at the same time. It was organised chaos as they milled about. For Bernard, who thrived on order, it seemed a hectic way to do business. He liked things neatly placed in boxes; it made for a comfortable life.

"Bernard," Nasra hailed him from the doorway. Bernard stood up and waved, then trotted over to meet her. They exited into warm sunshine.

"You cannot fly. I have arranged a boat." She looked at his face trying to judge if he was okay with the idea.

"A boat, but that will take days. We are in Marrakech, the middle of the country. Where is this boat?"

"Tangiers."

"But that's kilometres away. This is hopeless. I need to be in Paris today." He paced the floor. "I must be in Paris or..." he left the sentence hanging as he was not sure how far Saliki would go to carry out his threat.

"Bernard... that is not going to happen. We need to..." Nasra hesitated. Then smiling said,

"I am coming with you."

"We will have to go to Gibraltar and from there..." She grabbed his arm and hailed a taxi. Giving direction to the driver in Arabic, Nasra pressed some money into his hand and then sat back.

"Have you been to Spain?"

"Spain!"

"Yes, Spain. We will sail to Gibraltar and then..." Nasra looked at Bernard's luggage.

"Where are your gifts?"

Bernard explained he posted them and Nasra visibly slumped.

"What?"

"It's nothing," she said. "We have a bit of time. Would you like to go for coffee?"

Bernard agreed, realising he had skipped breakfast in his haste. They went back to the same cafe Nasra had taken him to earlier. It occurred to Bernard that Nasra must have been following him.

"How did you find me Nasra?" he asked when their coffee had arrived.

"Oh, I just picked you up. A bit of luck really."

Bernard watched her face for a sign of a lie. He wondered if she had micro chipped him or... he dared to think. Perhaps she wasn't working for NATA at all but the Israelis. Everything seemed so convenient – the pickup, the laser beam, the micro dot. *Hell,* he thought, *he didn't even know if there was such a thing as a micro dot.*

She saw the look of disquiet on his face. "We tracked you with your phone. Satisfied?" He nodded and sipped his coffee, not sure what to believe.

Nasra ordered some sweet sugared almonds and gave them to Bernard as a present saying they were a measure of goodwill. "You must trust me. I may be the only ally you have."

Those words echoed in Bernard's brain and he suddenly remembered that Duval had said the same thing. Taking a punt, he asked, "Do you know Duval?"

Nasra took an almond and studied its delicate pink skin, turning it over in her fingers. "Do you?" Bernard became insistent.

"He... he was my husband."

Bernard's brow furrowed with disbelief. "Your husband? What the hell is going on?"

"We work on the same side. That is all. It was all a long time ago." Nasra popped the almond in her mouth and bit down, the crack like the break in her relationship, hard and not repairable.

With this personal revelation, Bernard felt he knew the woman he had made love to and leaned over the table, "I trust you Nasra. I trust you with my life."

She smiled and offered an almond, pushing it into Bernard's mouth and pressing her finger to his lips. No more need be uttered as they sealed their fate with the sugary nuts.

Nasra looked at her watch and said it was time to meet their driver for the overland trip. She hailed a taxi and they sped off into the traffic to a rendezvous with a 4WD and a gun toting African.

The truck was well used by the look of the dents. The driver looked just as careworn. He wore a dirty pair of trousers and shirt and had a turban of sorts wrapped untidily around his head. But Bernard could not take his eyes off the automatic rifle slung over his shoulder. Nasra conversed in Arabic and their heated discussion took a good ten minutes as Bernard waited with his bag. Eventually, Nasra beckoned him over and they climbed aboard. They sat three-abreast on the front seat.

"Will he take us all the way?" Bernard asked.

The driver smiled. "Yes, my friend, all the way. I am Edward." He let go the wheel and offered his hand. Bernard shook it. Nasra sat between them, rested her head on the back of the seat, and closed her eyes. The truck threw up a cloud of dust as it left the city outskirts behind. Soon they were in the dry mountains heading for Fez, the radio trying to compete with the roar of the engine. The swinging baubles on the mirror were the only thing of colour to look at from the cab.

Bernard dozed in the warmth of the cabin. Every now and then, his neck snapping brought him back to life. About an hour into their journey, Edward pulled over onto the side of the road and cut the engine.

"Why are we stopping?" Bernard looked around at the desolate surroundings. He thought that if anything happened out here no one would ever know. A wave of panic swept over him as he cursed himself for falling for their trap. He had willingly walked right into their clutches and now he was going to be murdered, dumped in the desert sands and that would be that. Nasra woke up and followed Edward out of the cab.

"Any reason why we are stopped?" Bernard asked again. Nasra ignored his plea and walked along the road, following

Edward at a distance. Bernard looked for Edward's gun and when he didn't find it, he jumped out of the truck and followed the pair. They were looking at the ground. The tarmac road had been ripped away in several sections.

"What is it?" Bernard asked as he caught up to them and peered at the broken road.

"Tanks," Edward said matter-of-factly. Nasra squatted down and touched the gouge in the road.

"Look, I just want to know what is going on. For God's sake."

Nasra stood up and scanned the horizon. "We had better get going."

George grabbed her arm and spun her around to face him. "Are you going to tell me what is going on or do I have to beat it out of you?"

Nasra looked at her restrained arm and jerked it away. "We have a problem. There are army around here. Manoeuvres ... or something. We cannot be seen here," she said.

"Why? Can't anyone travel on the roads?"

"Technically yes, but we will be in their report. And it wouldn't take long for the information to be disseminated." Bernard now looked to the horizon, scanning for a dust cloud or any sign or army patrols.

"They are generally here for border patrol," Edward said, then added, "from Algeria."

"But aren't we a long way from the border?"

Edward looked to the road ahead and answered that people came over and camped in the mountains then filtered down into the city, "It is a tried and trusted method. Then they gradually make their way to Tangiers and from there it is just a boat ride to Europe." He looked around one more time, turned, and walked towards their truck. "Come."

Edward drove to the next turn off and decided to take a more circuitous route to their rendezvous in Tangiers and the waiting boat. The road was less used and the maintenance lacking. They passed a few desolate villages, but the road was mainly deserted. Bernard rested his head on the door frame and casually scanned the horizon. He saw a faint dust cloud in the distance and sat up to get a better look.

"Edward, look," he said pointing off to the right and some foothills. The cloud might have been a whirling wind, but Bernard had a gut feeling they were in for trouble.

"What is it?" Nasra opened her eyes and took a pair of binoculars from the glove compartment. She scanned the hills trying to keep a steady eye on the cloud as the truck lurched across the rough track.

"Patrol. Two. One truck and one tank." Bernard squinted at the menace.

"Can we outrun them?"

Edward grabbed the map from the dashboard and gave it to Bernard. "Find me a road. West."

Bernard twisted the map to try to get his bearings. He didn't know where they were to begin to look for an exit. "Where the hell are we?"

"Look, I will drive, Edward move over." Edward and Nasra changed places – the truck never losing a rev. Bernard spread the map out for Edward to see.

"We are here?" He pointed to a spindly little by road. "If we can get to Bin el Ouidane at the lake, then we can take the left turn to Afourart."

"But isn't that through the mountains?"

Edward nodded. "It is the only way. The patrol has no money for maintenance. They just might not make the road. It is steep." Nasra looked over to the advancing vehicles.

"But what about our truck?" Bernard asked.

Nasra laughed. "Edward loves this truck. It is the best kept truck in Morocco."

Edward smiled. He pulled out his gun from the back shelf and checked the ammunition. Then he put a few more cartridges on the seat. The truck hit a big pot hole in the road and the three were thrown together. They were just getting settled, when a shot rang out.

"They are warning us to stop," Nasra said, then went on, "It is decision time." She looked over to Edward and Bernard.

"Run," Edward said, picking up his gun and leaning over in front of Nasra. Bernard looked at the patrol getting closer. They would be on a collision course in less than ten minutes. He frowned.

"Well?" Nasra looked over to him.

"Run."

Nasra put her foot down and gripped the wheel a little tighter. "Hang on." She floored the truck and it took off with a roar. It picked up the dirt from the soft road edge and Bernard looked back to see a huge cloud of dust following them. Another shot rang out and echoed in the mountains. Nasra kept her foot flat and leant forward to better judge the road surface. She swerved several times and then they started to climb. The gears screamed as she took every change to the rev limit.

"I'm going out," Edward said. He motioned Bernard to move over and began to climb out the window. Bernard watched him deftly move to the back of the truck and safely sit in the tray amongst the jerry cans and tarps.

"Bernard," Edward yelled. "Pass me the cartridges." Bernard leant out of the window and looked down at the growing drop below. He swung his arm out, passed the clips over, and looked at the patrol truck. It was belching smoke as it tried to catch up. He watched as every gear change brought on more smoke. Edward was right. They might not last the distance. He retreated to the cab and watched the road. Nasra drove with an expert eye. She took the bends and sweeping corners at the optimum angle and took the engine to its limits. Bernard was just beginning to think they had outrun the patrol when a gun shot hit the truck. Edward returned fire and then a volley of shots rang out through mountains. The patrol was shooting aimlessly. Most hit the side of the mountain and the road.

"We are out of range," Nasra said, as she took a hair bend. "This will be tricky, look."

Bernard looked at the road. It seemed to double back on itself as it wound its way around the mountain. They would be in range and side on when the patrol truck turned the hairpin bend. Nasra pumped down the gears and then willed the truck to go faster; climbing up through the gears, hanging on until Bernard thought the engine might break up. They had gained a little speed when the Army rounded the corner. A bullet hit the door and Bernard jumped.

"Shit."

"Get down!" Nasra shouted. Edward returned fire and whooped as he hit the windshield of the truck. A bullet flew into the back window just above Bernard's head and he ducked. Glass exploded into the cabin and Bernard looked up to see Nasra had a trickle of blood from her ear. He went to wipe it with his shirt sleeve when there was a huge explosion behind them. He knelt on the seat and looked out at the road from the shattered window. The patrol truck was in flames – stopped in its pursuit once and for all.

"What the hell?" he said.

Edward smiled and poked his head through the window. "Gasoline and a bullet. Easy." Nasra slowed down and then pulled over. Everything was quiet. The towering mountains seemed to swallow up their deed and mock the three small, human figures.

"I just dropped the jerry can and aimed. Kaboom," Edward said reliving the moment. Bernard watched the fire burn. He didn't want to think about the men inside. Men that probably had families that now would be without the bread winner. He looked at Nasra and wondered at a woman who could just look and walk away. *All in a day's work for her*, he thought.

They followed the road to re-join the main highway just the other side of Oulad Salem. After the rigors of the mountains, the highway seemed tame and ordinary. The traffic was steady with trucks, cars, and buses.

The truck bumped and lurched for hours on end, Edward only stopping once to fill up from the jerry cans in the back. Bernard wanted to talk to Nasra, but felt Edward was always listening and so kept his thoughts and fears to himself. He wondered why he had put his faith and his life in her hands so readily. In the quiet of the cab, he thought about Gabrielle and his infidelity. Guilt was way down on his list of emotions as he pondered on the scenes in the Hilton Hotel. Gently he reached over and held Nasra's hand. She grasped it casually and smiled at him. *Yes,* he thought. *He did trust her with his life. He had no choice.*

The trip on the highway was just shy of three hundred miles, but Edward's detour over the Atlas Mountains made it seem the very long way around. It was well into the night when they finally drove into the bright lights of Tangiers. Nasra was alert, but Bernard was bone weary and yawned.

"It's very touristy isn't it?" he said looking at all the lights and street vendors. The smells of food wafting over the air made his stomach growl.

"Anyone hungry?" Edward drove through the bright lights and eventually stopped the truck in a small suburban street and turned off the lights.

"We are here." He smiled at Bernard and shook his hand.

"Good luck to you."

Bernard nodded and returned the well wishes. Nasra and he climbed down from the cab and stretched like a cat, rolling her shoulders and twisting her back.

"Who was he, Nasra?" Bernard asked as Edward walked down the street and disappeared into a house.

"Just a friend. He is discreet. We like that."

"We?"

"Oh Bernard, you ask too many questions. Let's eat."

"Where?" Bernard smiled at the joke. Nasra took his arm and led him into the same house, following Edward. Inside Bernard was greeted by a family of four adults and about a dozen children, all eating. They beckoned him to sit on their carpet and soon he was helping himself to lamb, goat, and vegetables – all with a distinctive spicy flavour, and, Bernard thought, absolutely delicious. He relaxed and enjoyed himself, forgetting about what might lay ahead, as his journey brought him ever closer to Paris. Nasra conversed in Arabic and Edward seemed at ease in the family situation.

"Is this a safe house or something?"

"Bernard, another question. This is Edward's family." She saw the unbelieving look on Bernard's face. Edward was a very black African and these people were definitely not African. "He was adopted. He came from Sudan as a boy and Ahmed and Sula took him in. He is family." Bernard smiled at Edward. He had heard of the lost boys of Sudan, but didn't realize some make it all the way to Morocco.

"Just one more question."

Nasra put her arm on his shoulder. "What?"

"Oh, nothing." Bernard stopped before he started. Nasra shrugged her shoulders and laughed, then planted a kiss on his forehead. Replete with food, Bernard stood up and thanked his host. He felt completely at ease in the family atmosphere – the parents, the children, the general clatter of family life. He thought about how Gabrielle had decided to forgo children and he had acquiesced. It was all so different in Paris. He had wanted to ask Nasra if she felt something for him, but the idea was a stupid one. She was doing a job and he was just collateral, nothing more.

The women cleaned up and put the children to bed and the house was quiet with just the men talking and drinking tea on the veranda. Bernard felt restless and offered a walk before they went to bed.

"No. We have to leave in ..." Nasra looked at her watch. "one and a half hours."

"Oh, I just thought that we would meet in the morning." Nasra shook her head.

"Get some rest. I will wake you. Edward will take us to the boat."

Bernard was offered a blanket and a cushion and he lay down on the carpet and tried to sleep, but his mind was racing. He closed his eyes and listened to the household. Hushed voices talked heatedly in Arabic. There words were unintelligible but the tone was menacing. Eventually, he dropped off to sleep only to be woken in what seemed like a few minutes.

Nasra shook his shoulder. "We must go."

Bernard shot up and rubbed his eyes. The house was dark and quiet. With Nasra leading, they tiptoed out of the room into the front courtyard and then into the street. Edward was waiting about one hundred metres down the road with the truck running and no lights.

"What about my bag?"

"Leave it." Nasra said striding in front. Bernard looked back to the house, but in the dark, they all looked alike. He hoped Ahmed and Sula could use casual trousers, cotton shirts and a used toothbrush. Once inside the truck, Edward moved off, slowly going up the gears until they reached the main thoroughfare, then he turned on the headlights and joined the traffic. Bernard looked at his watch ... 1:15. He was amazed at the traffic at this late hour.

"Is it always this busy?"

"Always," Edward said as he changed lanes. Nasra looked behind and then Bernard saw her stiffen.

"What is it?"

"Police."

Bernard turned around. Through the hole where the back window had been shot, he could just see a small car weaving in and out of the traffic in an effort to catch up.

"Hang on." Edward slammed the gears down into second and did a quick swipe of the wheel to the left. The truck veered into an exit and then did a lightening turn to the right and parked under an overpass. Edward switched off the lights and they waited. The police car turned down the left exit, and kept going, gained speed and eventually disappeared. The three waited a good ten minuted and eventually backed out of their hiding spot and re-joined the traffic.

"How the hell did they know we were here?" Bernard couldn't believe it.

"I don't know. I really don't know."

"You didn't miss a micro dot, did you?" Nasra shook her head and was about to answer when Edwards phone rang. He drove with one hand and listened to the call. His face dropped as he hung up.

"It is my family. They were interrogated by the police. They told them where we are going. They threatened my brothers and sisters." The three sat still thinking on the havoc they were causing.

"Bastards." Edward spat.

"My bag. It must have been my bag."

Nasra agreed.

"Shit, all this and they still know where we are. Why would it be the police?"

120

"Not the police, just people saying they are the police. The FFZ have..." Nasra drew a deep breath. "Resources."

Bernard drew back in his seat. Saliki had said the same thing,' resources'. He tried to judge Nasra's words as just a coincidence, but his doubts remained as to her integrity.

"I have to get back." Edward drove now with a determination to get the job finished. "I will drop you at the port and then I must leave."

"You can't go back Edward. They will be waiting." Nasra said, but they could see Edward had made up his mind.

The commercial port was lit up as ships loaded and unloaded. Cranes, trucks and men all worked through the night in the business of stevedoring. Edward parked the truck in a side alley and his passengers slipped out into the dark.

"Good luck," Bernard whispered and then the truck was gone. The narrow street led to a large wharf where a tanker was tied up. Bernard marvelled at its size.

"It that the one?"

Nasra laughed. "No." She led Bernard through a maze of small streets and passages. They eventually emerged at a little marina. Fishing boats bobbed up and down in the swell and one or two yachts swayed with the movement of the sea. "This way."

He followed her to a jetty and watched as she knocked on the hull of a Beneteau yacht. The rigging caught the moonlight and she looked magnificent with a patina of silver and white. They waited but no one answered.

"Shit." Nasra turned around, scanning the area. She quickly made the choice to leave. "Follow me."

Bernard lamely followed as they made their way back to the marina precinct and hid in the shadows. "What now?"

"We wait," she said looking at her watch. They stood still and watched the boat. Nasra put her finger to her lips and crouched down. Bernard pressed his body against the wall and wished he were invisible. He watched as Nasra took a gun from the holster at her back and poised herself. Bernard held his breath. There was the unmistakable sound of footfalls walking on the path just to their right. Bernard tried to squint, thinking the whites of his eyes would be a dead giveaway, his eyes were so wide.

The walking was getting closer. It stopped. Bernard thought his lungs would burst as he waited. He saw Nasra position herself for a shot. Then they heard the sound of feet turning and the intruder began to walk away. Bernard counted the steps until he couldn't hear them anymore. He dared to breathe again. Nasra stood up and put her gun away.

"I didn't know you had that?" Bernard whispered, pointing to the holster at the small of her back. Nasra shrugged. She looked up and down the street and when it was safe, they made their way back down to the boat. Bernard stopped at the spot where he figured the stranger had been. He sniffed the air. The unmistakeable aroma of a cigar lingered on the night. It was so familiar, Bernard, for the moment, forgot its sinister connotations. He caught up to Nasra as she climbed aboard the boat.

"We will wait," she said. It was all they could do as the next leg of the journey was out of their hands.

CHAPTER THIRTEEN

Nasra held out her hand and Bernard grabbed it as he climbed aboard the yacht. Bernard followed her down the companionway into the cabin

"It looks quite new," Bernard said. Everything was stowed in preparation for the journey and as Bernard looked around, he noticed the lack of charts or any sort of navigation aid. When Gabrielle and he had taken charter yacht holidays in the Black sea, the boat was loaded with all the latest charts, GPS, hand held GPS and radar. This boat seemed almost bare without any aid. He sat in the booth seat and ran his fingers through his hair.

"Nasra," he began, "I think we were followed. I..." he stumbled with the words, "I smelt a cigar. A Cuban. I know that smell and it came from someone I met in Israel."

"What are you saying?" Nasra kept watch up the stairs for their skipper.

"It's just that I was there when he lit his cigar. And I smelt it again this evening. I'm sure."

"Who?"

"En Saliki. From the Israeli secret service."

Nasra turned and stared hard at Bernard. "En Saliki?"

"Yes, I'm sure." He looked at Nasra and tried to fathom her tortured look. "What is it?"

"En Saliki... is the mole."

"But..."

"If he wants you to run, it can only be for one purpose. He wants..."

"What?"

123

"He wants the connection. You are the link, Bernard. Think about it. If he let you go when he could just have easily killed you... well, he wants you to..."

"To lead him to the big guys. But isn't that what NATA wants too?"

"Ssshhh." Nasra put her finger to her lips and slipped back into the cabin from her perch on the steps. She took her gun and waited. The boat rocked as someone came on board and then he stooped into the doorway.

"Tickets, please." The man smiled and held out his hands. "No guns." Bernard couldn't pick the man's accent as he jumped down the stairs and stood in the saloon.

"What cha. I'm Mike."

Nasra surreptitiously put her gun away and shook his hand, introducing herself and Bernard. Bernard took the hand and looked over the tanned skin and the blonde hair.

"Are you...?"

"Australian, yep," Mike said shaking Bernard's hand vigorously.

"So, shall we get underway? I'm being paid good money, so let's get the show on the road." Mike busied himself with the engine controls. Bernard and Nasra went on deck to loosen the dock lines. The engine beat a steady rhythm as the boat swung out of the mooring and made its way to the breakwater and the sea beyond. Bernard stood on the foredeck and looked ahead. At last, he felt free of the intrigue, the chase, and the threats. He breathed deeply and tried to enjoy the moment. The breeze felt fresh and the moon was high enough to cast a silvery shimmer on the water that made everything look magical. Nasra came and stood by his side and Bernard casually put his arm around her waist.

Mike hoisted the main sail and unfurled the headsail then cut the engine. The wind cracked the sails taught and gently the boat glided through the water.

Bernard looked up the mast and back at the boat and noticed there were no navigation lights. He made his way to the cockpit and sat down. "We don't have any lights."

"No. Not necessary. And not wise if you want to be invisible." Mike sat back and took the wheel with his feet. The only light Bernard could see was the red of the compass.

"You must know these waters. I didn't see a chart."

"Shut it. Too many questions mate."

Nasra joined the men in the cockpit and the three sat silently watching the moon reflect on the beginning of the Mediterranean Sea. Bernard yawned and closed his eyes.

"Look, there is a bunk down below," Mike said. Bernard took up the offer and was soon crawling into the aft cabin and oblivion. Nasra wasn't far behind.

Bernard's sleep was fitful and restless. He woke up several times, disorientated and sweating. After a few hours, he couldn't sleep anymore and scrambled out of the cabin.

The steering station was deserted and the sail had been shortened. Bernard shivered and looked at the rising sun that was just beginning to creep over the horizon.

Mike appeared. "Want a jacket?"

Bernard nodded and Mike went down into the cabin to re-appear with a red sailing jacket.

"It really is spectacular, isn't it?"

"Sure is." They looked at the sun rise in silence.

"You want coffee."

"Yes, that sounds great." Bernard wrapped the jacket around him and settled back into the seat. Once again, Mike shot down the companionway and Bernard was left alone. He mused on what had happened to get him to this point. It seemed an incredible journey. How he had managed to survive the ordeal was even more incredible.

"Morning, sailor." Nasra came and sat beside him. "Are we close?"

"I haven't asked yet. It was just a pleasure to sit still in safety and enjoy the scenery."

Nasra looked at the horizon and smiled.

"I totally agree Bernard." She snuggled up to him and he put his coat around her and kissed her hair.

"Where is Mike?"

"Making coffee, I hope."

Mike appeared, carrying a tray of mugs up the stairs. Nasra had hopped up to help him when he dropped the tray. Three shots rang out. Nasra stood for a moment in shock and then clutched her chest, the blood running freely through her fingers. Another three shots hit her. Mike aimed squarely at her chest. She staggered back and clutched the Bimini cover. Reaching for her gun, she managed one shot, which hit Mike in the shoulder, and then fell backwards overboard.

Bernard sat stunned. He watched the action as if it was in slow motion. No words could escape his throat as he saw Nasra get caught in the boats wake and bob on the water face down. Then a rage boiled inside him. The festering inaction that had lain dormant for so long rose like bitter bile and he lunged at the Australian. The pair fell down the stairs into the cabin and Bernard threw a punch in Mike's face. His fist hit Mike's eye and blood spurted from the raw wound. Mike rounded on Bernard and whacked the side of his head on the wooded steps. Bernard shook his head as his vision blurred. He grabbed a handful of the blood soaked blonde hair. He pulled until Mike's head was level with the table and then thumped it on the metal corner. Mike slumped over and lay still.

Bernard looked at his hands. They were matted with blood and hair. They began to shake. He leaned back on the settee and panted. It only took a second for him to remember Nasra and he hauled himself back out onto the deck. She was gone.

He frantically turned the wheel and the boat responded until the sails began to flog in the wind and the yacht began to slow. Bernard looked up, caught unaware, as Mike thrust a boat hook at him. The brass hook caught Bernard in the stomach. He doubled over in pain. Mike jumped on him, thumping him in the face with an iron fist. As the boat rounded up into the wind, the men scrabbled on the deck, blood splattering the portholes. Bernard grabbed Mike's shirt and shoved him over the compass binnacle. He knocked the depth sounder off the mounting. The men scrabbled for a foothold as the boat rocked from side to side.

As the gunwale dipped towards the water, Bernard wrestled free of Mike's grip and staggered towards the bow. He had seen some fishing gear stowed in a deck-box and figured there might be a knife. Mike chased after him and took him down with a tackle. He held Bernard down on the foredeck his fingers tightening around his neck. Bernard reached up and grabbed a winch handle. He brought the metal handle down on the side of Mike's head with such force he heard a crack. Mike's fingers let go.

Bernard gasped for air and swung the handle down for another attack, the star shaped end embedded itself in Mike's skull, and the Australian slumped to the deck. Bernard tried to pull the handle out, but it was stuck in its victim's skull and refused to relinquish its grip. A growing pool of blood raced to port as the boat heeled in the swell of the sea. The stream of red found its way to the scuppers, mingling with the water.

Bernard lay down and closed his eyes as the adrenalin leeched from his muscles. He could see the sun through his lids. Every now and again, the boat creaked and moaned and the main sheet shaded his eyes. How long he lay still, he didn't know, but when he finally stirred himself, the grizzly remains of the fight made him violently throw up. Wiping his swollen mouth with his sleeve, he looked at his victim.

127

The blood had congealed into a messy pool, which snaked its way down the boat to disappear over the side. Mike lay twisted around the rigging, the handle still embedded in his skull. Bernard raised himself and looked at the sails. The boat was heaved to into the wind and bobbing calmly in the water. He stood up and tried to make sense of what had happened. The only conclusion was that he had killed a man. He ran his fingers through his hair then looked at the blood stains.

Standing on the deck, he was trying to make some sensible decisions when the HF radio crackled into life. The sound of another human being spurred Bernard into action and he raced down stairs and grabbed the receiver. The radio had a myriad of numbers and dials. Without any knowledge, Bernard couldn't answer. He picked up the handpiece and pressed to talk.

"Mayday, Mayday, Mayday," he yelled. Silence. He tried again and then stopped. From where he stood, he could see the body on the deck. Questions raced through his mind as he played out different scenarios. He put the receiver back on its cradle and turned off the tuner. He knew what he had to do.

Bernard pulled down the mainsail and wound up the headsail. Without the steadying influence of the sheets, the boat began to roll and Bernard had to hang on as he walked around preparing things. The chain locker held a forty pound CQR anchor and he hauled it onto the deck. Next, he fetched several rolls of duct tape. The sea was calming as the midday sun shortened the shadows and Bernard worked in silence.

He dragged the Australian to the foredeck and began to lash him to the anchor with the tape. Round and around he went until all three rolls were done. He was sweating with the effort. Taking a short break, he went inside and grabbed a beer from the fridge. He drank greedily, until he spied his bloodied hands.

Rushing to the sink he scrubbed them with dishwashing liquid until they were raw, hoping to absolve his guilt with the soap. His clothes were stained, so he undressed and threw them overboard. Standing naked, he watched the last vestiges of his life float away. He thought that he could start again. A fresh start.

He once again looked at his hands and spied his wedding ring. How could Gabrielle love him now? He had killed a man. He wriggled the ring off his finger and looked at the gold band. She had loved him once. He had always loved her and probably always would, but... he threw the ring into the sea.

With Mike trussed up, Bernard manhandled the body to the side of the boat. The plan was to consign the body to the deep. He shoved and heaved but the bundle was unwieldy and the winch handle was caught on the life lines that surrounded the boat. Working naked, Bernard bent down and prised the handle out of Mike's scalp. It left a deep clotted hole that made Bernard gag. With the handle out of the way, the anchor and its passenger splashed over the side and sank without a trace. Bernard wished his part in the man's death would be as easy to absolve.

As the afternoon clouds gathered, the wind picked up and the yacht bucked on the choppy sea. Things seemed very quiet on the boat. Bernard slued the decks with sea water and then took a shower in the bathroom. The events whirled around in his mind and as he closed his eyes to let the warm water wash over him he felt sick. *Mike had obviously lived on the boat for some time,* Bernard thought, as he rummaged around for clothes. Suitably dressed, he made a coffee and took it on deck to start to plan his next move. The boat was scudding along with the small gusts of wind and going nowhere. Bernard took a bearing at the sun and went to find the autopilot. He ransacked the cabin and finally came up with a few charts, luckily one that included the coast of Spain.

In the night, the boat must have drifted, Bernard surmised, as he remembered the ferry only took about 35 minutes from one side to the other. He could see the shore. With a little perseverance, he found his rough position on the map. He was on the Atlantic side of the Straits of Gibraltar and the land he could see was Spain. Now with a purpose, he drew some navigation lines and plotted a course. It felt good to be doing something constructive. He threw himself into the navigation and then found the autopilot. With a bit of a crash course, he managed to set his co-ordinates and went outside to set the headsail. The boat appreciated the wind and the sail filled with ease, lifting the hull from the turgid wallow to crest the waves and sail along at a decent pace. Bernard pulled the sheet in tight and went to grab a winch handle to tighten it further. The only handle was still on the foredeck. Bernard locked the sheet rope off and made the hand over hand trip to the bow of the boat. The handle was still covered in matted hair and blood and Bernard wanted to kick it overboard.

He looked at the sail and realised it needed trimming if he was to make any speed at all. He tenderly picked up the handle, the blood, a sticky ooze, stuck to his hand. Mesmerized at the sight of the dried blood, Bernard didn't see the ship until it was on a collision course. He raced to the wheel, and disengaged the autopilot. He tacked to port, using the winches to pull the sail over to the other side. The enormous tankers wake rocked the yacht and washed the decks clean with clear water. After the near miss, Bernard shortened the sail and cruised taking control of the wheel and leaving nothing to chance.

Once inside the Mediterranean Sea, he relaxed a little and began to enjoy himself. He wished he could just sail away and forget it all.

The land was quite close when Bernard furled the sail and heaved-to. He needed time to study the map. He needed somewhere safe to land – somewhere where he would be inconspicuous. There were several ports and marinas along the Spanish shore that were small and off the main tourist routes. A small marina was just south of Santa Margarita. He estimated it would be a good three hours away with his short haul sail. He made a sandwich and settled back for the ride. As the winter sun dipped on the horizon, Bernard donned a jacket and started to pack a small carry-all he had found. There was money in the chart table and as much as he hated taking it, he shoved it in his pocket. He found Mike's passport and studied the photo. *He looked quite harmless, even a bit gormless*, Bernard thought. *Why would he want to kill Nasra? Why not me?* Bernard tried to figure it out. Then he pulled up his sleeves and things fell into place.

The clothes were way too big for Mike. When they were first on the boat things were a mess, almost as if a struggle had taken place. Mike wasn't sure where things were as he hunted for their jackets. He had made light of his ineptitude saying he liked to live in a pig sty, but he could *never find anything.*

Perhaps, Bernard thought, *Mike had disposed of the real boat owner and ...* he suddenly saw a clue. Perhaps Saliki and his Cuban cigar had come down to the dock to make sure Nasra and he boarded the boat. Mike was to kill them all along, only it went wrong. As Bernard made a few sandwiches for his journey, he wondered how Saliki knew they were taking a boat. Nasra has said she organised the boat when they were in Marrakech.

Bernard didn't want to think she was playing two sides, but alone in the boat, his scenarios began to all add up. NATA wanted the big guy, the bankroll in the defence of Tag. Nasra was conveniently placed to gain his trust. *Everything was just a little too convenient,* Bernard thought.

He could have been killed a dozen times, but he was still here. Why? Bernard had watched too many movies and thought it quite likely that once NATA had the top dog he wouldn't be incarcerated, but more than likely put on the payroll. A left wing fanatic could be an important ally on the killing fields, an easy person to blame.

"A patsy," Bernard said aloud. He wondered if he was their patsy. Was he disposable too? Then the FFZ wanted to stop Nozette and Simeoni at any price – and maybe Nasra too. They were the radical element in all this he pondered. The one thing Bernard did know for a fact was that if he didn't get back to Paris soon and warn Tag, it would just be a matter of when and where. Tag was a dead man walking.

CHAPTER FOURTEEN

The dinghy outboard spluttered into life and Bernard headed for the shelter of the Marina. It was dusk when he turned his inflatable side on to the wharf and tied up. Fishing boats hugged the walls and the walkways were piled high in nets and junk. He left the boat, and with his waterproof carry-all stepped ashore. He walked purposefully down the jetty, through the gate, and onto the deserted street. The first thing he needed was a phone.

"George?" Bernard asked.

"Yes?"

"It's me, Bernard."

"Where the fuck are you?" George asked then stopped. "No, don't answer that."

"Can you talk?"

"No."

"Ring Janelle." Bernard heard him hang up and stood at the booth trying to figure it out. *What did he mean, ring Janelle.* He stood there for a minute and finally it hit him. Janelle always kept a spare phone in the charger. He racked his brain trying to remember the number. He closed his eyes and pictured the office – the drawer with the charger in it, the spare phone. *God,* he thought, *he used to remember numbers.* Now he expected his iPhone to do all the work. He looked around in the glare of the one bulb in the phone booth then read the graffiti on the wall. It extolled the virtue of a Clarrisa on her birthday. *That was it.* Janelle had asked for their birthdays. Bernard typed in the numbers and they bounced. He transposed the numbers and heard a ring tone.

"Hello Bernard. I knew you would get it. Just give me a minute, I'm walking." Bernard waited and presently George came on the line. "How are you?"

"I'm okay. You?"

"I'm good, but it's been pretty full on here. I've got NATA breathing down my neck and the police are making it really difficult." George coughed.

"You sound dreadful."

"Just a virus I think. Oh, your cousin rang. Ira isn't it."

"Yes."

"Bernard, we have been trying to find you for days. Your mother, she..." George stammered. "She died three days ago." Bernard closed his eyes and banged his head against the glass.

"Are you there?"

"I'm here."

"I'm sorry. Really, I am so sorry Bernard."

"Thanks."

"Look, I'll have this number with me. Call me tomorrow. We will work something out where ever you are. Bernard..."

"Yes."

"Ira said she wanted you to know that she didn't need to wait any longer. And you would know what that means."

"I do." Bernard hung up. He slumped down on the cold concrete and buried his head in his folded arms. The cold seeped into his bones. Eventually, he took a deep breath and stood up.

With his bag slung over his shoulder, he made his way to the main road. He looked the seafarer with his jacket and boots and it wasn't long before he had hitched a ride with a truck going a good way up the coast. The driver was talkative, but as Bernard only knew a few words of Spanish and the driver knew about the same in French they confined themselves to listening to the radio and eating sweets.

The dark landscape flicked by and Bernard looked at his reflection in the window. He had a rugged look that was new and in his study, he saw strength. Was it because he had killed a fellow human? Was it because he had made a decision to divorce Gabrielle? He closed his eyes and tried to sleep, but every time he dozed, he relived his nightmare on the boat, and his conscience pricked him to remain awake.

It was around midnight, when the truck pulled into a sleeping town and parked in a truck stop. The driver mimed he was sleeping and Bernard was welcome to stay. The men settled down in the fuggy cab and once again, Bernard tried to sleep. Eventually, out of sheer exhaustion, Bernard did sleep, but his tortured dreams would not let him forget. Laying in the dark, he thought he would never forget.

The driver shook Bernard and he woke with a start and looked at his watch. The face was smashed and a big crack ran through the glass. He jumped up, defensive and disorientated. His watch said six am. His ride was going inland and he was told to leave. The air was cold and the truck stop dirty and deserted. There was nothing to do but walk back into the town and hope for a bus station or something to get his nearer him goal.

He had begun to walk when another truck stopped. The driver was French and going to Marseille. Bernard hopped up into the cab and introduced himself. Philippe was carrying air conditioners and often picked up hitch hikers for company. Bernard invented a plausible history and sat back satisfied that soon he would be in France. He knew the TVG train ran from Marseille to Paris. Things were looking better by the kilometre.

Philippe talked about his family, his hopes, his dream of running a restaurant one day and his love of food. His waistline, it seemed to Bernard, was already spreading the love. It was easy to let him talk and Bernard listened, immersing himself in Philippe's life. They passed villages and towns and soon came to the border. The Mercedes truck pulled into a weighing station and the men went for a meal. It felt strange to be so openly anonymous after the subterfuge of the last days. Bernard looked around at the faces in the cafe and took a seat at the rear of the shop. Philippe explained this would be their last stop and handed over a wad of Euros.

"No, I couldn't, Philippe."

"It is on the account. Please."

Bernard took the money and ordered a full meal. He hadn't realised how hungry he was until the food arrived. As he chewed his way through the steak, he began to relax. The small act of generosity went some way to restoring his faith in human nature.

"When will we be there?" he asked.

Philippe looked up from his chips, "Oh, about ten or eleven. If the traffic is bad; maybe midnight. I have to stop at Barcelona." He put his fork down and wiped his mouth. Bernard nodded and went to pay his bill. He stocked up on snacks for the trip and stuffed them in his bag, thinking of nothing but the high speed train to Paris in less than twelve hours.

The Mercedes truck was comfortable and the two men soon fell into idle chatter. Bernard dropped off to sleep and woke up with a start.

"Bad dream?"

"You might say that." Bernard wiped his face with his hands and tried not to think of his nightmare.

"Where are we?"

"Just coming up to Barcelona. I must report in and unload some pallets. About one hour." The truck rounded a corner on the highway and the exit appeared. Philippe manoeuvred the big rig with ease and stopped. "You can walk if you want. One hour."

Bernard smiled and jumped down, stomping his feet against the cold. The depot was busy with traffic and he watched with interest. Here was a world he hardly knew existed. A world that delivered the things he couldn't live without. It was an honest living, he decided.

The rest of the trip was an easy run on the highway. Towns, cities, and villages all slipped by as their final destination, Marseilles, became a reality. When it was time to go, Bernard felt a pang of regret. He had enjoyed the company and so he felt he owed Philippe some semblance of truth.

"Look, I'm a lawyer. From Paris. If ever you need any legal advice, please look me up." He wrote his name down on a piece of paper and handed it to Philippe. "Call me. I owe you my life."

The truck drove away and Bernard watched its red tail lights until it turned a corner, then he turned and walked in the direction of the train.

The TVG timetable stopped at midnight. He had ten minutes to catch the train and so found a telephone booth in the hope of talking to George. The number rang out. He was sure George had said he would be on the line. He tried again and someone picked up.

"Hello." Bernard said. The line disconnected. Thrown into a panic he rang the only other person he could remember.

"Gabrielle?"

"Bernard," she said sounding anxious. "Where are you?"

"Look, I can't explain now. I just need to know where George is right now. Can you call him, please, Gabbie?"

"Of course. Bernard, you sound strange. Are you ok?" Bernard pondered the question.

"Yes. Just find George and tell him I'm nearly there."

"Your nearly there," Gabrielle repeated the message.

"I have to go now. Love you," He said the words so easily, he wished he could believe them.

Once in his carriage he took off his coat and spread his meagre belongings over the seats. The last thing he needed was company. As the train gathered speed, the lights of Marseille were left behind and the view from the window became black. Bernard looked at his reflection. His looked unkempt and dirty. Gabbie had asked if he was ok. How could he tell her that things had changed? He had changed.

His fingers went for the wedding band and he looked at his naked finger. He was not the same man. He, who had tried to uphold the law and believed in man's right to justice, was now just one of the animals with base instincts. He glanced at his reflection once again and then leaned back in his seat and closed his eyes. Soon he would be home, in Paris, and in the glare of the city with all magnificence and its flaws.

CHAPTER FIFTEEN

The apartment was in darkness when Bernard opened the door. With the heavy curtains drawn, the lights of the city didn't intrude. The feeling that it was good to be home relaxed Bernard and he turned on the light to reacquaint himself with the familiar surroundings. The red light was blinking on the phone and he pressed the retrieval button and listened while he made a coffee. There were calls to Gabrielle about her work, a couple of hang-ups and one from George. He listened carefully as George explained he would be in the office or with Janelle. Bernard knew the shorthand meant to ring her mobile. He punched in the numbers and waited. The phone rang out. He called the office, and no one picked up. Then, thinking his wife might know where George might be, he dialled her mobile. It went to message bank.

The sun was just beginning to rise when Bernard, anxious to get to the office, called a cab. The traffic was building, even at this early hour, but after a few inventive turns and back-tracks, the taxi dropped him off at Rue De Maine.

The first thing he noticed was that the outer door was open. It was too early for customers and it should have been locked. With some trepidation, he climbed the stairs and pushed the reception door open. Papers lay everywhere on the floor. The place looked like it had been ransacked. Bernard opened George's office door and could see there had been a struggle. The one chair was knocked over, the desk was a mess of papers, and George's picture of his family had been smashed on the floor. On closer inspection, it looked to Bernard like someone had put their heel on the photo and ground it down. His office wasn't much different. The filing cabinet was pushed over and the intruder had thrown his files around. It was a mess.

It was obvious something had happened and now George was missing. Bernard figured the only thing to do was contact Duval. He might have an idea. The thought of Duval stopped him short. He would have to tell him about Nasra. What would he say? How could he explain that he was in love with his wife and now she was floating face down in the Mediterranean somewhere?

It was an impossible situation. He sat down and wrote some notes, then screwed the paper in a ball and threw it on the floor. Perhaps he would not have to say anything. Perhaps NATA already knew. He rehearsed a few words, but nothing seemed appropriate. Bernard decided to leave it up to chance and play it as it happened. He found Duval's card in Janelle's files and made the call. Bernard went to ask Duval if he knew about George when the agent stopped him.

"Say nothing. I will meet you."

"Where." Duval explained the directions to a cafe near an underground station.

"Half-an-hour?"

"Yes," Bernard said. He tried to tidy the room and then noticed his package from Morocco. It had been savagely ripped apart. Everything looked fine. Then he noticed the pendant was missing. Nasra had helped him pick it out and the memory stirred his sentimentality. He put the dilapidated box on the chair, looked at his watch, and with one last glance at the office, walked out the door. The cafe was only twenty minutes north. Bernard began to walk. He made good time and was seated at Cafe Bon when Duval walked across the road and joined him.

"Not here, follow me."

"Look, don't give me all this spy crap. I've come to see you, and a bit of civility would be preferable to a scrabble in the undergrowth." Bernard grabbed his glasses and polished them in frustration.

Duval scanned the street and sat down. "As you wish." He turned off his phone and ordered two coffees. "Now, Mr Simeoni, what do you have to tell me?"

"Well..." Bernard put his glasses on and began, "I thought it would be you who'd have something to tell me."

Duval looked confused. "Excuse me?"

"First." Bernard drew his chair in closer and hissed, "Where the hell is George?"

Duval remained stony faced. "That is what I was going to ask you? We have reason to believe..."

"Reason to believe," Bernard mocked his words.

Duval narrowed his gaze at Bernard. "We have a suspicion that Mr Nozette is talking to someone in the group."

"What fuckin' group, Duval. You're not making a lot of sense. I just about had a gut full of people telling me half-truths on a fuckin' need to know basis." Bernard slammed his hand down on the table. The waiter brought their coffees and diffused the situation.

"Look, we were watching him. Our man was compromised and we lost him."

"You lost him. How you ever get any results is beyond me."

"We have limited resources. We are not high on the list for..."

Bernard threw up his hand for Duval to stop. "Don't give me that budget, funds, money crap. The simple matter is that you failed. Failed, and now he is out there somewhere." Bernard waved his hand in the air. "And you don't know where." The two men sat stubbornly silent, sipping their coffee. Bernard began to think about Nasra. He had to tell Duval, it was only right, and so he softened his tone.

"Duval, I need to... I mean, I met your wife."

"Nasra? How?" Bernard rubbed his furrowed brow.

"She helped me in Morocco. She said you were married once."

"Yes, once." Duval twirled his coffee cup.

"Duval, there was an accident. Nasra..."

Duval cast his eyes down to the table cloth and picked at the threads.

"She tried to save me. She said you worked on the same side."

"We did. Then she went to the ISS, the Israeli Secret Service."

"What? She told me..." Bernard started then stopped.

"Yes?"

"Nothing. It's nothing. She just told me that she really loved you."

"Thanks." Duval pushed his cup away and stood up. "Don't worry, we will find him. It's only a matter of time."

Bernard nodded and watched Duval cross the road and walk away. *Time,* he thought, *was something they didn't have, as every day brought Tag closer to court and justice.*

He sat for some time, trying to gather all the information and make sense of it. He took a pen and paper and jotted down what he knew. He now knew Nasra was ISS. He knew the FFZ wanted him dead or to reveal the leader of Tag's group or both. ISS wanted that as well and Bernard drew a large arrow to link the two. NATA wanted the head of Tag's Neo-Nazi group, but didn't want Nozette and Simeoni dead, just as bait. He wondered briefly, why the head honcho was so important to everyone. If he were just a misguided individual then he wouldn't be vital to everyone. If he was a politician or a person in high authority, that would put a whole new ball into the game.

The other question concerned the final motive. Did they want capture or liquidation? Bernard shuddered at the thought. He ordered another coffee and some food and sat back to watch the human traffic walk by. It was good to just sit in civilized surroundings after the tumultuous events of the last week. He looked at the ordinary people with their ordinary lives. *Everyone has secrets he reflected. In all the subterfuge,* he thought, *everyone had dismissed the most salient point.* Nozette and Simeoni were Jews. He hoped his secret would remain just that as he ate his croissant.

CHAPTER SIXTEEN

George arrived at the office early in the hope of catching up on his other cases before Tag once again intruded on his time. He had been to numerous interviews and re-interviews and there seemed to be a stone wall blocking his every avenue of inquiry. The small bits of information he gathered were inconsequential in the scheme of things. He had met Tag on several occasions and tried to extract some remorse or empathy from the man. *But,* George thought, *Tag was completely brain washed and he just wanted to spit the rhetoric out, almost like a rehearsal for the real thing.*

The papers were reporting on another trial in Russia and all those Neo-Nazi supporters were imprisoned. No matter that their defence talked about destructive gangs and groups for disaffected impressionable youth and the likelihood of brain washing. George had read the trial with interest and noted the complete lack of moral education the accused exhibited. Tag was similar in so many ways.

He had started to plough his way through the correspondence, when there was a bang downstairs. He walked to the stairwell.

"We're not open for business yet" he said to the two burley men trudging up the stairs. "I'm sorry, but we are not open for another hour." One of the men produced a gun when he reached the top step. George backed off.

"There is no money on the premises. I don't have anything of value here." The gun toting thug waved the pistol at George's face and indicated they should all move into his office. Once inside George was shoved down on his desk and his hands were cable-tied behind his back.

"Fuck you. I told you, we don't have any money."

"Shut it." The larger of the two replied. George was picked up and manhandled to his seat. He sat down and took a good look at his assailants. The one with the gun was thick set and had a close shaved head. His neck and hands were heavily tattooed and as George looked at the designs, he thought they looked remarkably similar to Tags. The revelation brought the whole episode into perspective.

"You are here about Tag, aren't you?"

"I told you to shut it, fuck head." George looked at the other thug. He was smaller, of a solid build. He too had a shaved head and as George studied him, he remembered seeing him before. He watched as the fellow rooted through the files and ripped open a parcel that Bernard had posted. Rummaging about in the box, he came up with a pendant. He held it up and then slipped it into his jacket pocket.

"Thief," George said. The pistol whipped George's face and he saw a spray of blood on his desk. He swallowed hard as the pain began to bite into his cheek bone. Through the pain, he remembered where he had seen the small man. He was a prominent figure in the riots. The cameras had captured the fleeing Neo-Nazis and one of them turned just before they rounded the corner and gave a salute. This was that man.

With his mind racing through the possibilities, he fleetingly thought of asking this man to be a witness. If he was with Tag throughout the riot then he might be a good alibi. He watched as he swung around and around in the chair and realised it would be a stupid idea. The man obviously had an IQ of about fifteen if he derived pleasure from a swivel chair. George wiped his face on his shoulder and stared at the brute with the gun.

"Maybe I can help you. What do you want?"

"You are coming with us. But we have to make it convincing." He punched George in the stomach and then smiled.

"Is this your family?"

George didn't answer.

"Cooperate or ..." he said. He took the photo and gave the picture a grotesque lick then threw it on the carpet and stomped on the frame with his heel. Looking at the broken photograph on the floor George knew what they were implying.

"You fucking touch my family and it will be the last thing you do." George raged at the men. He didn't see the punch coming. The fist hit him square on the side of the head. Lights flashed before his eyes and he passed out.

When he came around, he was in a car, lying on the back seat. He could see the two men in the front and tried to sit up, but his whole body ached and his head throbbed with pain. He let out a moan and the smaller of the thugs turned around.

"He's awake."

George stared at him and committed his face to memory.

"We are nearly there. Get the bag ready," the driver said. The mention of a bag threw George into a panic. He tried to think rationally. They couldn't just kill him and put him in a bag. He would be missed. He wondered where the hell NATA was when you needed them. The smaller guy rummaged about and George could see through the seats to the front that he had a black bag. *Much too small for a body,* George thought. The car stopped and the men climbed out, leaving George on the back seat. He wriggled, trying to sit to see where he might be. When the side door was opened, he was unceremoniously dragged off the back seat and onto the ground. The thump hurt his back and he moaned. He looked up to see a factory building. Its red brick facade was old and the place smelt of something familiar. He scrabbled with his legs and felt a kick in his shins.

"Keep still," the driver said and then everything went black as a cloth bag was put over George's head. He was picked up and escorted into the building. George tried to remember the smells, the number of steps, and direction, but soon became disorientated and gave up. He was hurting all over and his head was throbbing. They climbed some stairs and George heard a door open. As they stepped through into a cavernous room, their footsteps echoed. The black bag was whipped off his head and he blinked in the white light.

"Mr Nozette, nice to meet you." A well-dressed man held out his hand.

George indicated his hands were still tied behind his back. "Well, you know me, but who are you?"

The big lug behind him gave him a less than gentle thump. George looked back at his aggressor.

"Go fuck yourself," he said, then took a step away from a possible punch. The middle-aged gentleman nodded to his lackey. George felt cold steel on his wrist as the strapping was cut away. He rolled his shoulders back and rubbed his reddened wrists.

"Mr Nozette please." The man indicated they should sit at the only table in the large room. George looked around at his surroundings. There were pallets stacked in one corner and what looked like boxes of wine on a conveyor belt. He quickly put two and two together and realized the smell was grapes. He was in a winery. The boxes had writing, a label of sorts, but with his blurred vision because of his beating, he couldn't read it. He walked towards the window, but when two henchmen took a step in his direction, he moved to the table and chairs that were offered.

"What the hell is all this about? And who the fuck are you?"

"I, Mr Nozette, am the man everyone seeks." The German accent seemed familiar to George and as he studied the fine features, the expensive suit and the manicured finger nails, he tried to piece the whole thing together.

"And just who is that Mr ...?"

The man smirked and took a cigarette from a gold case. He snapped the case shut and tapped the end on the box. "My doctor says I should give up. Do you smoke?" He held out his case to George.

"No, I don't."

"Ah well, you don't mind, do you?" He produced a gold lighter, and as he flicked the flint wheel George noticed a prominent ring on his little finger. It was some sort of black stone and had an inscription on it. George squinted a little and took a short breath. He recognised the two lightning flashes of the Reich.

"I'm sorry you had to endure my boys. They are brutish don't you think." George nodded.

"Now Mr Nozette, we need to talk. I represent a small dedicated group of people who are very interested in your recent rise in popularity, or is that notoriety?"

George swallowed. This man was charming and menacing at the same time.

"Of course, you will be paid handsomely for your efforts. My people come well connected and they have already deposited a substantial amount in your account for the trial.

"May I have a drink?"

"Of course." He looked over to his two brutes and they left the room. "Now, as I was saying, we would like your assurance on the matter of Mr Tag."

"Assurance of what exactly?"

"Ah, yes. Well. We have reason to believe that Mr Tag might not reach his potential."

"What?" George looked to the door as one of the men came back with a can of coke. He gratefully took the can and drowned the drink without stopping. The cooling effect it had on his lips and stomach brought his brain into sharp focus. He took in the man, the ring, the henchmen, and thought of the worst thing that could happen. He hoped they didn't find out he was a Jew.

"What?" he reiterated.

"Mr Tag is vital." The man stopped and drew heavily on his cigarette. He sat forward and looked at George. "Vital, Mr Nozette, to our... cause."

"And what cause is that?"

The man stubbed his cigarette out on the table and the smoke lingered in the air. It wended its way up in a perfect line as George watched.

"I represent a, shall we say, new way of thinking, or is it a very old way of thinking. Call it nationalism. Call it France for the French. I, and my cohorts, my influential associates, have an ideal. A way forward in this... mixed-up world. A coarse term I know, but it suits the mood here, don't you think?"

"I call it Fascism."

"Now Mr Nozette, labels are useless."

"Fascism," George repeated, and received a hit in the head for his insolence.

"Our nation requires strong leadership. If we have to wage war in order to find France's collective identity, and keep the nation strong, then so be it. We have a message that needs to be heard. A message that might be stifled in normal circumstances. So... Mr Tag is the messenger. He will be heard and you will give him the opportunity, Mr Nozette."

George furrowed his brow. "So you are saying Tag must be allowed to speak."

"Exactly."

"And that I have no control over what he says."

"I see you are a smart man, Mr Nozette."

"But what about Heinz? He will be slaughtered."

"I think they call it collateral damage."

***

George was dumped in a park. The car didn't stop, and he rolled into some bushes. He lay still for a minute or two, and then hauled his sorry body onto his feet, and surveyed his surroundings. The grounds were unkempt, with litter whipping around in the wind eddies, and there was graffiti on just about every surface. He dusted himself off and headed for a drinking fountain. Luckily, it was still working and he doused his face, washing off the caked blood from his moustache, and then ran his fingers through his hair.

The district was run down he noticed, as he walked looking for a taxi stand or a bus stop. The thugs hadn't taken his wallet and he had money enough to get a ride if he could find anything that would identify where he might be. He walked a few blocks and came to an overpass. The graffiti was in an Arabic script. He knew he must be in the ghetto. No sane person would go there by choice. George had read and heard of the tensions in the three kilometre block. He hurried along, not daring to look at the people on the streets. Women in black shawls passed him with their heads down and small gangs of youths lounged on street corners, their mere presence threatening.

George averted his eyes and soon came to a train track. Rubbish was strewn all over the lines, but he saw a P on the side of a signal and logically thought that the city was in that direction. Although his every bone ached, he broke into a trot, his breath leaving his body in a cold mist. He followed the line, his one thought to get the hell out of there before anything else happened that he might not walk away from so easily. Gradually, the squalor gave way to more regulated streets and houses. He had slowed to a walk, when he spied a taxi.

It was with leaden feet that he climbed the stairs to his office and plopped down on the reception settee. He closed his eyes and slept.

The phone rang on Janelle's desk and George woke up with a start. He fell off the settee and remembered why he was in the office. The phone spurred him into action and he picked up.

"Hello," he croaked not quite awake.

"George, is that you?"

"Yes," George answered rubbing the burgeoning lump on his head.

"It's me, Bernard. Where have you been?"

"Bernard, where are you?"

"Look, I'm coming in to the office. Stay there. Don't move. I will be around twenty minutes." George hung up and went to make coffee, then decided he needed something stronger, and found the whisky in Bernard's office. He poured himself a stiff drink and knocked it back in one gulp. The liquid burned all the way down. George poured another and went to the kitchen. He looked in the small mirror Janelle had hung on the wall and winced at his face. It was a mess. His nose was red and bruised, his cheek sported a large gash that was weeping, and he had a sizable lump on the side of his head. The first aid kit provided some stinging ointment and plasters.

George had set to work on his wounds, when there was a noise in the outer office. He picked up the hot boiling water and crept to the joining office doors. Someone was moving about in reception opening draws looking for something.

George threw open the door and made ready to throw the water, then he recognised Duval.

"What the hell." George put the kettle down.

"I didn't know you were here."

"That's obvious. What are you looking for Duval? Who gives you the right to just come in here and... take things?"

"We just wanted to check out your calls."

"You could just ask." Duval looked up at George as he shut Janelle's desk drawer.

"What happened to you?"

"I cut myself shaving. What the fuck do you think happened? While your NATA man was talking a piss or something I was kidnapped and..." George stopped his rant. He knew if he disclosed all the details, they would grill him for hours, maybe days to find the man with the ring.

Duval sat on the desk, "And...?"

"And some thugs said I had better stop the defence of scum like Tag."

Duval nodded. George thought he saw a look of scepticism in his eyes.

"Bernard should be here any minute. He rang just now."

"I've seen him this morning. He said he was looking for you."

"Well, now we found one another." George's sarcasm was evident as he dabbed his weeping facial cut.

"So, those phone records. Any idea?"

"No."

"Right. Well, if you think of anything you want to tell me, you know where to reach me." Duval held up his mobile phone," 24/7," he ended.

He left and George breathed a sigh of relief. He made his coffee and then went to see his office. He was picking up papers when Bernard rushed up the stairs two at a time and burst into his office.

"George,"

George stood up, "Bernard, you're late." Both men laughed.

CHAPTER SEVENTEEN

The whisky bottle stood empty between Nozette and Simeoni. They slouched in their chairs and fell silent. The shadows were long in the office and the men were spent after relating the recent events. George tilted his head back on his chair and closed his eyes. Everything hurt, in spite of the whisky.

"I need sleep."

"Me too. Why don't you stay over at the apartment? Gabrielle isn't there and..." he trailed off. George grabbed his coat and briefcase and it was decided.

"You know there isn't a hope Tag will get off," George said as he drove in the twilight. "The police want his guts and they will do anything to get him."

"I know. I think Tag is a suicide bomber without the bomb. He will be prepped to say things in court, and then they will dispense with him. I feel sorry for him in a way," Bernard said.

"No justice there at all. Just thinking of all that money in the account makes me nervous. It's like we are being paid to be part of their propaganda machine."

"I know you said your family is safe, but are you sure." George nodded and turned into the security driveway at Bernard's apartment building.

Once safely inside with the doors locked, they went through the motions of eating a meal, not caring what it tasted like, as the emotional rollercoaster ride finally came to an end, and sleep was their respite.

***

The phone rang at seven am and Bernard stumbled out of bed to answer.

A police sergeant began, "We have had an incident..."

"What?" Bernard couldn't quite grasp the situation.

"Your client, Mr Tag has been involved in an incident. We found your card in his pocket."

"Is he alive?" Bernard's brain began to tick over. He walked with the mobile phone into the spare bedroom and shook George awake.

"Yes. He was stabbed, but he is stable." The officer then gave the details of the hospital and hung up.

"What was that?" George touched his swollen eye, trying to gauge if he could see out of it at all. Bernard related the conversation, and added that their safety, and their family's safety, depended on Tag getting to court.

"I guess we could ask Duval for protection."

"I don't trust him Bernard. There is something just not quite right about that man. And besides, who would he protect; us or Tag. One is dependent on the other." George went to the bathroom and took a closer look at his face.

"So, we have to take Tag into hiding?"

"It seems so. I can apply to the court to have the firm as guarantor. He has had a threat to his life, so they might see the sense. And don't forget," George added coming out of the room with a wet towel on his face, "The court is cracking down on publicity beat ups, so they will want Tag's case to be low key."

"I don't like their chances, do you?" George shook his head.

"Not a hope in hell."

The men ate a hearty breakfast and packed a few things for Tag. George rang the court and pulled a few favours to get the order on the first session. The subterfuge needed to spirit Tag away was an elaborate plan and they rehearsed in the car on the way to the hospital.

"You know, I don't think Tag will be a very happy man. He is recalcitrant at the best of times. I think he only knows one or two words. Fuck and Fuck you," George said and Bernard laughed. They drove to the car park and immediately saw the gaggle of press camped at the entrance.

"So much for low key," Bernard said, as they walked to the double doors. A reporter recognised them and thrust a microphone in George's face. He recoiled and put his head down.

"You go, I will deal with this," Bernard said. George hurried past and Bernard held up his hand. When he had their attention, he explained that their client was under sedation and until he could see him, he would not be answering any questions. The press threw a barrage of questions at Bernard as he walked through the doors. He made his way to the lift and saw George sitting on a bench in the corridor.

"Forget it Bernard. He's gone."

"What? Who?" George shrugged his shoulders.

"Let's hope it's the right side."

"And which side is that, I wonder."

They waited half an hour and then left the hospital and drove to the office. George opened the door and went to look for the appointment book on Janelle's desk.

"It's got to be here somewhere. She always writes everything down." He stopped and corrected the present tense. "She always wrote everything down." Bernard ran his fingers through his hair remembering Janelle.

"You don't think Duval has it do you. You said he was looking for something." George shook his head.

"I didn't see him leave with anything. Ah, here it is." He pulled out a small diary and opened the pages. "Thank God she was thorough." He flicked through the dates and came up with an entry.

"Look, here it is. A phone call. The number." Bernard looked at the number and picked up the phone.

"Hello," A German accent answered.

"This is Bernard Simeoni. May I speak to someone about a money transfer?" Bernard winked at George.

"Is there a problem?"

"Well there might be, and that depends on whether you have Tag."

"Ah, I see Mr Simeoni," the voice said, "How astute of you."

Bernard motioned for George to pick up the extension in his office. "The courts have awarded Tag to us. If he breaks bail, he will be in gaol." There was silence on the other end of the line. "Well?"

"He will be delivered on time."

"Well, we need him now."

"I'm afraid that isn't possible."

"What do you mean? Do you have him or not." The phone went dead. George walked back into the reception.

"They don't have a bloody clue."

"So where is our Mr Tag?" Bernard sat on the edge of the desk.

"And who is he with?" George asked knowing that if Tag was missing his own family was on the line.

George drove through the streets of Paris, listening to the GPS and following every turn and twist to Tag's last known address. They eventually drove down a dead-end street.

"Number 16," Bernard said looking at the shabby housing estate. There was rubbish in the streets and the clatter of a train overhead.

"I've been here before." George looked at the graffiti on the walls and the gangs of ethnics on the streets.

"When?"

"I was dumped here. After the interview," he touched his cheek where the pistol had hit him. "I'm sure this is the place."

"Pretty convenient, isn't it," Bernard said. "Do you think you could recognise anything to get you back to that factory? Anything at all?" George stopped across the street from the house and they sat in the car.

"All I can remember were the walls. They were brick, and inside everything was white. I think it was a winery or something."

Bernard looked at number 16. The building had been derelict for some time and all the windows were broken, the front door was listing on its hinges and some of the tiles on the roof were missing

"This is it." They sat, looking at the false lead.

"What now? He obviously has duped the courts and us," Bernard said.

"He always wanted me to drop him at the railway station. There has got to be something in that. But God knows what?"

"Look, we are wasting our time here. I think we need to see some acquaintances of Tag's. What about that guy you said you recognised. We could get a police match on him and..." George grabbed Bernard's arm and he fell silent. They watched as a man came out of the house and look up and down the street. He started to walk in the direction of the train overpass. George pulled out his mobile phone and took a hasty photograph.

"Who do you think that was?" Bernard said. George flicked through the files on the phone and they looked at the picture of the man. He was tall and thin with a swathe of black hair and looked like he was carrying something under his leather jacket. George shrugged his shoulders,

"I don't know, but I think we should have a look inside. Don't you?"

They studied the few people on the street, and when it was relatively empty, walked casually to the house and slipped inside. It smelt of urine and years of neglect. The weak winter sun cast a dull light over the destruction. The walls had been punched full of holes, the light fittings were hanging like criminals from their fixtures in the ceiling, and the once bright wallpaper fell off in great strips. Downstairs was evidently used as a shooting-up haven by the number of syringes lying around on the greasy floor. The two men made their way upstairs and Bernard pushed open a door. The room had a bed and a desk. The curtains were blowing in the breeze from the broken window. George walked around the room and looked at the papers strewn about.

"Look here." He pointed to a notepad. "The writing is Tags. I recognise the way he has done the letters. Very primitive."

Bernard looked at the paper. "What does that mean?" He pointed to a scribble in the corner.

"I've seen that before. It's the lightening flash of the Reich. The SS had it on their insignia and on their rings."

"Well, it is keeping in character." Bernard picked up the notepad and flicked through the pages. Some were scribble or doodles and then he came to an address. "Rue de Montparnasse, 12. 16th 2:30" he said. Bernard looked at his watch. The broken watch brought back memories and he closed his eyes and took a breath. "That's today. It's 11:30 now so we have time. What do you say?"

"I say we should go for it." They picked their way out of the rubble and drug paraphernalia. Once outside, they came up against a small group of youths.

"What you want here, you dicks?"

George took his hands out of his pockets, "Just leaving fellas. Nothing here for us."

"What's your hurry?" The obvious leader grabbed George's wrist and twisted it behind his back.

"Look, we are going, okay," Bernard said. He was pushed from behind and the menacing group came in close trying to intimidate the pair of lawyers. Bernard grabbed the leader by the arm and aimed a punch straight at his nose. The unexpected violence gave George enough time to twist from his hold. He kicked the young thug in the shins. A long lanky boy jumped on George's back and thwacked him in the ear. George threw him to the ground for his efforts. The fight was heating up, as the gang swarmed over the men, trying to get them to the ground with gouges, punches, kicks and any other means. Bernard backed into the front yard of number 16 and picked up a brick. The first to follow him received the brick on his shoulder and fell down. Bernard hoped it was broken or dislocated at the very least. He stooped to pick up a wooden stake. A boy jumped on him from the low brick fence. He shrugged him off and kicked him in the back several times, until he lay still. George, meanwhile, was being punched by two young men. Bernard took his stake and whaled into the assailants. They fell off George and began running down the street.

"You OK?" George wiped his bloodied nose on the sleeve of his coat.

"I'll live – although my nose can't take much more." He dabbed at his face and winced. "How about you?"

Bernard felt for his ear, which had been ripped in the fight. "I'm fine. That's nothing, compared to what I have been through. A walk in the park." They walked to the car and noticed a big scratch right along the side.

"Will you look at that! Fucking bloody vandals."

"Let's go. I've had enough of this neighbourhood." Bernard looked at his watch. "We have two hours." They climbed into the car and he punched in the address on the GPS.

George wiped at the blood still trickling from his nose. "Grab me a wipe, will you? In the glove compartment."

Bernard opened the little door, pulled out some baby wipes, and began to administer first aid as George pulled the car out onto the street. The GPS directed them to the other side of the city. Before they had gone too far, the traffic was banking up because of an accident.

"We might be late."

"Just forget the GPS. I think I know where it is." George swung the car across the traffic and up a side street. "I have a hunch that this address is where Tag is getting his idealist brainwashing. All that bullshit."

Bernard watched as they passed the smart suburbs and started to drive into an industrial area.

"George, where do you think he is now?" he asked, as he helped himself to some children's sweets.

"I'm not sure, but I think he was taken for prepping. I don't think Tag has the brain capacity to just do it off the top of his head. He didn't strike me as being the top shelf."

"So that Mr Big you saw is calling the shots. Then this is a set up. If he has Tag, they just want us to panic. I don't get it."

"My guess; and it is only a guess," George began as he took a sharp left onto a main road, "is that there is a double-cross somewhere."

"What?"

"Well, just think of this. We are chased all over the place. NATA want to find our Mr Big. They think we will lead them to him. Your Israeli people just want anyone dead who is associated with Tag and his cohorts, and yet they don't kill us. Why? I think they want Mr Big too. But Bernard," George slowed for a stop light, "I think the man I saw wasn't Mr Big. I think Mr Big is really big."

"How big?"

"Really big. I'm talking politics big."

"How do you know?"

"Because I think they are letting us play out the game. We will find the truth for them. We are the stumbling innocents. And along the way we and Tag are just pawns."

Bernard digested the revelation. "It's all conjecture at this stage."

"I know, but that gold cigarette case man I saw said, 'he and his influential associates'. Do you remember that politician who they called xenophobic? He used the same phrase... 'France for the French'." George pulled the car to the curb and turned off. "Is that a coincidence or not?"

"Not," Bernard said and looked out the window at a large building in the deserted industrial estate. Weeds grew through the sidewalk and the place had an air of neglect. The front had been painted years ago and now all that remained was the reminder of the colour red in the brickwork mortar. A flapping sign thrashed itself against the eves and George could just discern the logo of a small winery.

"Looks like they went broke and just walked away," Bernard said as he looked up at the big iron double door with a padlock and two small blackened windows either side. They stepped out of the car and looked around. A Citroen was parked at an odd angle in one corner of the quadrangle that formed a car park. Bernard pointed to the car and they walked over and stooped down to looked inside.

A corpse was sitting in the driver's seat his hands cable-tied to the steering wheel. His neck had been sliced through. The blood had stained his clothes and was now a black congealed mess.

"Shit." Bernard staggered back.

George looked in and grimaced. "I think he's been dead for some time." He opened the driver's door and the stench was sickening. He slammed it shut again and retched onto the ground.

"Fuck, that's disgusting." George said wiping his mouth with his hand. They looked at the body through the

162

windscreen. "Any ideas?" George shook his head. "Well, I guess he might have ID." Bernard took a deep breath and opened the car door again. He fossicked around in the dead man's jacket and pulled out a wallet. It was sticky with blood and as Bernard opened it a paper fluttered to the ground. He picked it up and read,

"2:30 appointment. Hell, what now?"

"What day, don't you mean?" George looked at the paper. "There is obviously something happening at that time." Bernard looked at his watch.

"2pm. We should get out of sight." Bernard said thinking of their clue. They leafed through the wallet as they walked back to the car. "Michael Jardanne. Oh my God."

"What is it?" George asked.

"It says here he is a journalist." Bernard took out the union card. If he is here, then someone knows something." Bernard started to walk faster, "Come on," he said as he broke into a trot back to their car. Once inside, Bernard flicked through the wallet and found a drivers licence and a few coins. He took a baby wipe and cleaned his hands, putting the wallet in a plastic nappy bag.

"You seem to have everything in this car George."

"Just left over family stuff. Do you think we should go to the police?" Bernard considered the question. There were a lot of variables in the answer.

"Not yet. Let's just park out of sight and wait for 2:30. Then I think we should try to go inside." George looked over to the building.

"Okay," he said.

With the car parked out of the way, they walked back to the warehouse and skirted around the outside. The back entrance had a loading dock and George looked at the building with his mouth open.

"This is it. This is the building they took me to when I met the cigarette guy."

"Are you sure?" George smelt the air, and then touched the side of his face. "I'm sure."

Once inside, they cautiously made their way upstairs, looking for possible signs of occupation.

"What was that," Bernard whispered when he heard a loud bang. George beckoned him to a window and they watched two men jump from a van. The well-dressed visitors opened the main door and stepped inside, as two more men walked over to the Citroen. Nozette and Simeoni watched as they poured petrol over the car from a jerry can and then stood back. One threw a cigarette and the car burst into flames. It burnt quite well and as the arsonists walked away, it blew up. The sudden explosion made Bernard jump and he hit his head on the window.

"Shit," he said and stood back.

"They don't like people snooping, do they?" Bernard shook his head.

An old service elevator clanked into gear and began its accent, the noise making the lawyers take up a hiding position. They crouched down behind a derelict bottling machine in the corner of the room and waited. The lift stopped and they heard two men talking.

"I can't stay all day. If he is not here in ten minutes I'm going."

"I'm sure Tag won't be long. I have everything under control."

"Don't reassure me with your platitudes. If you had control, we wouldn't have been tracked by that reporter. I hope it is taken care of now."

"Yes, of course."

Bernard looked at George at the mention of Tag.

"And what about his legal representatives? Are they...?"

"Yes. We made sure of it. They will co-operate. Family men always do." The man laughed.

George nudged Bernard and pointed to his little finger. He mouthed the words,' the man with the ring'. Bernard risked a quick look to confirm George's fears. He spied the ring and nodded.

"I don't want any slip ups. The court case is in a week." There was the now familiar noise of the elevator on the move and the men stopped their chatter.

Tag was thrust into the room and manhandled by the thugs from downstairs.

"Fuck off," he said and shrugged his arm away from their grip.

"Let him go. Mr Tag, we need to make sure you are the right man for the job. You do know what we are talking about here?" Tag smirked and wiped his nose with his sleeve.

"Yeah, I know."

"We understand your rage, Tag. People need to be taught a lesson and you are the man to do it."

"Attention." One of the men barked the order. Bernard watched through a crack in the bench as Tag stood to attention. He took on a military stance and seemed to be in a trance.

"Good. He will do."

"We still need a few more days. Herr Doctor is very good, but these things take time."

The other man snapped his fingers and Tag slumped to his normal posture.

"You will be a wealthy man, Tag, when all this is over." Tag smiled and the thugs escorted him out of the room.

"What will we do with him after?"

"I think we both know the answer to that question, don't we?"

CHAPTER EIGHTEEN

"How did he know the trial date?" George asked Bernard as they drove back to the office. They pondered the question.

"I mean, we haven't been advised yet. Well not that I know of." Bernard looked at the wallet in the bag.

"They don't care who gets in their way. I don't think Tag has a chance. Did you see the way he sort of snapped?"

"I've seen that before. It's like auto suggestion. They say a word and it is associated with what they have to do... or say."

"Hypnotism."

"Yeah, and Tag's got it bad." George drove to a shopping centre and parked the car. They decided they needed to eat and talk, and the centre was a noisy, busy precinct where they were unlikely to be heard. The conversation ranged from Tag to the man pulling the strings – and what they should divulge to the police and Duval. Then, as they relaxed, Bernard related his adventures in more detail and George sat back and listened.

Bernard fingered his cracked watch.

"And that's about all of it." George looked at the watch. Its face was a constant reminder to Bernard of his culpability and it burrowed into his conscience and wouldn't let go.

"It was you or him Bernard. Anyone would have done the same." George put his hand on his partner's arm. Bernard pursed his lips and nodded, although he wasn't convinced.

They drove back to the office and George rang his wife. He didn't want to alarm her, but suggested that they move somewhere else.

"Don't you have an aunt in Switzerland?" He tried to persuade her that it was a judicious decision in the circumstances and it would take the heat off her parents.

"I can't leave my parents. They are worried, and the children are happy here."

"Well, just be careful. Tell Franc and Claudine to shut the lower gate. Things are..." George left the adjective hanging in the air.

"Audrea," he hesitated, "I love you."

Bernard rang Gabrielle with the same advice and cajoled her into going to the Alps for a week or so. The crowds were just beginning for the snow and the holidays, "And you could do some skiing," he said. She wasn't so easy to convince and Bernard promised to visit for a honeymoon when it was all over. His looked at his empty finger and wondered if he really cared about her. Perhaps they could start again. He thought he might try.

Now, with Tag being manipulated, and then possibly assassinated, they had to find him and fast. Their whole defence rested on his vulnerability at being brainwashed into the destructive cult. If he came across as articulate and spouted well thought out rhetoric, it wouldn't look good.

"You know Bernard; I think they have had Tag for some time. Perhaps it was a standing appointment at 2:30. You just don't do that to someone's brain overnight." Bernard thought the reasoning sound, and postulated that whoever did it, knew what they were doing. He found a phone book in a public booth and skimmed the pages.

"Psychotherapist?"

"Maybe."

"Hypnotherapist?"

"Possible." George said. They each picked a page and rang around looking for someone that was busy at 2:30. After about a dozen calls, George put the phone down.

"Got him."

| | |

Dr Arlan Cadieux's offices were in a smart district right in the centre of Paris. Bernard read the directory in the modern, glass walled building's foyer. Dr Cadieux was a master in numerous sciences, and by the look of the directory, had the whole of the top floor.

George had already found an expert witness for the trial who was well known on the circuit, but if Dr Cadieux could be persuaded to appear, then Tag's weak-will might be established.

"After all," Bernard had said in the car on the way over, "he's a doctor – he must have ethics."

The interview didn't go well. The doctor was bound by patient confidentiality and seemed to be overly demonstrative about Bernard's attempt to enlist his expertise. The men left the office in no doubt that the doctor was scared. Someone was either threatening him or paying him a large amount of money. George thought the latter was more likely. They could see Tag's case becoming a sham and justice for him virtually impossible. Bernard even wondered if the date had been set for the convenience of the people who seemed to be running the show.

George knew the doctor was busy at 2:30 all week and so the men decided to stake out the office in the hope of kidnapping Tag.

"Where are we going to keep him?" Bernard wondered aloud.

"I was thinking about that. What if we give him to NATA?"

Bernard thought about it and it was set. They planned to snatch him by following the doctor. It seemed so ridiculously easy. Then they would ring Duval and broker a deal – keep Tag safe for the trial, and Nozette and Simeoni would hand over any information they gathered in their defence research.

"We shouldn't ring Duval until we have Tag. No use getting him worked up," Bernard suggested. George agreed.

It was a filthy day. The sky was leaden and the sleet and rain came in patches with a biting wind. Bernard had offered George the apartment, and now, as they stood at the window in the lounge room and looked out, it seemed that the weather was a portent of things to come. They surveyed the car park and remained vigilant on the drive to the office. George parked outside and let Bernard open up as he went to the underground car park. He parked the car in his usual spot and was gathering his bags, when he saw movement in the side mirror. Instinctively, he stayed low and watched as a figure darted into the shadows. Thinking fast, he texted Bernard and hunted around for a weapon in the car. In the console was a can of baby air-freshener. George grabbed it and opened the car door. A shot rang out and hit the side panel. George put the car into gear and rammed his foot on the accelerator. The vehicle careered back and trapped the assailant up against the wall. George though he saw him drop the gun as the man's leg was crushed. He jumped out of his seat. With a cigarette lighter and the spray aimed at his attacker, the contents of the can became a flame-thrower. The fellow screamed as he was enveloped in fire and slumped – unconscious.

Bernard appeared around the corner in time to see a ball of flame. He ran down the ramp.

"What the..." he said puffing from his run. George dropped the spray can and began to shake.

"He was shooting at me – he was shooting at me, Bernard." George tried to assuage his guilt.

The victim of the attack groaned.

"Ring an ambulance, George. Now!" Bernard surveyed the devastation as George fumbled with his phone. "Anonymously, George."

George put the call through while Bernard grabbed a fire blanket from George's car. "We need to move him." He moved the car forward to free the man, then wrapped him in the fire blanket.

"He tried to kill me. It was self-defence."

"I know, George, I know."

The men cleaned the crime scene before the emergency services arrived. They drove the car out of sight and then walked back to the office from a different direction. Neither was under any illusions as to their culpability, and it sat uncomfortably on their shoulders.

"We need to..." George's mind wandered.

"To forget that and concentrate on Tag." Bernard finished his sentence.

"Bernard. I..." George started, but he knew Bernard was right. If they had any hope of finding Tag, he needed to concentrate.

They drew their plan on a piece of paper and made allowances for every eventuality. When the time came to leave the office, Bernard looked at George.

"Well, this is it. I never thought I would be kidnapping my own client." George looked at the cable ties in his hand.

"Neither did I."

The drive to the Cadieux office block was in silence, each man in his own thoughts. Bernard parked a short way down the street. With a view of the main entrance, and the car park entrance, they sat and waited. Around 2:20, the men sat forward concentrating on the building. Bernard looked at his watch at 2:22. Then a huge explosion rent the air. The top floor of the building blew apart and the masonry began to rain down on the street. Car alarms sounded and people screamed as they ran for cover. The whole of the penthouse suite was gone and in its place, a fire took hold.

"Fuck," George said, as he opened the door and stood on the street looking up. A window on the floor below gave way and fell out, the glass shattering on the ledges on the way down and showering glass over the road. Bernard got out of the car and looked at the building opposite. Its windows were broken from the blast and people were beginning to look out at the devastation. The wailing of sirens had begun, adding to the cacophony of sounds when there was another explosion in the already destroyed building. People were screaming in the upper floors, hanging onto balconies and waving curtains or anything that might attract attention. The people on the ground seemed to be rooted to the spot. No one was walking or moving and the traffic in the normally busy street was at a standstill, hindering the police as they tried to get through. Burning papers began to flutter down with the new shower of rain. It was chaos. George saw a woman who was hit by glass, bleeding, and pulled out his nappy wipes. He cleaned her up and saw Bernard tie a tourniquet around a man's leg with his daughter's skipping rope. The traffic thinned and several ambulances arrived, the medics throwing themselves into the job at hand. It wasn't long before the press arrived. The whole scene resembled other terrorist attacks that had been broadcast on the television. Now it was the turn of Paris to bear the brunt of terror. Bernard comforted a young woman and watched as the police cordoned off the area. He yelled to George,

"We should go before..." he cast his eyes to the police with the barrier tape. George nodded and stood up. He left the wipes with his victim and they walked back down to their car. Another sheet of glass groaned and cracked, then fell.

People were screaming, running in all directions as the glass hit the ground. The men turned and took one last look at the mayhem then drove away. They were in no doubt about the motive for the attack.

"First the journalist – now the doctor. It seems that anyone who gets in their way is disposed of, no matter what the consequences." Bernard tried to wipe the blood off his hands with a tissue. "Do you think we are next?"

George gained speed and hit the ring road, "I don't know Bernard, I really don't know."

He drove sedately through the Paris traffic and they ended up back at the office.

Bernard looked at the cable ties, "I guess it was a stupid idea anyway," he threw the ties in the office bin. George turned on the television and they watched the blast on the newsflash. The reporter said that no-one was coming forward to take responsibility and they likened the attack to 9/11 and the London bombings.

George sat down in his office chair and pulled on his moustache. "If only they knew. Shit." He banged his fist on the desk. "Where the hell is Tag?" The phone rang and Bernard answered. He listened, said "Yes", a couple of times, then hung up.

"Duval wants to see us. Now."

"Is he coming here?" George asked. Bernard shook his head.

"No, he said to meet him at the Sorbonne University cafe, near the psychology faculty.

"Why there, I wonder?"

"Who knows, but it sounded urgent," Bernard said. The two men walked to the car looking around the street for anything suspicious. The ambulance had gone and there was no trace of the recent incident in the car park. George wondered did it really happen when the area was cleaned and life went on so easily.

"I'll drive," Bernard said as he looked at George, who was still under the influence of his attack. George handed over the keys. As they made their way across the city there was no conversation. The events of the afternoon had shocked them into silence. Bernard drove to the university car park and turned off the engine.

"Are you okay?" He looked at his partner.

"Fine, just... just a bit shocked."

"I understand," Bernard said, knowing full well what George was going through, while trying to forget his own demons. They walked through the courtyards, past the jostling students into the colonnade. The archway shadows flickered in the weak late afternoon sun as they strode to the cafe.

"This takes you back a bit doesn't it?" Bernard said. George looked around at all the young faces,

"It makes me feel old."

"Remember when we met Gabrielle in the library?" George grinned. Their time at the Sorbonne was a happy one and their friendship had the cement of times shared.

"Come on." Bernard led the way to the little café, almost hidden in the corner of a much grander building. The cafe was thick with students trying to get into the warmth of the coffee house, and Bernard and George stood back, hunting for Duval.

"I don't think he's here, I can't see him." George pushed through a group of people to get inside the door. He looked around the crowded room, and then at Bernard waiting outside, shook his head, turned and pushed his way out.

"Not here. He did say this cafe?"

"Yes, I'm sure." They stood to one side watching the comings and goings in the hope of spotting Duval. Bernard looked at his watch and twisted it to see the face when there was a tap on his shoulder. He swung around to face Duval.

George turned, "We thought you were a no-show." Duval beckoned them to follow and they all walked along a cobbled path to a small building with a low wooden door, tucked into an alcove.

"This way." Duval opened the door with a large key. They stepped into the gloom and he shut the door. "Up here." They climbed a set of spiral stairs, until the landing opened out into a little room.

"Where are we?" George looked at the tiny room with a desk and computer.

"The Chapter house. But this is not what I wanted to show you. Look down there." Duval pointed out the window to a courtyard below. The quadrangle was a small oasis of garden populated with bare trees and empty flower beds, plus a garden table and chairs.

"In," Duval looked at his watch, "fifteen minutes, three men will sit at that table. We know you have been in contact with Tag's benefactor. You have been busy." He looked at the two men. "Now we need to know if you recognise any of these gentlemen."

Bernard looked out the window at the garden.

"But..."

"Save it Simeoni. We don't sit around all day waiting for something to happen. Oh, and by the way, nice job on that guy in the car park."

George bit his bottom lip. "Who was he?"

"Minor player. Hired to give you a scare."

George winced at Duval's callous disregard for his so-called collateral damage. "Well, he did that all right." The three men shifted in the confined space and George asked, "Why here Duval?"

Duval looked at this watch. "The Sorbonne has a recruitment cell. We have been watching and waiting for quite some time. How do you think we gather intelligence?

This organisation is very sophisticated. The Sorbonne has a wealth of young militant impressionable minds. They use subtle ways to infiltrate the curriculum. Professor Dupone is..." Duval stopped.

"Professor Dupone? He has been at the University for years. Surely he..." George posed the question.

Duval raised his eye brows. "Not all professors have altruistic motives."

"Why do you let it happen?" Bernard said, as he pressed his forehead against the glass to watch below.

"How do you stop the debate of ideas? How do you challenge the exchange of information? Isn't that censorship?" Duval said.

"But there must be a way?" George asked.

"Not with limited resources … limited people in the right places."

"You mean politicians and lobbyists with deep pockets." Bernard stepped away from the window.

"So it all comes down to money in the end," George said.

"That's about it." Duval walked to the window. "Look." He pointed to the scene below. They watched as two well-dressed gentlemen in coats strolled out into the late winter sunshine and sat at the table. Then they looked to the door and said something to someone out of sight. Bernard watched them talk but he couldn't hear the conversation.

"What are they saying?"

"They are brokering a deal."

"What deal?"

"We think the third man will be running for election."

"But if he gets in on a fascist ticket..." Bernard said, "he will have one foot in the door with his..."

"Exactly."

"Who is he?" George watched the exchange below.

"That is the million dollar question? Do you see anyone you know?"

George looked down. "That one... in the grey coat. See his ring. I recognise it. Who is he?"

"Conrad, Vincent Conrad. Do you see anyone else?"

"No," George said, watching the meeting.

"Simeoni?" Duval asked. Bernard swallowed and watched. He had seen one of the men before and chilled at the memory.

"Simeoni?" Duval asked again.

"That one," Bernard said, "The one smoking the cigar."

After Duval left, Bernard led George to the nearest bar. Three good stiff drinks later, he began to talk.

"I didn't think I would ever see him again. Especially with them."

"So who is he?"

"En Saliki. He certainly has connections. Nasra said he was the mole in the Israeli Secret Service. He was with the FFZ." Bernard looked around the bar hoping no-one overheard. "I wonder..."

"What?" George asked.

"Well, perhaps he has infiltrated their ranks. George..."

"What?"

"He knows we are Jews."

CHAPTER NINETEEN

With five days to go before the trial, Nozette and Simeoni calculated they had assembled all they could in relation to Tag and his mental state. He was still missing, and they would have liked to get him independently assessed, but time was running out. Bernard had amassed Tag's history and the story was one of low socio-economic abuse. *Heinz was a perfect candidate for recruitment,* Bernard thought. *It was almost his destiny.* George had pursued the police witness and those in the crowd that could be contacted, and by the end of the third day, holed up in the office, they had done the job. Now it was up to the jury and Judge to decide.

The press were in a frenzy, digging up any bit of dirt on the players. George and Bernard watched the television as a debate raged on the freedom of the right to associate. It seemed the whole country was watching.

"We haven't heard from Duval in three days, George. Is that a good sign or a bad sign?"

George shrugged his shoulders. "I don't know. It's been remarkably quiet. After all we have been through it's almost too quiet. Makes me nervous." He pulled on his moustache and sat back in his chair.

Bernard stood at the door and contemplated the words. "Well, I'm done for the night. How about you?"

"Bernard, I was thinking. If we make Tag out to be brainwashed and then he starts his..."

"I know, but what can we do?"

"Perhaps we should visit a hypnotherapist. He might be able to counteract the damage done." George drummed his fingers on the desk and looked at the television.

"See that," he pointed to a politician on a talk show. They listened to the man speak. "...and if we allow this flood though our border, who is going to pay? Where will France be in ten, five, two years? Is not France for the French?"

George looked at Bernard. "Did you hear that? France for the French. That man Conrad said that. He said he had friends. Bernard..."

Bernard looked at the television. "That's the opposition Minister for Foreign Affairs, Theodore Voisard." They listened to the debate as Voisard became agitated and started to shout.

"And who is going to stop this wave of illegal immigration. We need more than legislation and rhetoric. We need action. We need the youth to make their mark for France." The audience booed and cheered in equal proportions and the programme went to a commercial break.

George turned off, "What does that sound like to you?"

"It sounds like he is inciting radical nationalism."

"Surely Duval can put two and two together. Do you think we should tell him?" They considered the question and the probable outcomes.

"Duval might throw the whole idea out, or he just might think it is a worthwhile hunch, either way," Bernard said, "he has to listen to us." He pulled out Duval's card, dialled the number, and waited. The phone went to message-bank.

"Hello, Duval. Look, it's Simeoni here. We need to discuss something with you. Can we meet?" He hung up and immediately received a text message.

"Well at least we know he's still alive Bernard," George said. "And that's a good sign." Bernard answered.

George took a train to the Louvre and waited on the concourse. Bernard elected to stay at the office and look into the winery. The men figured if they used the premises twice there must be a sympathiser somewhere in the ownership.

George stamped his feet against the cold and shoved his hands deep in his pockets watching the human traffic. There was a biting wind and eddies of light snow whirled around the few people who were scuttling across the pavers. A figure hailed him from about one hundred metres away and he recognised Duval. George raised his hand and made a move then felt a searing pain in his arm. It felt hot and cold all at once and he looked down to see a small hole in his coat sleeve. The slow realisation dawned as he felt a warm trickle down his arm and into his glove.

George staggered and grabbed his elbow then looked up to see Duval running to the northern end of the building. The pain was kicking him and he forced himself to walk to a bench and sit down. Blood was dripping on the virgin snow from his sleeve and he felt faint. He sat and tried to breath and remain calm. The pain crept along his shoulder and he felt paralysed to do anything.

"This is not a game. This is not a game," he said to himself to try and stay focussed. The snow fell on his face and he roused himself to fossick for his mobile phone. He couldn't think who to call and then decided on Bernard. Bernard's number rang, but when he picked up George didn't answer. He had fainted and was out cold.

George woke up in hospital. He tried to turn over and a sharp pain reminded him of the recent events. He felt around for his arm and was surprised that his whole torso was bandaged. Every muscle in his body ached as he lay still and closed his eyes to the glare of the overhead light.

Bernard stood at the side of the bed and whispered, "George, are you awake?" George opened his eyes and smiled at his friend.

"The doctor says you will be okay. The bullet went through your upper arm, nicked your rib and came out. You are one lucky bastard." Bernard sat down and folded his coat over his lap.

"How long have I been here?"

"Oh, about 24 hours. You were sedated." Bernard looked at his watch. "We only have two days to go before the trial. While you were sleeping like a baby, things are getting serious." Bernard pointed to the door, "We have protection, 24 hour protection, courtesy of Inspector Pallis. Duval is missing and so is Tag. The media are just about falling all over themselves with conspiracy theories about us, the shooting and Tag, and Audrea is coming back to Paris. She should be here by the early afternoon." Bernard saw the look of consternation on George's face and tried to reassure him,

"Don't worry. Pallis has sent a man to escort her."

"Well, that brings things nicely up to date." George tried to sit up.

"What are you doing?"

"Well, we can't just wait here." He swung his legs over the side of the bed and winced.

"Look, big fella, you aren't going anywhere. The doctor said a week at least." Bernard stood over his friend. "I can take care of things."

"But..."

"You wait for Audrea. After that, I may need you. There are just a few loose ends before the trial – besides losing our client." Bernard laughed at the situation. "And by the way, I looked up the winery records. It seems Black Chateau Wines was," he corrected himself, "is owned by three people, one of whom is our Mr Voisard." Bernard raised his eyebrow and smirked. "How convenient, don't you think?"

"Absolutely."

George lay back on the bed.

The hospital front reception was crowded with the press. As Bernard left the hospital and approached the crowd with his police minder, they sprang into action thrusting microphones in his face and following his every move with cameras.

"How is Mr Nozette?"

"Do you think your client has a chance?"

"Will you still be taking the case?" The questions were thrown at Bernard as he walked. He stopped and faced the barrage of reporters.

"Yes, we will be taking the case. I believe a legal system that meters out justice is crucial in a democracy. I'm talking about justice, not politically correct attitudes that undermine the law. My client deserves that justice. He deserves to be judged by the law, not by scaremongering rumours and fear." Bernard pushed through the throng and walked away, his principles held out for all to see.

Back at the office, Bernard left his minder outside in reception and sat down at his desk, put his head in his hands and closed his eyes. He was contemplating the list of impossible tasks when the phone rang. They had changed the number when all this began and only special clients knew the new code.

"Hello, Bernard Simeoni speaking," he said trying to sound businesslike.

"Mr Simeoni, I have rung to allay your fears." Bernard swallowed as he recognised the German accent.

"My fears? What do you know about my fears... Mr Conrad." He slipped in the name hoping for a hit.

"Ah, I see you do some homework. Well done, Mr Simeoni. I wish to assure you that your client will be presented on time in Court the day after tomorrow. Nine am isn't it?" Bernard detected a hint of sarcasm.

"It is. And where will Mr Tag be?"

"We have arranged for transport. A car containing Mr Tag will pick you and your partner up and transport you to the Chambers."

"Look Mr Conrad, I..." But Conrad had hung up. Bernard slammed the phone down on the receiver.

"Damn you," he shouted and threw the phone bodily at the wall. The police officer came in, but Bernard's anger had dissipated and he was on his hands and knees picking up the broken pieces. He threw the smashed phone into the bin just as his mobile phone indicated a text. It read, 'GET OUT BOMB'.

"Bomb!" Bernard shouted and thrust the phone in the Gendarme's direction. The two men dropped everything and ran for the street. Once downstairs the officer called in the threat and tried to get people off the streets. Bernard ran down the road and stopped the traffic. He explained his panic with a gas leak and the cars backed up. The faint unmistakeable sound of sirens could be heard in the distance as the two men frantically tried to clear the area. A patrol car skidded to a halt at the street's top entrance and the road was quiet. Everyone looked to the building. A pigeon flew down, landed on the window ledge, and began to preen itself. Bernard watched transfixed. An enormous explosion shook the pavement. The audience in the street all ducked involuntarily at the noise. The blast demolished the front of the old building and the bricks came flying out like a freight train.

Bernard watched his offices go up as if in slow motion. The window frames blew out, tumbling onto the street and a gaping hole next to his office showed the interior. Dust and papers flew around in the wind as the building started to collapse. Bricks cascaded down to the sidewalk, their clattering mingling with the sirens and screams.

After the initial shock, a fire took hold. Flames licked the upper floor and sent a column of smoke high into the sky.

Police appeared from every direction. Soon the whole street was swarming with gendarmes. Bernard sat down on a door step and ran his fingers through his hair. He wondered who could do such a thing, and then the enormity of the situation became apparent. Someone must have found out they were Jewish.

Rue de Maine was awash with flashing lights and emergency services. The fire raged through the building, but the fire service managed to contain it from catching neighbouring buildings alight. Bernard looked up at what was left of the firm. He and George had been so proud the day they signed the lease to the offices. Nozette and Simeoni were not going to set the legal world on fire, but they steadily carved out a comfortable living. Now, as the black smoke billowed all around, their living was being torn apart. Gradually the fire was contained and put out. Bernard stood up and looked at the charred mess, the twisted and mangled windows. He just felt like closing his eyes and hoping it was all a dream. He stood up and surveyed the scene.

A policeman came over to him. "Mr Simeoni?"

"Yes," Bernard answered, studying the fresh-faced Gendarme.

"We understand you had prior warning."

"Yes." Bernard produced his mobile phone and looked at the message. It struck him as odd that someone could plant a bomb and then let the victim know.

"We might need your phone, Mr Simeoni, for further investigations."

"What?"

"Your phone." The Gendarme held out his hand. Bernard looked at his empty upturned palm and decided to withhold his co-operation.

"Mr Simeoni?" Bernard took a step back and shoved his hands in his pockets. He had rushed out without his coat and now, as the adrenalin wore off, he shivered.

"I will bring it down to the station." Bernard began to walk away.

The officer grabbed his arm. "This is an ongoing investigation, Mr Simeoni. With respect, we would like your co-operation on this."

Bernard backed away and then turned and walked purposefully down the street. He didn't know why he felt suspicious, but the feeling remained.

The press had arrived. A police barrier contained them. Bernard ducked into a side lane and made his way to the main thoroughfare without being seen. It was only when he hailed a taxi that he stopped and contemplated his next move.

"Where to?" The taxi driver asked. Bernard considered the question.

"Rue de la Victoire."

The Synagogue was empty in the early afternoon. Bernard found a seat and relished the quiet. His ears were ringing from the explosion and he needed to think. He looked up at the architecture of the building and thought of his mother. She would have approved, he knew that as the one certainty in his hectic life. With his eyes closed, he tried to think clearly. There was a tap on his shoulder.

"Excuse me," an elderly gentleman said. "You look very cold, would you like a hot drink and..." the old man smiled.

Bernard followed him into an office and took a hot chocolate between his hands. The old man had put a rug over Bernard's shoulders and now he sat at a large desk and watched as Bernard hugged his drink.

"Is there something on your mind?"

Bernard looked up. He presumed the man to be a Rabbi. *Where to begin*, Bernard thought.

As if reading his mind the man said, "Just start at the beginning." Bernard took a long draught of his drink and began to talk.

It was dark when Bernard stopped talking.

"So, now what?" The man asked.

"I don't know. I really don't know. How can I protect my client when I don't even know where he is hiding? And how can I reconcile my job with my religion?"

"Perhaps you should do your job, the religion will follow."

"But..." Bernard started. The old man held up his hand.

"Tomorrow is another day.

"What is your name?"

"Nicholas Roquet."

"We should ring George. He will have seen the explosion on the news."

"I will ring. What could be more natural than his Rabbi calling?" Bernard nodded and relaxed. His jangled nerves began to subside and he fell asleep in the chair.

CHAPTER TWENTY

The day before the trial, the papers were gagging on the news. The editorials were thick with revenge, vengeance, and vitriol. It seemed the world had Tag convicted and people were baying for blood. George read the editorials and threw the paper down in disgust.

After the explosion, George had feared Bernard was dead. He had raged at the injustice until the call came through. Now George was waiting for his wife. He sat on the end of the bed and flicked through his phone. Early on in the firm's history, Nozette and Simeoni had elected to back up their files off premises. Now he accessed the case notes from his phone and sent them to his home. When his wife arrived, they would pick up Bernard and drive to the suburbs to finalise their case. He moved and winced as a sharp pain reminded him of his near miss.

The morning wore on and Audrea still had not arrived. George looked at his watch and his packed bag. He tried to call, but the phone was out of service. *He might have expected no signal in the mountains, but she should have arrived by this time*, he thought. He walked to the corridor and nodded to the policeman on the door, checked the time and went back to sit on his bed. Half an hour passed and she was still missing so George called Bernard.

"It's not good. I can't get her on the line." They discussed the plan and revised it. Bernard would pick up George from the hospital and when Audrea did arrive, she was to call them.

George looked at the bomb warning text when he was in the car.

"It's a blocked number. Any ideas?" Bernard shook his head concentrating on the road. The traffic was busy but moving fast. They took the freeway, George turned on the radio, and Bernard engaged cruise control.

"I'm sure she is ok. Just held up in the traffic." Bernard tried to allay his friend's anxiety. He drove sedately through the late afternoon traffic.

"They said it might snow tonight. I guess this traffic is just people trying to get home before it starts." Bernard looked around and saw a black Mercedes coming up fast in the left hand lane. The car slowed to match their pace and Bernard looked over to the occupants.

"Shit."

"What?" George asked.

"Look." Bernard pointed to the Mercedes in the next lane.

"Audrea. It's Audrea." George scrambled into the back seat and then saw the look of fear in his wife's eyes. She seemed to be pleading for him to stay away. He watched, helpless, as a passenger in the Mercedes put a gun to her head. Audrea bit her lip and George could see her trembling. She put up a hand written sign against the window. George tried to focus on his wife's eyes. She stared at her husband and pointed to the number to make him look.

"It's a number. Can you remember it?" George yelled out the numbers and Bernard consigned them to a tune. He found he could remember anything as long as it was set to a simple tune.

"Got it. What's going on, George?"

"Keep up, Bernard," George said as he watched his wife going through agony. He opened the window and shouted, "I love you."

The black car gathered speed and zoomed away, cutting off other drivers. Bernard stamped his foot down and his car jumped into action. Weaving through the traffic, they sped after the kidnappers, trying to keep up. George climbed into the front seat and strapped himself in for the ride. He spotted gaps for Bernard as they put the car through its paces. The Mercedes had about a 10 second lead, as it flicked through the thickening traffic.

"I think they might take exit 12. I know this road," George said. Bernard narrowed his focus and hunched over the wheel of the Toyota.

"I can't see them," Bernard said. George pointed out the topography of the three lane freeway he travelled every day.

"There is a bend, but no exit. We have about seven kilometres to go. They can't get off. Can't you crank this thing up?"

"I'm doing the best I can." The Toyota picked up as they went down a slight hill and then the momentum carried them to 140km/hr on the flat.

"Four to the exit, Bernard. We have to catch them."

The radio went to the news. "*The coming trial of Neo-Nazi Heinz Tag has a new twist. Unconfirmed reports have suggested Nozette and Simeoni are Jewish. More later...*"

"Fuck, that's all we need," George said, then added, "One to exit, Bernard." His friend gripped the wheel a little tighter and kept his eye on the black car. He saw the brake lights flick and knew their path was set.

"Hang on." Bernard swung into the emergency lane and passed on the inside. Gravel flicked up as he put his foot down. Other cars honked the Toyota as it used the unoccupied lane. They were gaining on the Mercedes when it took the exit.

"Damn, damn." George hit the dash with his fist.

"What?"

"There are three roads off the exit. If we don't see them choose then it will be impossible to get back quickly. Bernard pumped the accelerator and pushed the car to its limit. He swung off the freeway and followed, closing the gap. Then they came up behind a truck. The Mercedes shot past the Mac and Bernard was stuck.

"Do something," George yelled. The Toyota veered off to the left and hit the side barriers as it squeezed past the monster truck on the exit lane. Bernard caught a glimpse of the Mercedes as it moved to the third road.

"Where does that road over there go?" Bernard asked.

"To the Lake Estate."

"Do you know it?"

"A bit. Let's go." Bernard turned off and chased the black car down the exit and under an overpass. The traffic was much heavier as they neared the housing estate and he kept losing the vehicle as it began weaving through the other road users.

"Keep your eye on it George, I'm having trouble." George spotted a gap three cars in front and directed Bernard to go for it. He slammed down a gear and pushed his way through the lane to the blare of horns of irate drivers. The Mercedes was pulling away when George had an idea.

"This is a two lane dual carriage way for about two kilometres. No turns or anything. Do you want to risk the other side?"

"You mean..."

"Go for it, Bernard."

The Toyota mounted the median strip and bumped down on the opposite side of the road. The traffic was much less, yet it was still a driving nightmare as he dodged oncoming traffic. A break in the chaos gave Bernard the opportunity to floor it. He held on tightly, as he gathered speed, and they made real progress towards the kidnappers.

"Truck, Bernard, truck."

Bernard steered to the median strip and jumped the curb just as the truck thundered past, its horn blaring.

"Shit, that was close," Bernard said. He spotted a gap in the inside lane, crunched down a gear and took the opportunity. George hung on as the Toyota swung wildly through the cars, his only thought for the safety of his wife. With one last lane change, they were just one car length away from their quarry.

"What now?" Bernard asked as he gripped the steering wheel and hunched over.

"Push them off the road."

"At this speed?" Bernard looked at the speedo. "150km/hour, you must be joking. We'd all be killed."

"Bump them."

Bernard nodded and crept up on the back end of the kidnappers. He nudged the bumper of the Mercedes. The driver braked and skid-steered to the outside lane, but the manoeuvrer set up a chain reaction. Cars spun out of control as the Mercedes crashed across the median strip. The traffic began to disintegrate. People braked in panic. A truck skidded into the back of a Skoda trying to avoid the Mercedes. Three following cars crashed into the back of the light truck. A Volvo skidded across the inside lane trying to avoid the chaos, but created a pile up of its own.

The Toyota was pushed along in the chaos and rear-ended. Bernard lost control. He skidded along the outside barrier. George watched in horror, as their chase ended in defeat. The Mercedes recovered, and with a wheel spin, it sped away in the direction they had just come.

"Shit, shit, shit." George hit the dash as he watched the car disappear. He looked at the pile up. Cars were at all angles across the two lanes, pinning Nozette and Simeoni in the emergency lane, blocking any chance of moving.

"We have to call the police." George began to make the call.

"Wait, George, listen to me. They have her for a reason. Let's find out what it is."

"Do you remember the number?" George asked. Bernard nodded and sang the numbers back. George rang on his mobile and heard a message that chilled his bones.

"What is it?" Bernard asked when he saw the look on his friend's face.

"Audrea is insurance. If Tag fails she..." he swallowed hard, "dies. We have to get him to court, Bernard."

"First we have to get out of this mess." They waited as the drivers began to unravel the gridlock. Bernard saw a gap and swung the car around, driving away before the police arrived.

They parked in the suburban driveway and walked into George's house. He checked the alarm system. When it responded with the all-clear message, they entered. Slumping wearily into the nearest chairs, they contemplated the predicament.

"Who knew Audrea was coming?" Bernard began.

"I can't think of anyone."

"What about the police?" Bernard asked.

George thought on the question. "Only Pallis and his escort."

"What do we know?" George fetched a brandy bottle from the sideboard and poured two drinks. Bernard grabbed a handy piece of paper and pencil.

"You and your lists Bernard – always with the list." George chided.

"It works. I've done this before and it puts things in order. Okay let's start. Duval is missing. The FFZ are affiliated with the Israeli Secret Service via Saliki who has infiltrated the Nazis. Duval knows Saliki, Conrad, and the mystery man are Neo-Nazis. Audrea is their insurance for Tag."

"It just gets better and better." George pulled his moustache. "But all this is just supposition really."

Bernard agreed, "But it makes sense doesn't it?" he said.
"That is the scary part Bernard."

The two sat back and looked at the list on the coffee table.

"Where do you think she is, Bernard?" Bernard shook his head and chewed on the end of his pencil,

"I don't know." He thought for a minute and then something clicked.

"That number. We might be able to trace it. I know a guy who does that sort of thing."

George handed him the phone. "Do it."

***

It was snowing when they walked up the flight of steps to an apartment block. The snow blanketed the ground and the streets seemed eerily quiet. Bernard pressed the buzzer for number six and a voice answered, "Lennard, here."

Bernard introduced himself and soon they were climbing the stairs to the sixth floor. The whole place was run down and graffiti tags covered every wall of the stairwell. George pressed the bell for apartment six and a thin man opened the door. He was pasty and wore an overcoat and fur-lined slippers.

"Come in," he said with an Eastern European accent. Lennard shut the door and ushered Bernard and George into a grubby little apartment. The windows were lined with aluminium foil and the one electric heater was having little effect on the chill of the room.

"I need the phone number," Lennard said holding out his hand. Bernard cleared his throat and sang the number as Lennard wrote it down.

"It works for me," Bernard said and gave a little laugh. Lennard lit a cigarette and beckoned the men to follow him to another room. The second room was full of computer paraphernalia. Wires draped from computers to other outlets with still more black boxes and about seven flat screen monitors.

"This is some set-up." George walked around stepping over the mess of many take-away meals strewn on the floor.

"It does its job." Lennard sat down, dropped his cigarette on the floor, and stubbed it out with his slipper. He punched in the telephone number and the lawyers watched as the screens went through an elaborate de-coding sequence.

"Will it take long?" George asked. Lennard grunted and watched the screen, tapping in something when the prompts came up. Names started to appear on the screen and they scrolled unending through the alphabet.

"Getting close now." Lennard leaned in closer to his monitor and watched the names. He kept a second screen downloading and moved easily back and forth checking and re-checking. Another screen started scrolling and he moved over and seemed to be engrossed.

"What's he doing?" George whispered to Bernard who was watching the screens.

"I never ask. I just pay up and walk away."

"How the hell do you know about this guy?"

"He was introduced by that private detective, Johnsson. The Swedish one." Bernard put his finger to his lips. They watched in silence as Lennard had all the screens working. Then one by one they flicked over to a screen saver and he only had one left. He pressed the enter key and a name appeared. All three men leaned forward and read the name.

"That's not right," George said and looked at Bernard.

"It's got to be a mistake," Bernard replied.

Lennard shrugged his shoulders. "I don't think so gentlemen." He rubbed his hands together and sat on them to get them warm. Bernard looked at the screen and frowned. He wrote Lennard a cheque and they left the apartment. The snow was deep on the steps as they crunched their way to the car. Their new footprints were quickly covered as they drove away into the night with the disturbing information.

"How can that be Bernard?" George asked as he opened the door to his house.

"I said we couldn't trust him. Didn't I say that right at the beginning?" Bernard leaned back against the kitchen bench. George nodded and sighed.

"But why?"

"I don't know. Why string us along with all that bullshit. You don't think he has infiltrated the group, do you?" Bernard rubbed his brow.

"Well, that would make sense. If Duval is in, then he is playing a deadly game. NATA must want the top man really badly."

"Why don't you ring his number?" George picked up the phone and pulled Duval's card from his wallet. He waited as the call rang. He was just about to hang up when it diverted and someone answered.

"Ya."

George hung up and looked over to Bernard.

"What?"

"Conrad."

"Then he's in." Bernard said.

"And we are out … out on our own."

CHAPTER TWENTY ONE

"Look, I just can't sit here. Let's go back to that winery," George said after collecting the case notes he had transferred to his house. They collected a couple of ski jackets and thick boots and hopped in the car. It had been snowing steadily for hours, and the drive was torturous. Traffic was slow, and as the night air froze the compacted snow, cars started skidding and careering out of control into one another. George elected to drive and took a few pain killers before he started. He proceeded with caution and took the main thoroughfare hoping the snow ploughs and grit truck had been through. His hunch was right and they picked up speed to the dangerous part of town.

It was only when they reached the overpass, that Bernard asked, "George, do you have a gun?" George looked over to Bernard and wondered at his friend's capacity to change. Bernard used to be the safe as houses, quiet, negotiation option partner in the firm. And now he was asking for a gun.

"No, I don't." Bernard took the answer stoically and watched the road. The streets were deserted and looked clean with a covering of snow. The grit trucks hadn't bothered with the smaller streets and their car crunched the snow into the few frozen ruts in the road.

"Good thing no-one is about," George said, and Bernard agreed. They drove to the warehouse and parked down the street, under a light.

"It's very dark." Bernard said, looking up at the windows. They walked towards the front of the building. The only noise was their footfalls on the snow. The car that contained the reporter had been towed away and now the quadrangle was a huge expanse of white.

"Look at that." Bernard pointed to track marks in the snow leading up to the double doors. Fresh car tracks disappeared into the building.

"They can't be too old." George squatted down and studied the tyre tread marks.

"You're not going to tell me you can read tyre treads."

George looked up from the ground and shook his head. "No." George smirked. "Come on." They quickened their pace and walked along, shaded by the wall. A lone light illuminated the corner of the building and they slipped past its halo of light and turned the corner into the dark.

"Up here," George whispered and Bernard followed him up a flight of steps. A small window at the landing yielded to a gentle push and George flicked it open. He peered inside, and then with a leg up from Bernard, hoisted himself onto the ledge.

"Ow," he gasped as the ledge bit into his chest wound. He was hanging there on the windowsill catching his breath, when they heard a door open below and an oblong of light shone on the snow. A man stepped outside and lit up a cigarette. Bernard watched as he stamped his feet against the cold. Then he looked up. Bernard froze, not daring to breathe and George hung half in and half out of the window. The snow was easing off as they waited. Then Bernard sniffed the air. The aroma of a Montecristo was unmistakable. He looked down and studied the figure in the doorway.

Saliki stubbed out his cigar in the snow, and then turned and went back inside slamming the door. Once again, the stairway was dark.

"They are here," Bernard said, as he lowered George back down onto the landing.

"Who was that?"

Bernard explained what he saw. He frowned in concentration for moment. "What if we can get to Saliki? He is bound to know about Audrea."

"Let's get inside first," George said.

This time Bernard hoicked himself up and through the window. Once inside, he opened the door and George walked through. The upper floor was dark and small banks of snow had formed where the skylights were broken. The men were creeping across the expanse of wooden floor, looking for a way down, when they heard voices below. Through the planking gaps in the floor, they saw a light. Bernard motioned to kneel down and he applied his eye to the crack. Saliki sat on a sofa and someone's legs crossed to his left. They were talking. Bernard heard a moan from somewhere off to their right. He moved away and George looked through the crack.

"I can only see two," he mouthed to Bernard and held up two fingers. Bernard put his finger to his lips and they listened.

"We only need them for the trial, and then I don't care what you do." Saliki stood up and paced in front of the sofa. The men heard a muffled reply and Saliki laughed, "If you like, after all she is only a Jew." Bernard felt George stiffen and put a restraining arm on his friend.

"We have to find her," George whispered. "She must be here." They stood up and Bernard remembered a small torch he had on a set of keys. He pressed the button and swept the beam of light around the top floor.

"There." George pointed to the elevator. "We can climb down the shaft." Bernard looked at the open pit and nodded his head.

"Come on." George shimmied down onto the bracing and began to climb. He reached the roof of the elevator and beckoned Bernard. Once they were standing on the roof, they could see into the ground floor. Saliki was sitting, reading the paper. They watched as another man came in pushing Audrea in front of him. The oaf grinned and pressed his hands against her buttocks and breasts, then rubbed her neck. George swallowed hard to contain his rage. Her hands were tied behind her back and she staggered and slopped from one foot to the other. George began to breathe faster as he watched his helpless wife being pushed around. Bernard took George by the arm and held him back. He wagged his finger in front of George's face and made him watch. Audrea seemed drunk as she swayed to and fro trying to keep standing.

Saliki looked up, folded his paper, and greeted Audrea, "Good evening Madame Nozette. I trust you are comfortable." Audrea tried to speak but all she could manage was to twist her mouth to form the words that wouldn't come.

"Yes, it's not a nice drug is it?" Bernard watched and knew what she was going through. He remembered his time in Israel and how hard it had been to speak. Audrea shook her head, her eyes wide with fear.

"Your husband is a good man I'm sure, but we don't want him to get any ideas, Mrs Nozette. You will be comfortable here until we have a result." Audrea looked around like a caged animal.

"Bastard," she managed spit at Saliki.

"Take her away." Saliki waved his hand at Audrea and added, "Jewish filth."

George could not contain his anger. He sprang from the elevator and sprinted through the packing room to Saliki. He forgot his ribs, his pain, and his safety, as he landed a punch square on Saliki's face. Saliki staggered back and clutched his nose as he braced himself on a pillar.

"Fuckin' bastard," he said as he looked at the blood on his hands. The brutish moron who had brought Audrea in ran into the fight. He grabbed George by the hair and landed a punch on his ear. George reeled back and hit the floor with a thud.

"Guido, get him." Saliki yelled, then he began to run to the door. Guido bent down to pluck George from the floor. Audrea took a run and head-butted him, making him lose his balance. He staggered and dropped to one knee. Bernard came at him with an iron bar from a broken conveyor roller. He took a good swing at the big man and hit him on the shoulder blades. Guido groaned and then pulled himself up and turned with rage in his eyes. He lunged at Bernard and missed his mark. Bernard side stepped his grasp and ran to George. He pulled him up, waited until he was steady, then grabbed a wine bottle, and hit out at Guido as he charged into the man. He fell with a vicious hit to the head and lay still. George looked over to his wife. Sobbing, Audrea staggered to her husband and they hugged. Bernard hunted around, found a piece of glass, and began to cut Audrea's cable tie to her wrists.

"Are you OK?" he asked.

"Yes." Audrea nodded. There was a loud bang from downstairs and the noise of voices. George grabbed his wife and they looked out of the window to see several cars parked in front of the building.

"Shit, we have company." He pulled Audrea away and the three made their way to the elevator. The pulley started to move.

"What now?" Bernard looked around the room. There was only one entry and exit and that was bringing people. He spied the conveyor.

"Through here." Bernard led his friends, on their hands and knees, along the track which disappeared into another room. They listened as the crowd entered the room and sized up the situation.

"Find them," someone yelled.

George, Bernard, and Audrea scrabbled off the conveyor and looked at their surroundings. The room was furnished with long stainless steel benches and wine testing paraphernalia. Vials and bottles stood on the benches and a large vat occupied one corner.

"Over there." George pointed to a small hatchway in the wall. They had begun to run for it, when the door to the lab opened. Two men stood in the doorway.

"Here," one of the skinheads yelled as the other smirked and began to walk towards the three fugitives. Bernard looked around for a weapon. He picked up a corkscrew.

Then, thinking better of his choice, he grabbed a large long glass tube. The skinhead lunged at Bernard with a flick knife, as George took on the fight. He picked up the discarded corkscrew and punched it into the attacker's neck. Bernard staggered back as the man fell clutching his neck. His mate came to his rescue. He was armed with a menacing metal bar and now he swung it wildly about, in the hope of hitting anyone close. The bar smashed the glass on the bench, the splinters flying off in every direction. Audrea threw a bottle of wine at the thug and it hit him on the head. Dazed, he stopped his attack, shook his head, then dropped to the floor.

"Go!" George yelled to Audrea. She crawled into the hatchway and dropped into the next room.

"Bernard, go." George pushed his friend to follow Audrea. George watched as Bernard slid through the hatch. Then, George took the thug's bar, and with some rope that was hanging on the vat, he trussed up the man, threading his arms through the bar at his back. With the free end of the rope, he tied the man to the vat. When he was satisfied, he ran for the hatch and dived through.

Audrea and Bernard were being held by two skinheads. Their mouths we taped and their hands tied behind their backs. George stood up and the two Neo-Nazis jumped on him. He received a punch in the stomach and doubled over. The pain came not from the gut punch, but from his still fresh gunshot wound in his chest. Gasping for air George felt the warm trickle of blood on his shirt. Another punch landed on his ear and he fell to the floor.

Audrea watched; a look of horror in her eyes, as George lay still.

"Things could have been so simple Mr Nozette," Saliki walked into the room nursing his bloodied nose. You are lucky you are still alive." He directed a swift kick at the prostrate figure. George groaned and closed his eyes. Saliki walked over to Bernard. His trussed arms were being held by a skinhead. Saliki spat at his face.

"Jew." Saliki sneered. "Ah, I see. You were under the misapprehension that I was, as you say, on your side." Saliki smiled and licked his lips. "But as you can see, things are not always what they seem.

"It was necessary you see… if I wanted the names in the FFZ. I see you are beginning to understand Mr Simeoni. You know, the world is a different place now. Times have changed and we need a leader who will lead. Someone who will give the people what they want. The great majority want change. They don't want the dirt of the world on their door step. Tag is just the beginning of the revolution."

"Now Mr Simeoni, you have a job to do. We will keep the Nozettes here so that you can do your job." En Saliki pulled out a cigar and made a show of clipping the end and lighting it. Then he grabbed the tape on Bernard's mouth and ripped.

"We expect a result Mr Simeoni. I think you know what we mean."

""There are some things a decent human being just will not do, and I think you know what *I* mean." Bernard looked Saliki in the eye.

"Oh, a decent human being, Mr Simeoni. And you count yourself in that number. But what about your precious justice, Mr Simeoni?"

Bernard studied Saliki. He wondered if he knew about the Australian. He seemed to be playing word games with him and it made Bernard wary. He looked at the face, the gold tooth, and the dark skin. Saliki returned the stare. Then, when he had his full attention, Bernard head butted him. Saliki's nose cracked and he reeled back, tripped over George, and fell down. Audrea, taking up the fight, grabbed for the man standing behind her and found the prize. She squeezed his testicles. He screamed, but she wouldn't let go. Bernard threw his head back. It smacked his guard, making him let go and drop to his knees. George managed to rouse himself. He picked up a box cutter and stabbed Audrea's victim in the leg. He yelled and fell down, clutching his balls and his leg. The box cutter was used to break the cable ties on Bernard and Audrea's wrists. As they ran out of the door, Audrea ripped the tape from her mouth. The drug was wearing off now and she felt in control.

"There is a man. He is in a room. They beat him. It's bad." She saw the look on Bernard's face,

"I don't know where it is. It was small, with no windows."

As they ran down a flight of steps, George had to stop. "I'm done." He opened his coat and they saw the blood on his jumper.

Audrea put her arm around her husband and helped him move. "He needs attention. Now, Bernard." She looked pleadingly at Bernard as they shuffled with George to a fire exit.

"This room, was it a long way from the elevator?"

"No, just a short walk. I don't think we even went outside." Bernard looked around and saw an old evacuation map on the wall. It showed all the corridors and rooms on the ground floor. At the far end was a bond storeroom.

"No windows?"

Audrea nodded her head.

"That must be it." Bernard pointed to the small square at the end of the building. "Look, here are the car keys. The car is down the street. Take him." Audrea nodded and roused George to walk.

She looked back as she pushed the fire door open to the cold air, "Be careful," she said then they walked out into the snow. Bernard took one last look at the mud map and then pushed the door open and walked into the corridor. He listened for any noise, but the place was eerily quiet. The bond store was off to the left at the end of the building and Bernard found it had been signposted. He tried the door handle, but it was locked. The iron clad door was to stop theft and it seemed to Bernard that they had made it bullet proof as well. He banged on the door, but all was quiet from inside. Saliki must have the key he reasoned. Bernard retraced his steps and crept up to the first floor of the building. He listened, and heard a few low moans, but nothing else. The floor near the door was blood stained with drips leading off to the elevator. Someone had left. The trail led him to the outer door. Bernard looked at the spats of blood and thought it had to be Saliki. He opened the outer door and saw it was snowing. The track was rapidly disappearing as the thick flakes fell.

With a wine bottle in his hand, Bernard walked outside and scanned the area. A van stood off to one side at the southern end of the quadrangle. The exhaust had a plume of gas. Someone was trying to leave. Bernard hugged the shadow of the wall and soon came level with the vehicle. It was Saliki. Bernard ran for the van and pulled the driver side door open. He grabbed Saliki by the coat lapels and pulled him out into the snow. Saliki grappled with the car door, trying to hang on. Bernard landed one punch to his temple and knocked him out. Saliki slumped to the snow and

Bernard rummaged through his coat pockets. There was nothing. Sitting back on his heels, Bernard closed his eyes. He felt like giving up. Then he remembered the van. The keys were dangling from the ignition. He grabbed them, ran back to the storeroom, and fumbled with each key. One slipped in and turned. He pulled the large heavy door open and saw a figure sitting at a table with his head down, resting on the table-top. Bernard tried for a light switch and hoped it would work. A single globe illuminated the scene.

"Hey." Bernard shook the fellow. "Hey, you." He knelt down and then gasped.

Duval's face was bloody and puffed up. His eyes were just little slits, his lip was split, and his nose was a pulped raw wound.

"Duval?" Bernard shook the man. He let out a long groan.

"I'm going to get you out of here." Bernard put his hands under Duval's arms and tried to lift. He was a heavy set man and Bernard couldn't move him.

"You're going to have to help, Duval. Can you help?" Bernard tried again but he couldn't budge the man. He took a breath and tried one more time – then he saw it. He lurched over to the corner of the room and threw up. After wiping his mouth, he walked over to take another look at Duval.

"The bastards," Bernard said. They had used a nail gun and pinned Duval to the table through his elbows.

"Wait here. I'll get help." Bernard locked Duval in and ran back to the van. Saliki was lying in the falling snow, out cold. Bernard tried to think what to do with him.

As he drove the van into the street, he was glad to see that Audrea had driven away. Bernard glanced over to the slumped Saliki in the passenger seat and took the quickest route to the police. The snow was steady now as he negotiated the traffic. After a twenty minute drive, Bernard skidded to a halt outside the police station and ran inside. The police took control of the situation. They rushed out to the van just in time to see Saliki foaming at the mouth and his body going into rigors. He stiffened and jerked once, and then he was dead.

"Shit, shit, shit." Bernard thumped the van. Saliki was the only link they had to the group.

"You had better come inside." A gendarme took Bernard by the arm. He let himself be led back inside and sat down.

"Coffee?" someone asked and Bernard nodded automatically. He took the cup and began to shake and then he remembered Duval.

***

Detective Inspector Pallis walked into the interview room and nodded to Bernard.

"The ambulance attendant said Duval was lucky. He hadn't lost much blood and he was alive." Pallis sat down and poured himself a coffee.

"I would like you to..." Pallis stirred his coffee, "to enlighten me."

Bernard hugged his drink and closed his eyes. "Tomorrow, Inspector."

"I'm not sure we can do that, Mr Simeoni. A man has died and another is in hospital. I am looking for answers."

"I have none." Bernard opened his eyes.

Pallis sat back and narrowed his gaze. "Why don't I believe you Simeoni?"

Bernard shrugged his shoulders. "Look Inspector, I have to be in court in less that twelve hours and I need to sleep."

"I cannot charge you, Mr Simeoni. But I can give you protection. "

"Protection?" Bernard queried. "Your protection didn't help Mrs Nozette. I think I can look after myself." He sighed and rubbed his eyes. "Or perhaps your protection is a minder. Who can trust who Mr Pallis?"

"Either way." Pallis stood up. "Just do your job Mr Simeoni. Just do your job."

CHAPTER TWENTY TWO

The press gathered at first light in front of the hospital. They had grabbed the story and now were inciting the public to vilification and a frenzy of hate. It was six-thirty. Day one of the trial. Bernard had rung the hospital. George was being discharged at eight. As Bernard showered and dressed, he reflected on his encounter with the now dead Saliki. He had said to Saliki, 'There were some things a decent human being will just not do', but did he really believe it. Tag needed a defence. It was his duty, his moral obligation to defend Tag and yet he felt morally bankrupt. He had done things that he could never erase. Things that made him a hypocrite. How could he possibly hold his own credentials out as pure? He wondered if George was wrestling with his conscience.

Bernard looked at himself in the mirror. He used to see a decent man, a decent human being. His watch flared in the morning sunshine reminding him of his culpability. He took it off and threw it in the bin. Then he looked at the pale ring of skin where his wedding band should be. What would Gabbie think of him if she knew? The Rabbi said to do his job and the religion will follow. *How*, Bernard thought, *could it follow when he had let it go so long ago?* The events of the last few weeks welled up and cast doubts over his ability to be objective. His ability to be sincere and uphold the law. *He was the criminal,* he thought. *He was the one who should be on trial.*

The day was grey and cold as Bernard stepped out of his apartment and greeted his minder. The young Gendarme nodded and they travelled down in the elevator.

"You're the one who is defending that Nazi?" The Gendarme let Bernard exit first and they walked to a waiting car.

"I had the car waiting," the officer said when Bernard looked around.

"I have to go to the hospital." He stooped down and sat in the car. The driver pressed the central locking, turned around and smiled. Bernard felt uneasy at his scrutiny. "The hospital," he repeated. They drove out of the underground car park and through the gates then headed south. No-one spoke and Bernard looked out of the window at the grey streets on the grey day. He pulled his coat a little tighter and adjusted his briefcase.

The car pulled into the hospital car park.

"The door?" Bernard asked as he tried the knob. The door remained locked.

"What the fuck?" He looked around at the Gendarme and the driver. "Who are you?" The driver turned around and smiled, "We will be watching you Mr Simeoni. Always." The electronic door opened and Bernard jumped out of the car. He turned to take a last look at the men and saw they were watching him as he hurried away.

The press weren't so easy to evade. They spied Bernard and rushed forward, pressing him with questions. He kept his head down, barrelled through the crowd to get to the relative peace of the hospital foyer, and made his way to George's private room.

"You made it." George was sitting on the side of the bed dressed in a suit.

"What are you doing?" Bernard indicated the clothes.

"I had Audrea go and get it. You don't think I'm going to miss the first day, do you?" Bernard shook his head.

"You're an idiot, George Nozette." George slowly levered himself off the bed, in obvious pain.

"Hold on George. I have to tell you something." Bernard explained the latest developments.

"I don't know what happened to the officer that was supposed to be protecting me. I dread to think after what they did to Duval. George..." Bernard stammered, "I don't think we should trust anyone. You agree?" George nodded.

"I'll call Audrea. She has the car." George made a quick call at the reception desk and then they waited.

The press swarmed over the two lawyers as they left the building asking questions and pressing in on the men.

Bernard stopped and held their attention. "Our client will attend court today. All that we have to say will be said at that time." He grabbed George's arm and they walked to the waiting car.

Audrea smiled at Bernard, kissed George, then drove them to the office.

"And you're saying that man, Duval, is ok?" Audrea asked as she drove.

"Yes. Detective Inspector Pallis said he was lucky, if you can believe that." Bernard said. George furrowed his brow. "Audrea, you're sure you weren't followed?" he asked.

"I don't think so. I've been watching and it doesn't look like it." She glanced in the mirror. Bernard swivelled around and looked out the back window. The peak hour was horrendous. *If anyone was following they would have a hard time,* Bernard thought as he looked at the wall to wall traffic. Audrea swung the Toyota into Rue de Maine and slowed as they pulled up next to the office. The burnt out building was a stark reminder of the power of hate. Bernard walked George and Audrea through the events, pointing out where the bomb went off and the surreal feeling he had as he watched it all go up in smoke. The area had been taped by the police and now the banners fluttered in the cold wind, making the scene look even more desolate.

"They certainly did a good job." George stood on the pavement and looked up. The blackened facade painted a grim picture.

"You can rent something else, darling." Audrea hung on her husband's arm.

"Let's go up." Bernard opened the stairway door and began to climb. "Come on, we have two hours before our rendezvous with Tag." The stairs groaned and creaked as they climbed. The reception area was a mess of shattered glass and splintered furniture. Papers and files littered the floor and all seemed a sodden mess. Audrea frowned and held George's hand.

"It's too awful. Let's go." The men agreed and turned to leave.

"Hang on. I just need to see if something is still here." George walked over the debris and entered his office. Most of the contents had been strewn about in the blast and wet by the fire brigade, but in one far corner stood his filing cabinet. Bernard and Audrea stood at the door and watched as George flicked through his files and found what he was looking for.

"Have it," he said holding a file up high, "now, let's get out of here."

Once back in the car, George opened the file and looked at the photographs of the riot. He thumbed through the pictures taken from the television and the papers.

"What is it?"

"Look." He pointed to a grainy black and white photograph. They leant over the picture and followed George's finger. What they saw put their defence into context.

***

The television began with live coverage. A Somalian was murdered in the street, shot by the police, the report began, and his death had sparked riots in the outer suburbs. George and Bernard watched the television at Bernard's apartment while Audrea made coffee. A picture of the chaos looked more like a war zone. People were banding together to loot and rage against the system.

"The man, an illegal immigrant," the reporter said, "was being questioned by police when a gunshot was heard, eye witnesses reported. An officer was shot and Mr Mogadu died at the scene. The public perception is that Mr Mogadu had done nothing wrong and now the public are rising up against those in authority." Bernard sipped his coffee and watched as the camera panned to the streets where people were looting and smashing the very infrastructure they needed to eke out a decent living.

"This is madness," he said.

The reporter went on, "The influx of refugees and illegal immigrants to this neighbourhood of Paris has created an artificial ghetto atmosphere." A brick hit the cameraman and the telecast went blank. The three stared at the black screen.

"It's xenophobia of the worst kind. Muslim gangs of disaffected youth roamed the streets baying for justice," George said to no one in particular.

"This is bad." The screen resumed transmission and showed the police in riot gear charging the gang wielding iron bars, chains, and anything that might be called a weapon. Audrea sat down next to George and watched as the news went live to a different location.

"That's the courthouse." She pointed to the screen.

"Live at the court where the case begins today into the death of Mr Darlan who was assaulted and murdered at the Rue de la Victoire riots. The firm of Nozette & Simeoni will be defending the self-confessed Neo-Nazi."

George interrupted the report, "That's not right. He isn't self-confessed anything. God, how can we get a result when the press already have him guilty?" Audrea rubbed her husband's shoulders and they listened once more as a politician came on the screen.

"We must send a significant deterrent to this small faction of society. We can never excuse this level of carnage." The news went back to the courthouse where a large crowd was gathering for the beginning of the trial.

"There is a swathe of spreading unrest here," the reporter started, "as we wait for the appearance of the accused and his lawyers. A general disillusionment with the justice system is the pervading mood. I can see placards for both sides of the argument, which at this stage seems to be about the growing non-indigenous population and the demands they make on the nationals."

Bernard looked at George and then held his head in his hands. "They want to crucify him...and us."

"Or put him on a pedestal. He is the standard bearer for intolerance and racism and by the look of that crowd, they think his way is the right way," George said.

"Ssshhh." Audrea indicated the television.

"Mr Voisard, what do you think of this unrest? Does this minority have a point to make?"

Voisard looked right into the camera, "I'm not sure we are talking about a minority. The French are restless. And who can blame them. Unemployment; the GFC has all but destroyed the Euro; waves of immigrants demanding their rights. Not their inalienable rights, mind you, just their rights, when they haven't contributed to our society one centime. When is enough enough? We will be fair, but when will these people be fair. Do we have to liberate ourselves once again? Liberate ourselves from, not the yolk of tyrants, but from the grip of a so called moral obligation. Do we not have an obligation to be true to ourselves? France is for the

French." Voisard stared at the camera and blinked. His grey eyes burned with an inner fire and then he was cut for a commercial break.

"It's a compelling argument." Bernard sighed.

"I thought in this, the twenty-first century, we would be past all the tribalism bullshit. He wants us to close our borders and become isolationists."

"But if we did, would that be so bad. We might just turn a profit if we were a closed system. What's made in France stays in France."

"That's communism Bernard."

"Well, it hasn't hurt the Chinese. That's all I'm saying."

"Boys." Audrea stepped in to quell the growing argument.

"George, I'm just playing devil's advocate, that's all." Bernard chuckled and stood up for a coffee refill.

The morning television continued with the live coverage of the outbreaks of unrest, with the clashes being reported on several fronts across the city. The courthouse was massing a huge, angry crowd and scuffles had already broken out. The police Commissioner came on the screen to implore people to stay away, and for calm. Then he admitted his resources were stretched to their limit.

"We have to walk into that." Bernard pointed to the seething crowd on the steps of the court. We have an hour and a half George. Do you think we should ring for the Gendarmerie?" George considered the question.

"And who do you suggest?" Bernard took his drink from Audrea and let the question remain unanswered.

"It's been like this for weeks now," Audrea said as she looked over George's shoulder. "Everyone hates the immigration," she said, "Voisard has incited the people with all his 'France for the French'. We live in a multi-cultural world. It's a fact."

"Still, he has a point."

"Bernard Simeoni, I never would have thought it of you." Audrea looked at him and scowled.

"But look, where does it end? We can't feed, clothe, and house all the world's poor and outcast. Can we?"

"But we have an obligation." Audrea challenged. Bernard sipped his coffee to sidestep the argument.

"Right now we have bigger things to worry about." George interrupted the growing argument. "Audrea, I don't want you near the court today. The press will be on the hunt, and who knows what will happen. I want you to stay here. Lock the doors and..."

Audrea cupped her husband's face in her hands. "I know," she said, and kissed him silent.

"What we do today may change the perception of who we are as a nation," George said, "And I think the world may be watching that change."

The taxi was waiting outside the apartment when George and Bernard walked through the security gate to their appointment with Tag.

"He said this morning, didn't he? Bernard asked, trying to remember the instructions for picking up Tag. He looked down the street and scanned the building opposite but everything looked ordinary and normal. The men had just closed the taxi's doors when a photographer appeared and started to reel off about a dozen shots. He chased the taxi down the street. As they turned the corner, he gave up.

"You see that. It won't be long and they will put two and two together and come up with a confirmed report that says, Jew." Bernard looked out the window at the gathering clouds.

"So what, Bernard? Does our religion preclude us from defending someone? Does it stop us from seeking the truth and from delivering justice?" George looked at his friend, but Bernard was silent.

214

The taxi drove away to another call and left the men standing in the street with their briefcases. Bernard looked up and down the street, his paranoia evident in his actions. He glanced at his wrist and remembered he had thrown his watch away.

"What's the time?"

"Listen Bernard, we have plenty of time." George looked at his watch, "Plenty of time." George fingered his moustache. Bernard paced the pavement until he saw a car turn the corner. It was an Audi A4 and seemed out of place in the little street.

"They're here," he said. The car cruised down the street and stopped in front of the chiropodist next door to the office door. George stooped down and looked at the driver.

"Where's Tag?" he asked as he peered into the back seat.

"Get in," the driver ordered.

"What? You must be fuckin' joking." George stood up and looked to Bernard for confirmation.

"We were expecting Tag," Bernard said.

"Get in. I will take you to him." The men resigned themselves to their fate. The driver sped away from Rue de Maine with two uneasy passengers.

"Where is he?" George tried to question the driver but he wasn't having much success. No answer was forthcoming. The car joined the ring road and Bernard noted the markers as they made their way across the city. With a quick swing to the left, they exited the main road and soon were lost in the maze of back streets and alley ways. The Audi finally came to a stop.

"Here." The driver sat and refused to be drawn in.

The area was surrounded in high rise buildings and they were right on the river. Bernard looked up at the modern architecture and recognised the location as the new reclaimed land with at least a million Euro price tag.

"I know this place." He pointed to the high rise apartment block with its distinctive swirling outer structure. "It's millionaires' row." He reiterated the name the press gave the precinct.

"Let's go." George led the way to the foyer and pushed the door open. A concierge greeted them and it seemed they were expected. He ushered the men to the elevator and pressed the penthouse suite button. George raised his eyebrow at his partner in a silent exclamation. The ride to the top was quiet and quick. As the elevator button flicked to the penthouse, the doors opened, and the men stepped out into a private reception area.

"Hello?" George called.

A woman appeared, "Hello, we will be with you shortly." She smiled and walked away.

"What do you make of all this?" Bernard indicated the luxurious surroundings. "Tag has friends in high places."

"We are quite high aren't we?" A well-dressed gentleman held out his hand as he approached.

"Pierre Nadeau."

"Where is our client, Mr Nadeau?" George was getting agitated at the delay.

"He is here. Just a bit of last minute grooming. Adele has done wonders."

"Adele?"

Pierre nodded preferring not to add an answer.

"Look, we don't have a lot of time. We have to sign him in and there are procedures to complete," Bernard said.

George added, "And the crowds are tremendous. It's going to be a struggle as it is."

"Yes, yes, procedures. Will you wait in here?" Nadeau led them to a spacious lounge room with windows on three sides and left. The view was panoramic and all of the southern side of Paris seem to stretch before them.

"Look at this." Bernard went to the window and looked down at the Seine. "Spectacular."

"But look at this." George walked to the sideboard and pointed to a cluster of photographs.

"Voisard and..." He swallowed. "Conrad." Bernard ran his eye over the photos and picked out half a dozen dignitaries.

"This is bigger than we imagined. Than even Duval imagined."

"Look, it's the Chancellor of the Sorbonne." He pointed to a picture of Voisard with his arm around the Chancellor. George looked closer.

"Is that a ring?" He pointed to the Chancellor's hand resting on a table." Bernard had picked up the photo, and was examining it at the window, when they heard the door.

"The view can be quite nice in the sunshine. Of course, now it is dull and grey," Nadeau said.

Bernard put the photo in his coat pocket. "It's spectacular." They stood and admired the view for a few minutes. The sound of door opening made them all turn.

"Ah, here he is." All three looked at Tag. He had been totally reformed and now looked like a stock broker, albeit with tattoos.

"Is that a..."

"A very expensive suit? Yes." Nadeau walked over and pulled an imaginary piece of fluff from the lapel of Tag's suit. "So now you have your man."

Heinz walked into the room with a slow gait and held out his hand. "Mr Simeoni." He shook Bernard's hand.

"Mr Nozette." Tag took George's hand and smiled. George let his mouth drop in amazement, trying to remember the last time he had seen Tag. Then, he only had a vocabulary of two words.

217

"Now gentlemen," Nadeau interrupted, "It is imperative that Tag be presented in a favourable light. He must be allowed to speak. I think we know the consequences of ... well, I will leave that up to you."

George looked at Heinz then back to Nadeau.

"You so much as touch our families and..." Bernard threatened.

"I'm sure it won't come to that, Mr Simeoni. We both have a job to do."

"We?" Bernard asked Nadeau.

"Mmm," Nadeau started, "Yes, it is we. You see some ideals have a resonance that sets up a note of harmony. That one note can spread and soon, well you have your symphony." Nadeau felt pleased with his analogy.

George countered, "But there will always be the odd wrong note."

"Yes, of course, but like the bad apple in the barrel, it can be taken out."

"And disposed of?" Bernard asked.

"Any new or very old idea will have its detractors. It's inevitable, but with the world changing so quickly we... my associates and I, have very few opportunities to get the message across. Modern technology has helped immensely. Twitter, Facebook etc. Subtle language is a very persuasive tool in the right hands."

"I think you mean propaganda."

"Of a sort, Mr Nozette. Who are we to deny the people what they want."

"Or what you think they want," Bernard said.

"Isn't that democracy, Mr Simeoni? You vote for your man and place your trust in his judgement, whatever that may be. We are the voice of the disaffected."

"It's a very exclusive club, Mr Nadeau."

Nadeau shrugged his shoulders. "Exclusive or inclusive, Mr Nozette. We employed you, and as I recall, you have our funds in your account at this very hour." Nadeau walked to the window. "Napoleon thought Paris the centre of the world. It can be again. We can make it happen."

"By using people?" George looked at Tag who was standing apart from the group and looking into space. "He's not drugged is he?" George asked. He felt Tag wasn't spontaneous or quite normal and all his actions had a measured, calculated feel about them.

"I am fine," Tag answered. Bernard raised his eyebrow in George's direction.

"Mr Tag is a soldier, gentlemen. He is the vanguard of our politics. Be under no illusions. Mr Tag is fully aware of his role."

"Tag?" Bernard asked.

"I have a job to do," Tag said the words, but the conviction was missing.

"And what was Doctor Cadieux. Was he just a soldier?" Bernard turned on Nadeau.

"Gentlemen please. This is neither the time nor the place." Nadeau fidgeted with his cuff links. "There are winners and losers in every game. The people of France will be winners when this is all over."

"I'm not so sure about that, Mr Nadeau. But what I can tell you is that Heinz Tag will have his day."

"That is all we ask, Mr Nozette, that is all."

Bernard glanced at the clock on the wall. "Oh, that doesn't work. Chinese rubbish I'm afraid." Nadeau brought his hand up and looked at his watch. Bernard watched the movement and noticed the ring on his little finger. The implications of the ring brought the whole deal into sharp focus. Now they were displaying their allegiance openly, it could only mean that Tag was the catalyst they wanted. How many were waiting for the call no one could guess. But with

219

their rhetoric appealing to the masses and their phobias, it was an age-old ploy that seemed to work every time. Bernard hoped he was wrong, George hoped history didn't repeat itself.

"Shall we go?" he said.

The Audi was waiting for them as they exited the building to make the journey to court. Snow flurries busied themselves around the men and the leaden sky had the promise of more to come. Bernard mused on the connections they had seen in the apartment. He knew he should tell someone, but the list of reliable law enforcement was getting a bit thin. Anyone of the people he had met could be affiliated with Tag and his twisted ideals. The only man that might help was in a critical condition in Intensive Care with a ruptured liver. He instinctively looked for his watch and then remembered why he had thrown it away. The secret burned inside his mind eating at his morality like a cancer. Bernard looked at Tag. He was the dupe. What riches did they promise him to bring him to this point? Or was he so brainwashed that he really believed the rhetoric?

"Tag?" Bernard looked into his face.

"What?"

"You don't have to do it you know. It's not too late to plea bargain." George turned and looked at the two men in the back seat.

"We have a compelling case. We know who was there at the riot. You know too, don't you?" George asked. Bernard stared at Tag, trying to gauge what was going on in his brain.

"But I..." Heinz faulted. "I must. I must, I must." He repeated it as if saying the mantra would fix everything.

George tried once more, "You know they are just using you Heinz. They will discard you once you have done your duty." George was hoping the shock tactic might snap his client out of their mind games.

"We have to cleanse. It is the only solution." Heinz pulled himself up in his seat and set his jaw. "It is a necessary step."

The Audi pulled up half a block away as protesters and the media crowded the sidewalk.

"We will walk," Bernard said, then looked at George and added, "We must steer the questions from the obvious. You and I know who was orchestrating the event."

The three began the long walk to the steps of the court house. Some protesters saw them and began to run.

"Filthy Jews." Someone shouted and spat at them.

"Traitor to Jews," another yelled. The chant was taken up as the men quickened their pace. The media pounced on them as they were swamped by protesters. The police stepped in and a fight ensued. Punches were thrown and placards smashed as the Jews fought with the police and the media. And then a group of Muslims waded into the fray. They shouted 'Allahu Akba' (God is Great), and carried banners declaring their right to call France home. Bernard looked up to see a barrage of pictures of the murdered Somali next to a sign of a Swastika. The sheer force of the mob drove the police-line further up the steps. Then the riot police ranks were broken. A wave surged forward and the fragmented police forces clashed with the gangs in a frenzy of fighting. Bottles were thrown at the journalists and the cameramen trying to film. There was a real sense of danger as the crowd lost any semblance of decency and began pelting the gendarmes with missiles. The hordes moved as one entity, pushing up the steps. Someone screamed and the Gendarmes put up their riot shields and donned gas masks.

"Come on." George grabbed Tag's arm and started to drag him through the crowd. The police tried to rescue them. They made a cordon around the three men as they climbed the front steps. The angry mob began to throw missiles at the group. Bernard ducked an orange. A shot rang out. For that one split second, the street was stunned into silence. Tag staggered back and fell. George felt blood splatter his face. He looked down his hands shaking in shock. Tag had a large hole in the side of his head. He was slumped on the steps. Bernard knelt down and went to cradle Tag, but it was a lost cause. Tag was dead. The media went wild. Bernard took off his coat and covered Heinz – trying to give him for some semblance of dignity.

"Get down." A policeman pushed George to the ground and covered him with a riot shield. The crowd pushed and shoved. People were running in all directions in panic. Screams, shouts, and anarchy took over the street as a human wave tried to disperse. Bernard sat down on the cold steps, put his head in his hands, and closed his eyes. What had started with a riot now ended in a riot. Gradually the chaos subsided and the police let George and Bernard stand. The area was strewn with litter. Broken banners, rocks, papers, the odd shoe, all told the story. George looked down at the sprawled figure, and watched a large pool of blood slowly trickle down the courthouse steps. *The stain of intolerance and injustice,* he thought. The media scrum was quiet now, talking amongst themselves. One reporter asked for a comment.

"Just a man in the wrong place at the wrong time," George answered as the snow began to fall.

CHAPTER TWENTY THREE

Nadeau's words echoed across the two lawyer's consciousness. "I think we know the consequences of failure."

Bernard looked at his bloodied hands and then up at George.

"This is bad." George looked at his watch and then at the last of the media camped out on the steps. "It will be on the news already," he said. "We..."

Bernard gave his partner a look of understanding. "I know." He pulled out his iPhone and rang Gabrielle's number. It rang out. George grabbed the phone and rang Audrea. It too rang out.

"Shit." The men looked around and began to descend the steps as the paramedics started to swarm over the scene. George pulled his coat a little tighter around his body and broke into a trot. The snow was a thick carpet on the ground, making their progress difficult in office shoes. Bernard slid to the car door and grabbed the handle before he fell down.

"Let's get out of here," he said and stood up to dust himself off.

"Should we call the police?" Bernard asked as they drove away. "We could get protection."

"And who do you think we should call? Duval, Pallis?" George eased the car onto the gritted main road. "Pallis doesn't know anything. Why would he believe us?" George said. Bernard pondered the problem.

"Well, why don't you drop me off at the hospital. I could speak to Duval. He might have contacts."

"Okay." George swung the car around and backtracked to the Municipal Hospital.

"Listen," he said to George, "pick up Audrea, and meet me here in one hour." Bernard stood back as the Toyota drove away. He gave Gabrielle one more try on the phone, but there was no answer.

Duval was in a single room with a man standing guard at the door. He took Bernard's credentials and called them in to a higher authority. While Bernard waited, he looked through the observation window in the door at Duval. He was hooked up to tubes and both his arms were bandaged. Bernard shuddered at his memory of how they had impaled Duval. The all-clear was given and the guard opened the door.

Bernard leaned in close and whispered, "Pierre."

Duval opened his eyes and tried to smile.

"We need your help Duval." Bernard gave a quick glance at the door. "Tag is dead." He watched as Duval's eyes grew wide and then he frowned.

"They are coming for our..." Bernard choked, "for our families."

Duval's eyes registered the dire situation and he began to speak. The words were croaked out one at a time. "I have gun." He swallowed hard and Bernard saw for the first time a horrible black bruise on Duval's throat. *They must have tried to choke the life from him,* he thought.

"Locker Gare du Nord. 12." Duval closed his eyes and sighed. "Kill," he ended, the word whispered and lingered in the air.

"What about the key? I need a key."

Duval opened his eyes, "4790."

Bernard repeated the locker number in a sing-song lilt then asked, "It's a combination isn't it?" Duval nodded.

"Thanks." Bernard touched Pierre's shoulder and left. With half-an-hour before George would arrive, he hailed a taxi to the train station. The snow had eased and the traffic increased, but the taxi weaved it's way though the mess in ten minutes. Bernard told him to wait and he ran into chaos. Trains were delayed, others late, and passengers were camped on the concourse with their luggage everywhere. He sprinted over bags, legs, and people and headed for the locker area.

The electronic system had only one terminal and it was being used by some back packers. They dallied about as Bernard waited stomping up and down. He had left his coat over Tag and now was feeling the cold. Eventually, the tourists paid and left. Bernard punched in the numbers. He sang the combination and looked down the line. Number 12 popped open.

Kneeling on the ground, he looked inside at a large carry bag. Bernard carefully unzipped the bag in the locker and felt around. It was a gun. He zipped up and pulled the bag out, trying to act casual. The luggage was remarkably light, he thought, as he made his way back to his taxi. Once in the car, he sat back, nursing the bag on his lap for the short drive to the hospital.

George and Audrea had just driven up when Bernard paid his driver and walked over to the car.

"Where have you been?" George asked as Bernard climbed in the car. The back seat was full of skiing gear and Bernard gratefully found a jacket.

"Just an errand for Duval. Are we going on holiday?" he indicated all the equipment.

Audrea swivelled around in her seat, "It may be snowing hard when we get there."

George interrupted, "Have you managed to get in contact with Gabrielle? We can't raise Franc and Claudine in Bonneville at all."

"No." Bernard took his iPhone and sent a text. "What is your parent's address Audrea? I'm sending Gabi to their house." Bernard began texting as Audrea dictated the address. He wondered how to say all he wanted to say with just a few characters.

"Good idea." George looked at his wife, "It will be ok." It was one thing to say it, but believing it would be an act of faith.

The three passengers in the car were tense and conversation was sparse. Audrea looked out of the window at the blanket of snow. Bernard kept his thoughts to himself as the kilometres ticked away. The snow had eased off and the steady traffic had scrubbed two tracks in the road. George followed the endless line watching for any suspicious signs of tailing cars.

"Bernard," George began as he engaged cruise control," I think we need some sort of..." He wasn't quite sure what he was asking.

"A gun?" Bernard finished the thought.

"Well, yes a gun." Audrea looked at her husband and then to Bernard in the back seat.

"I have a gun." Audrea watched as Bernard reached over and opened the travel bag. He pulled out a Styer A3 sniper with a telescopic sight.

"What? How?" Audrea stammered. Bernard brought the gun up to his shoulder and cocked his eye to look though the sight. It was a remarkably well built weapon.

George looked via the rear vision mirror, "Whose is it?"

"Duval. He said we might need it," Bernard answered, being modest with the details. If he told the Nozettes that Duval wanted them to kill, it might jeopardise the rescue.

"Do you have ammunition?" George asked. Bernard fossicked around in the black carry all and came up with a stash of magazines.

"I think this is enough to stare down any Nazi, don't you?" He laid the magazines on the back seat of the car and counted twelve. As the freeway swept through the foothills to the Alps Bernard familiarised himself with the gun and was soon proficient in the loading and unloading.

"Can you stop that," Audrea asked Bernard as he shoved home the cartridge one more time. "I don't like it."

"Sorry, Audrea." Bernard stowed the weapon and sat back. He tried Gabi one more time, but the intermittent signal made any connection tenuous at best.

"It's no good. I just hope she received my message before we were cut off." The statement silenced any further conversation in the Toyota as the car began to climb. George turned off the main road and they began the drive on the smaller roads to his in-laws, and an uncertain reception.

"Do you think we should have rung Pallis?" Bernard asked, then realised it would be too late. Only a land line would work now. He slumped back in the seat and closed his eyes.

"Hell," George said and twisted the rear vision mirror for a better view.

"What is it darling?" Audrea looked around at the road behind.

"Fuck," George said. "Wake up Bernard."

"I'm awake, what is it."

"Look," George thumbed the trailing road. The headlights of a vehicle were winding their way up the road and gaining on the Toyota.

"Are you sure they are for us?" Audrea watched the road.

"They have turned the last three junctions. I deliberately went round in a circle and they are still there."

"Shit." Bernard swivelled in his seat and watched the headlights.

"We have binoculars, in the glove compartment." George said, indicating Audrea to get them. Bernard watched through the Steiner Admiralty binoculars.

227

"These are good." He tracked the car as it followed their every move on the steep road.

"A present." Audrea touched her husband's leg. "He wanted them for our holiday." She smiled remembering their promised holiday on the Black sea. "What do we do now?"

"We lose them." George revved the engine and the car skidded on the icy road, then with the 4 wheel drive capacity, he sped up the incline and turned sharply onto a side road.

"Where does this go?" Audrea said hanging onto her seat belt.

"Don't know. Find it on the GPS." Audrea pressed the homing button and found the cursor.

"There is a turn off going down in one kilometre. It's a 4:1 gradient." She bit her lip and frowned.

"Take it." Bernard snapped. George changed down the gears and pushed the rev counter up, trying to wring the most from the car in the icy conditions. They slewed across the road and back again, and lost the following car for a minute.

"Are they gone?" Audrea asked, as the GPS said, "500 metres. Turn left."

"Hang on." George pulled the steering wheel hard over. The car lurched onto the corner and then righted itself, and they zoomed off down the slope.

"Right turn 700 metres," Audrea said then continued, "It goes to a mountain pass. Only passable in summer." She held onto her seat belt.

"We can do it." Bernard watched as the following car gained speed. He steadied himself on the back seat, "It's a Range Rover." They all knew the implications. A Range Rover would be just a capable as the Toyota in the rough and it had the Land Rover's high-tech "terrain response" system.

"Tyres?"

"Road, as far as I can see, George." Bernard tried to keep steady as he watched the car. George knew he had the winter tyres and that was to be their only advantage. He pulled up sharp at the corner and pumped the accelerator to drive through the right turn. Bernard lost his grip on the binoculars and then decided to get the Styer.

"Bernard?" Audrea watched as he loaded a clip.

"I'm not aiming to use it. It's just in case." He rested the gun on the headrest on the back seat and positioned himself to use the sight.

"Three kilometres, then the track starts." Audrea read the GPS and looked at the leaden sky. "I think it is going to snow again." As if on cue light flakes of white fell from the sky. George hunched over the wheel. The car thumped over the last bit of tarmac and then began to crunch the road. There were deep frozen ruts, which wanted to grab the wheels and steer them in strange directions. George clenched the wheel and ran up and down through the gears. They rounded a corner and the Toyota was hit with a stray bullet.

Audrea screamed. "George, George," she yelled as another shot hit the back window.

"Duck," George yelled back. "Bernard, fire for God's sake." Bernard let off a volley of shots. Then their assailants were out of sight behind a sharp corner.

"Are you alright?" George looked at his wife. She nodded. The cold air rushed in from the broken window as Bernard's hands turned blue. He gripped the Styer tight and trained the sight on the road. The snow was falling steadily now and as it rushed towards the windscreen George tried to focus on the treacherous road.

"Wait for it..." Bernard watched as the Rover came into view. He let off several shots missing the car completely as the Toyota bumped over the uneven ground.

"Shit, they are gaining. Down!" he shouted and all three took cover. A shot hit the side door its glancing blow puncturing the air bag.

"Hang on," George said, "I'm going to try something." He looked over to his wife. "Tight."

Audrea grabbed the seatbelt on her shoulder and shortened the strap. She looked through the falling snow at the precipice on her right. The Rover seemed to gain traction and sped towards them.

"Now." George hit the brakes. The Toyota skidded to a halt and the Rover smashed into the back of them. George slammed his car into reverse and began to push. The Rover airbags had deployed and as the occupants tried to gain control, they were slowly being pushed to the edge.

"It's working," Bernard said, as he realised what George was trying to do. "Faster," he said with the gun trained on the other car. George put his foot down and swung the wheels to the right. The Rover jack-knifed on the icy road and its back wheels jumped over the edge and were hanging in the air.

"A bit more, slowly..." Bernard issued the directions. "Shit." He saw two men open their doors and try to get out. Bernard fired a shot above their heads and they retreated to their car.

"Fuckin' shove it, George." The Toyota found grip on the mountain track and with one final push, the Rover toppled over the edge. All three watched as it slid down to an outcrop. The impact made it roll over onto its side, gaining momentum until it careered down the mountain side and disappeared.

George stopped the engine and the snow swallowed up any noise save their breathing.

Audrea spoke first, "Do you think they're dead?" The men didn't speak. Their silence on the alpine road confirmed the answer. They walked around the back of the car and surveyed the damage.

The fuel tank had been ruptured. Their one hope of getting to safety was gushing onto the ground. The Rover had smashed any hope of driving to Bonneville and now the foolhardiness of the action came to bear.

"What now?" Audrea looked at the two men.

"We will have to ski." With the pronouncement, they began to assemble their gear. The GPS had an eight hour battery life and now George looked at their route to the farm house.

"It will take about three hours."

"Like the Transjurassienne long distance ski race. No worries." Bernard pulled on ski trousers and flicked over the braces, donned a jacket, and lastly, slung the bag carrying the gun over his shoulders.

"Can you do it?" George asked his wife.

She smiled, "It's you I worry about. Will you be able to ski, George?" Audrea watched George wince as he put on his jacket and began to kit up for the trip.

"I'm alright." George took four painkillers and pocketed the rest. "Right." He stood with his stocks looped over his wrist. "All set?" He positioned his goggles, stomped the loose snow off his boots and pushed off. Audrea followed and Bernard took up the rear. They had fluoro jacket tabs that were a boon in the worsening snow fall, and George had the GPS. Their trek took them down the track they had traversed in the car and then up the gradient that had seemed so easy when travelling in comfort. George's injury plagued him with pain and after a solid hour, he stopped.

"What is it?" Bernard asked coming along side.

"I need to rest." George lent up against a tree and tried to breathe through the pain.

"Are you alright?" Audrea took off her goggles and stared at her husband. He unzipped his jacket and looked at his dressings. A dark stain showed on his shirt and jumper.

"Shit, I'm bleeding."

Audrea took her glove lining and padded out the wound.

"That will have to do," she said. She found a piece of chocolate in her coat pocket. George ate it gratefully, hoping for a sugar rush and a bit more energy. They set off across the frozen landscape, each cocooned in their thoughts, with eyes set on the jacket in front. George set the pace making good progress. He stopped at the second hour and took their position.

"We can go down there." He pointed to an easy gradient, sloping off into the distance and ending in a valley. "That should get us on the right side of the road." Bernard took off his goggles and looked at the lay of the land. The slope was littered with boulders, which were not quite covered in snow. A line of fir trees dissected the run half way down. "We should take the left side, I don't like those rocks."

Audrea nodded, "I'll go first." She pushed off and cut across the slope with ease. George followed. Bernard looked around, and then started. All three were exposed on the mountain side when a helicopter shattered the peace and quiet. Bernard glanced up, and through the light fall of snow saw it heading their way. He crouched low and took a more direct route to catch up to George, but he had already made the connection and was racing for the trees. Audrea reached the cover and stopped. She watched the two men turn and run down the mountain head on, gaining speed. It was a dangerous manoeuvre and Audrea held her breath.

The chopper caught sight of the two figures on the slope and started to double back. George was the first to break into the trees. He slid his skis at 90 degrees trying to slow. He hit a tree and tumbled to a stop. Bernard flew into the cover, dodged trees until he found a deep drift, and plunged into it, landing on his side. He watched the sky, covered himself in snow, and then lay still.

Audrea raced to George and dragged him further under a tree, then squatted down and waited. The helicopter hovered over the area circling and hunting for the fugitives for ten minutes then moved off and was gone. The snow had stopped falling and the mountainside was still.

"Bernard," Audrea whispered as loud as she dare. "Bernard," she repeated a little louder. Bernard sat up and hunted for the voice.

"Over here." Audrea waved her hand. She was cradling George in her lap and he was moaning.

"Are you ok?" Bernard skied over, then unclipped his boots, and knelt down to look at George. He was pale but breathing.

"I'm alright. Just winded." George took a deep breath and sat up. "How did they find us?" Audrea scratched her head and the action jogged Bernard's memory.

"Audrea, when they had you, did they... touch you?"

"No. Well, yes." She looked at George. "Just a filthy grope. Why?" she said, then she frowned and she shivered at the memory of the lecherous thug.

"I saw it. He must have put a homing device on you. Think," Bernard said.

Audrea unzipped her jacket and pulled down the neck of her jumper, "Here." She pointed to her neck. Bernard came in close and took off his gloves to scrutinise her neck. He worked his way all around then up around her hair line.

"Hey, that's my wife your man-handling there," George remonstrated.

"What are you looking for?" Audrea submitted to the inspection.

"It's a... here it is." Bernard picked off the micro dot and put it on his thumb nail.

"What the... What the hell is that?" George and Audrea peered at the tiny dot. Bernard explained its deadly capabilities.

"How the hell did you know about it?" George asked taking the dot.

"It's a long story. But now, what are we going to do with it."

"Throw it away," Audrea said.

"No. We have an opportunity here." Bernard said. "We need to send it on a long journey. Away from us."

"I could do it." Audrea looked at her husband. "I could ski down to the road. Once I get to the turn-off I could put it on a car or something."

"No." George took his wife's hand.

"It's a good idea, George. Audrea is an excellent skier. She could be there in an hour, less as she is travelling alone." Bernard looked at George and they all knew what he was thinking. George winced at the thought that he was a burden and slowing them down.

"I could do it." Audrea stood up. "Give it to me darling?" She held out her hand. George looked at the dot then handed it over.

"Be careful. You are the only wife I have."

"Look Audrea, just go to the turn off, plant it, and head for the farm." Bernard took the GPS and they worked out a route. If you take the road, we should be there around the same time. We will find the kids, don't worry."

They watched Audrea weave her way through the woods and then turn and continued down the mountain to the valley. Bernard had worked out that they only need to follow the stream, and then climb around the base of a large hill, and the farm would be above them. He looked at George who was breathing hard.

"You ok?"

George nodded, and wheezed, "Okay."

The men dug in and trudged through the deep snow, the effort making any conversation impossible. When they reached the other side of the hill, George signalled he needed to rest. He sat down on a rocky outcrop and leaned heavily on his stocks.

"It's killing me." He moved about trying to get comfortable.

"I know." Bernard looked up at the copse of trees above. He could just make out the roof-line of the farm and a column of smoke from the chimney. "We are going to have to walk." He bent down and unbuckled George's skis then did his own.

"I'd love to leave these here, but I think we may need them again." He tied George's skis to his back then asked George to do the same for him. Once strapped, they set off up though a natural break in the trees to the farm. George found the short climb extremely difficult and had to stop every few paces to catch his breath. He put his hand inside his jacket and felt the cold wet patch on his clothes. He was bleeding constantly.

"Nearly there," Bernard said. They had reached the outer edges of Claudine's garden when a shot rang out.

"That wasn't close. It was down there." Bernard pointed to the road below.

"Audrea!" George gasped.

"Come on." Bernard pulled his friend through the fence and they ran to the house and skidded onto the veranda.

"Franc, Claudine!" George called as he came close. He looked inside through the window, but the place looked deserted. Bernard ran around to the side and saw Gabrielle's car. He smiled to himself at the thought she had taken his advice.

"I can't see anyone around. They must have gone somewhere. Somewhere safe, I hope." Bernard said as he came back to George. "Gabrielle's car is around the side."

"Franc's car is still here." George pointed to Franc's car in the barn. "Come inside, there might be a message or something." George led Bernard around to the back door and they walked inside not caring to take off their boots.

The table was laid for a meal and the stove was burning bright. George looked around then went to his children's rooms. They were neat and untouched.

"It looks like they just walked out," Bernard said.

George ran his fingers through his hair and leaned heavily on the table. "But where? Audrea and the kids – I should never have gotten them mixed up in all this. These people will hunt them down, Bernard."

"Well, George, we will be waiting." Bernard sat down and then picked up the bread knife and drew it across his throat. "Keeeeeeeek," he said, "Kaput."

"I've got to go Bernard. I've got to find them."

"Think about it George. You're injured. You don't know where they are or what direction they went. We need to think things through."

"You're right. I know you're right. But I just can't sit here."

"You will, George. Look at you. You need treatment," Bernard said.

George found the first-aid box and Bernard made him sit still while he tended his wound. The bleeding had stopped now George was sitting still, and with some sutures and a large sticking patch, which was used for horses, he stemmed the weeping. Bernard gave him an anti-bacterial table then made him a hot chocolate and handed it to his friend. "All we can do is wait. My guess is that our pursuers are in the dark, like us, about Audrea, Gabrielle and the rest." He sank into a chair by the front window.

"I think Franc has a gun somewhere. He used to go hunting." George sipped his drink and winced as his emotions caught in his throat.

"If it would be anywhere it is probably on top of a dresser. They usually are." Bernard looked out of the window and then put his finger to his lips. He pointed to the tree lined driveway and held up one finger. George peered through the lace curtain. They both watched a figure trudging up the drive. The person stopped and checked behind, then continued.

Bernard pulled out Duval's gun and loaded the magazine. "I'm not taking any chances." He cracked open the window and lay the barrel on the sill, training the sights on the lone figure. It was only when he had a telescopic view did he relax. "It's Audrea."

When she was closer to the house, Audrea broke into a trot, clumping along in her boots. She saw the men in the window and waved, then ran in the front door where Bernard was waiting. "I thought I'd never make it." She hugged Bernard and then looked over to George sitting down. Concern clouded her face.

"I'm okay. Are you?" he said standing up and holding out his hands.

"Okay," she replied, coming swiftly to his side.

"We heard a gunshot. Was that you?"

"Yes… and no. I was down at the road. A dog ran out and was knocked down. He was in a pretty bad way. A man came up and asked me if it was mine, then he shot it." Audrea sat down and sipped George's hot chocolate. "Poor thing."

"This man just happened to have a gun?" Bernard asked.

"He was ok. Just a hunter I guess."

"Did he ask you any questions, Audrea?" Bernard looked at her and frowned.

"Well, he was just ordinary. We had a little talk. I think I said I grew up here, you know all the usual stuff..." She trailed off and then her mouth dropped. "You don't think..."

George took his wife in his arms.

"It wasn't your fault. How could you know?" Audrea sat back and put her face in her hands.

"Oh God, what have I done? I practically drew him a map." Then she looked around. "Where are the kids? Where are papa and mama?"

"We don't know. They were gone when we arrived."

Audrea looked around the room trying to make sense of the situation. She stopped and lifted her head and stared at Bernard. "You're going to use them as bait, aren't you? They will come looking for them."

"No. How can we, we don't know where they are?" Bernard looked at the floor.

Audrea turned to George, "Tell me it's not true, George. Tell me."

"They will be coming. We should be ready Audrea." She began to sob and bent down to cover her face. The men watched her then Bernard asked, "Have you any idea where they might go. Gabrielle is with them." Audrea sat up and frowned, in thought. She looked around the room at the familiar objects, her father's collection of bird eggs, collected feathers in a large jar, and watercolour paintings of his favourite birds – things she had grown up with and never taken notice. Then a thought jolted her to stand. "The hide. They have gone to the hide."

"What's that?" Bernard asked looking out the window.

"It was built by Papa to watch birds. It is about a kilometre away down the hill." Audrea looked around the room. "His walking stick is missing, and... I think he has a gun in his room." She raced to her parent's bedroom and pulled up a stool. She reached on top of the wardrobe and felt about, but only came up with a wad of newspaper. "It's gone. The gun is gone," she yelled from the bedroom.

The three debated what to do. Bernard was for staying in the house and letting them come. George and Audrea wanted to run to their family.

"Perhaps we should separate. I could stall them here and you might be able to protect them at the hide." Bernard watched the driveway as he talked.

"I think we should stick together," Audrea said.

"I agree." George took his wife's hand.

Bernard nodded. "That's settled then. We all go."

With their skis snapped on, the three started the trek down the hill, Audrea leading the way. They left the yard and took a track through a line of trees. A sharp piece of wood hit Audrea in the face. Confused, she stopped and rubbed her cheek, then looked at the tree trunk next to her. It had been splintered. It only took a second for Audrea to understand what was going on. "Gunshot," she yelled to the others. She squatted down and searched frantically on the horizon for a shape.

The men scrambled into the thicket and crouched low. Bernard twisted the Styer around and looking through the scope, scanned the woods. The only sound was the occasional snapping of a branch in the cold afternoon. The three remained still, squinting into the reflected white of the new snow. George was to first to spot a figure. He signalled to Bernard to look about 200 metres to his left. Bernard trained the scope and waited, holding his breath. The figure moved and Bernard squeezed the trigger. The jolt made him lose his balance. He fell on his hip, as a bullet narrowly missed him and lodged in a tree just behind and to the right. Audrea screamed. The men looked around to see a white clad man bearing down on her and making ready his gun. Bernard swung around and aimed the Sniper gun, but the shot was off the mark. The man pressed on, then fired a volley of shots. Audrea threw herself down into the snow and lay still.

"Bernard," George yelled and pointed to two men racing in their direction. Once again, Bernard let off a few rounds and the men skied for tree cover. George stood up and salaamed towards his stricken wife, not caring for his own safety. Bernard covered his friend's back. He began firing blindly into the woods, then followed George, still trying to get a clear shot at the attackers.

Bernard was 20 metres away and covered by a thicket of bush when the man came to a stop and stood over Audrea's prostrate figure. George was desperately trying to cover the remaining metres, when Audrea raised her stock and in one swift movement plunged it into her attacker's neck. He reeled back, then seemed to recover and lunged at Audrea who was still on the ground. She took her other stock and thrust. The man fell heavily on top of her, dead. She slithered out from under the body and pulled off the stock strap from her wrist. Her pole had impaled her assailant's through the mouth and out the back of his neck.

George reached the scene and fell down to comfort his wife. Another shot rang out in the woods. The two instinctively ducked as Bernard turned and let off a magazine, raking the air. He re-loaded and repeated his fire. The volley gave Bernard enough time to ski the remaining metres to Audrea and help George get her up. She was shaking, crying, and leaning heavily on George for support.

"I think they are gone." Bernard looked around at the trees and they listened.

"Nothing?"

"No. Come on. We need to go." Bernard pulled Audrea's stock from the corpse's neck and handed it to her. She recoiled, then with a deep breath looped it over her wrist.

"Which way?" Bernard pushed her to move and George followed.

Audrea led them through the trees with an expert eye. As a girl, she had been to the hide many times with her father. She stopped at a rocky outcrop and the two men came to her side.

"I can't see it," George said, looking around.

"Me neither," Bernard turned around in a circle.

She pointed to a large boulder just over 100 metres away. "Over there, near that boulder, see." The men looked and then Franc opened the door.

"Papa," Audrea pushed off to cover the distance.

"Audrea," George yelled as he saw a crouching figure in the trees, "Watch out." A gun shot split the air and George fell awkwardly in the snow. Audrea turned and skied back to her stricken husband. Bernard twisted around. Putting the scope to his eye, he saw his target and gently squeezed. The man dropped with one shot. Franc, seeing the danger, ran to his daughter. Claudine came to the hide doorway and surveyed the devastation. A single shot came from the rise and she fell, hit in the chest. Bernard fumbled with his gun as Franc stopped and turned to see a lone figure on the rocky outcrop.

"Mama!" Audrey began to move to her mother when Franc yelled.

"Audrea, get down!" He drew back his bolt action Lebel rifle and fired, shouting, "Nazi pig." The lone gunman was no match for his years of rage. The man fell, tumbling down the rocks to land at the base. It was over.

Franc threw his gun down and ran to his wife, knelt down in the snow and cradled her in his arms. Her breathing was laboured in the frigid air. He could see that she struggled to live, but the effort was too great. Claudine slumped in her husband's arms and died.

"No!" Audrea screamed, and fell to the snow sobbing.

Everything was quiet in the woods, giving a false sense of what had just happened. Then the world caught up. Everyone was spurred into action. Gabrielle came to the door with the two Nozette children who were crying. Immediately they spied their mother, they ran. Audrea held out her arms and enveloped the children, crying into their shoulders as her family was reunited.

"Bernard!" Gabriel cried and ran for her husband. In that instant, Bernard knew she would forgive him anything.

It began to snow again as Bernard, with his arm around Gabrielle, looked at the devastation. *What price justice,* he thought. He watched as Franc covered his wife's body with a knitted blanket. Then, in one last act, Franc walked over to the dead gunman at the base of the rock and spat at the body.

CHAPTER TWENTY FOUR

Audrea read the paper to George as he shaved. The paper reported: *The riot at the courthouse on the first day of the trial was called a stain on our secular society and the French should be ashamed of their actions.* She flicked through the pages and then an item caught her eye.

In two separate incidences, the paper said, the Chancellor of the Sorbonne and prominent and outspoken politician, Theodore Voisard, were killed in car accidents on the outskirts of Paris.

"Is that a coincidence?" she looked at her husband.

"I doubt it," he said.

"What do you mean, George?" Audrea watched him shave.

"Well, I just think it's a bit too convenient. They were in the higher echelon and now..."

"Does this mean it's ended?" George stopped his toilette and stared at his wife. He debated whether to tell her what had transpired at the university and what Duval had said.

"Audrea, there will always be people like that. Like Tag, like Voisard. I think it is a bit like snakes and ladders. Sometimes we go up and then sometimes we go down."

"But..." Audrea continued the conversation, "we should be able to stop them."

"How? With freedom to associate, people with different ideas, different morals will always seek out each other. "

Audrea shook her head. "Well, it's over for us. For Nozette and Simeoni at least. Isn't it?" George nodded and continued shaving.

Audrea turned the page and saw the firm's name in the paper.

"Look, here it is," she read, "*In a gracious act, the law firm of Nozette and Simeoni have donated the bulk of the funds from their defence of the murdered Heinz Tag to Mrs Darlan, the widow of the victim in the Rue de la Victoire riots. Mrs Darlan was overwhelmed by the generosity and planned to erect a memorial to her late husband's memory.* That's nice isn't it?" Audrea said. George finished shaving and gave his wife a kiss. She ran her finger over the scar on his flank and made him shiver.

"Don't get shot again George, or I will personally kill you." She playfully tickled him and gave him a kiss. His children barged into the bathroom and their intimate moment was over.

It was a cloudless day no rain the radio announcer had said. George and Audrea buckled up their children and began the drive into the city. The traffic was thick by the time they reached the inner suburbs and slowed to a walking pace. *Life carries on as normal, people living ordinary lives*, George thought, as they ground to a halt in a traffic snarl.

Audrea looked across at George, who was pulling his moustache and asked, "George, who was that man in the photo you saved from the old burnt offices?"

"Oh, that photo. It was Detective Inspector Pallis."

"So was he at the riots?"

George shrugged his shoulders, "He... ", George began, "He lied to us. He claims he wasn't there.

"Why would he do that?" Audrea looked at her husband.

"Don't worry about that now," George said as he looked at this watch. The traffic eased and they hit the ring road, then made progress to arrive at Rue de Maine just as Bernard drove up to the kerb.

"You're late," Bernard said to George by the way of a greeting.

"Well, it was bound to happen sooner or later." George smiled at his partner and slapped him on the shoulder.

"Duval said he was coming, didn't he?"

"Mmmm," Bernard answered, "They said he is to receive a bravery award or something."

"Yeah, I know." George looked down the street to spy an Audi TT coming his way.

Bernard turned and nodded, "That's him." They waited at the kerb until Duval had parked his new car and then walked over to the NATA Agent.

"Good to see you, Duval." Bernard held open the door and George gave Duval a helping hand.

"You look well." Duval smiled at George.

"And you." George said knowing what punishment their bodies had been through in the last month.

"Well, come on." Bernard led the way and the men walked over the road to their new offices above the accountants. They looked up at the small sign erected to announce they were back in business.

"You're coming up for a drink, I hope?" George opened the ground floor door and ushered the small party inside.

Once in the reception area, Audrea cornered Duval, "Pierre, I'm so glad you are ok." She held Duval's hand and squeezed.

"You were very kind to me in that room, Audrea. Very kind."

"It was nothing really." She blushed, and busied herself with her children and the drinks.

"Well, here's to a new beginning. Here's to ordinary people with ordinary lives." They toasted the new premises and talked of grand plans for the future and no-one mentioned the past.

***

It was a month later when Audrea, who was the new secretary, escorted Detective Inspector Pallis into Bernard's office and shut the door.

"What can I do for you, Inspector Pallis?" Bernard indicated a chair. Pallis sat down and in a practiced motion rubbed his shoes on the back of his trousers to keep the shine.

"Just wanted to know if you were interested in taking a case?" Pallis crossed his legs and stretched out his feet. "He is a Muslim"

Bernard watched the relaxed attitude of the Inspector and wondered at his almost cocky manner.

"Ah, I see. What did this Muslim do?"

"What does it matter? He doesn't need a defence, he needs a bullet." Pallis looked Bernard straight in the eye and held his gaze with an intensity that left Bernard in no doubt. The words didn't need to be uttered, as he heard the crowing of the beast.

47439412R20141

Made in the USA
San Bernardino, CA
31 March 2017